THE
MODERN CHRIST

BY

DAN HAMBRIGHT

Copyright © 2021 by Dan Hambright

Published by Purpose Press

Author Website: www.danhambright.com

Cover Design: www.ebooklaunch.com

Library of Congress Cataloging-in Publication Data has been applied for.

ISBN 978-0-578-96775-2

To my amazing wife, Courtney.
I couldn't have done it without you.

PREFACE

Several years ago I had a random thought pop into my head: *what would Bible stories look like if they happened today instead of thousands of years ago?* It was an intriguing question I spent a lot of time exploring. I envisioned Pharoh chasing down the Israelites in Humvees, David's army battling the Philistines with assault rifles, and the prodigal son blowing his inheritance in Dubai before crawling back to his father.

As these modern-day stories played themselves out in my head, the one I couldn't get enough of was the story of Jesus. I spent countless hours imagining what his life would look like in today's society. Then I came up with the ultimate plot twist. What if he had been born in the United States instead of Israel?

I was hooked. My mind was creating endless "what if?" scenarios that left me wanting more. Not only that, but I was connecting with God in a new and profound way. Something about bringing these stories into a world I could relate to was impacting me on a spiritual level like never before.

Then God put it on my heart to turn the idea into a book. It sounded crazy when I said it out loud; I was an accountant, not a writer. I'd always enjoyed writing as a hobby, but I was anything but qualified to publish such a unique story. The idea was great, but it belonged in the hands of an established author who could do something amazing with it.

Whenever I tried to push the idea out of my mind, it came roaring back with a vengeance that left no doubt it was God telling me to write the book. So I gave in and began the daunting task with nothing more than a vague idea and a blank Word document. Five years later, the book you hold in your hands is the result of that leap of faith.

I'm incredibly honored that you've decided to join me on this journey, but before we begin, I think it's important to establish what this book is, and what it is not.

This book is a work of fiction I hope will entertain you and give you a whole new perspective on Jesus's life. If it helps even one person grow in their relationship with Jesus Christ, then all the years that went into it were more than worth it.

This book is *not* a replacement for the Bible in any way whatsoever, and it's not intended to be 100 percent accurate. While the story stays true to the original gospels, I had to take certain liberties in order to move it to the modern-day United States. You'll also notice stark differences between the United States we live in today and the one that exists in this book. In order to keep the main plot points as accurate as possible, I needed a certain amount of world-building to make that happen.

In the end, I hope this book will lead you back to the Bible, where you can read the true story of Jesus's life with a whole new appreciation.

ACKNOWLEDGEMENTS

So many people have played a huge role in making this book a reality, and I am forever grateful for their contributions. Words can't even begin to express how thankful I am, but unfortunately, words are all I have within the confines of this novel.

To my wife, Courtney. I already dedicated this book to you, but you deserve an additional mention here as well. Satan did everything he could to stop me from writing this book, and I'm certain he would have succeeded if it weren't for you. We've endured some hellish storms over the past few years, but we've come out the other side stronger than ever. You've been my rock every step of the way, and it thrills me to know how angry Satan must have been watching you carry me over the finish line. I don't deserve you, but I am forever grateful that God brought us together.

To my dad, Dennis Hambright. You've been one of my biggest supporters, and you've never wavered in your belief that I could do this. Thank you for always encouraging me and pushing me to keep going.

To my mom, Cheryl Spiva, and my stepdad, Robert Spiva. You always made God the number one priority in our family. As a young and combative teenager, I often fought you on that, but you always stood firm in your beliefs. Thank you for teaching me what it means to put God first in your life. I'm thankful for all the sacrifices you made while I was growing up. I didn't appreciate them back then, but I sure do now.

To my grandpa, Roy Culp, who I hope is looking down from Heaven with a nod of approval. You taught me the importance of God, hard work, family, and pursuing your dreams. Without you, I wouldn't be the man I am today, and I hope I've made you proud.

And lastly, to my editor, Briana Farr. I'm embarrassed to think about what this book would have looked like without you. Thank you for breathing life into my story and taking it to the next level.

PART I
THE BIRTH

You will conceive and give birth to a son,
and you are to call him Jesus.

-Luke 1:31

CHAPTER 1

Mary vomited into the toilet, clinging to the bowl with one hand while holding back her long, dark hair with the other. She flushed the toilet and carried herself to the sink on trembling legs. The pipes in the wall groaned like an angry ghost as she turned on the faucet, and a trickle of water belched from the spout.

"Not again."

Mary had an on-again, off-again relationship with the water in her apartment. Sometimes it was on, but most of the time it was off. The landlord had been promising to fix it for over a month, but after talking to some tenants who'd lived there for years, she realized the only thing the landlord was good at delivering was excuses.

She looked in the cracked mirror at the image staring back at her. Mary's brown eyes looked dull and empty. A thin sheen of sweat covered her olive skin.

Mary had been sick for a week. The vomiting had been a daily occurrence, and the nausea was constant. She needed to rest, but rest didn't pay the bills. Past due notices were already scattered across the tiny apartment like uninvited guests. She had no choice but to power through her 12-hour shift at the laundry plant.

Mary wiped her mouth with the back of her hand and went to the only other room in the apartment. The tiny room held a twin bed, a beat-up dresser, a refrigerator, a microwave, an ancient television, and a faded couch with more stains than stuffing. Cyndi Lauper belted *Girls Just Want to Have Fun* from the radio on the dresser.

Resisting the urge to climb back into bed, Mary put on her white linen uniform, grabbed her sack lunch, and walked into the warm Pennsylvania morning. The laundry plant was a forty-five-minute walk from her apartment. Owning a car was impossible at this point in her life, and taking the bus was a luxury she could rarely afford. She normally enjoyed the walk, using it to spend some alone time with God. Today, however, was not one of those days. It took all her focus just to keep the nausea at bay.

She arrived at the back of the laundry plant with ten minutes to spare. The front entrance was reserved for customers and employees with a desk job; Mary was neither. She pushed her way through a set of glass doors that winked back at her in the morning light. The coolness of the break room greeted her like a welcoming friend, the air kissing the sweat on her face. She walked past tables of people sipping coffee, leafing through the morning paper, and sharing the latest gossip with their coworkers. Mary opened the locker that had belonged to her for the past eighteen months and tossed her sack lunch in the back. Just thinking about the food inside of it made her stomach turn.

"Honey, you look terrible."

Mary let out a small cry. She whirled around to see her friend standing beside her. Jackie was a tall, heavyset woman with fair skin and kind, green eyes.

"I'm sorry, sweetie. I didn't mean to sneak up on you like that. I thought you heard me comin'." Jackie frowned, making her wrinkles more defined. "You look worse than yesterday."

"I *feel* worse than yesterday. I don't know what's wrong with me."

Jackie raised a plump hand to Mary's face and placed it against her forehead. "No fever, that's for sure. A little clammy, but no fever. Why don't you go home and rest? When my shift's over here in a few hours, I'll bring you some of my homemade soup that'll do your body better than any medicine ever could."

Mary smiled. Jackie was old enough to be her mother, and in many ways, she was. She had taken Mary under her wing from the moment they met. Jackie was very protective of her and was always there to give her advice or lend an ear when needed.

"That's sweet of you, Jackie, but I can't afford to call in sick. I need the hours."

"Oh, honey. You know Miss Jackie would help you if she could, but I'm just shy of stealin' pennies out of the mall fountain myself. Lord, now wouldn't that be a sight? My big booty wadin' through the fountain in front of Radio Shack lookin' for change." She gave that sweet, southern laugh that always warmed Mary's heart. "I reckon I'd scare the children. Might get a wink or two from some of the old men, but . . . oh goodness I'm ramblin' again. What I mean to say is I'll still bring you that soup when your shift's done."

"You're one in a million, Jackie. Really." They walked over to the time clock.

Jackie tucked a strand of brown hair behind her ear. "Aw shucks. You're gonna go and embarrass ole Miss Jackie, and I'll be redder than a ripe tomato. Then that old pervert down by the foldin' station's gonna see me and think I'm blushin' because of him. That man don't need any more reasons to think I like him."

Mary couldn't suppress a smile. "But you do like him, don't you?"

"Girl, you're a load of trouble, even when you're sick as a dog. Hush that pretty little mouth of yours and let's get to work." Jackie stopped at the door and winked. "Well, maybe I like him a little."

CHAPTER 2

The next twelve hours felt like the longest of Mary's life. Her sickness had made her mundane job even more excruciating. She worked in the sorting station, which required her to sort, inspect, tag, and weigh the laundry. Management tracked their output and fired anyone who failed to meet the minimum requirements. Mary had seen countless people come and go during her time at the plant. Immigrants were a dime a dozen, and there were plenty of people to take the place of someone who couldn't pull their weight.

Most of the employees were immigrants because they were easier to take advantage of. Due to a shocking constitutional amendment in the 1950s that removed naturalized immigration, along with a Supreme Court ruling that determined only citizens had constitutional rights, immigrants had very little recourse to the abuse they experienced in the United States. Citizens had rights, immigrants didn't. It was a cruel reality, but a reality nonetheless. Sadly, the problems immigrants faced in the United States paled in comparison to the horrors they had experienced in their native countries. As a result, there was little choice but to endure the hardships.

The company paid little but demanded a lot. They would work someone to their breaking point and then bring in a replacement. Management treated the employees like cattle rather than people. Although they had gone through countless employees over the years, Mary had refused to let them break her. With her wedding only several months away, Mary and her fiancé, Joseph, both needed stable jobs in order to support a future that would someday include children.

All this kept Mary going despite her illness. Her hands worked on autopilot as she prayed for enough strength to make it through the day.

Mary breathed a sigh of relief when the whistle announced the end of her shift. Feeling exhausted, she allowed herself the luxury of taking the bus home. She dug two crumpled bills from her pocket and placed them in the holding container next to the driver.

The ride only lasted a few minutes, but Mary was already dozing when the bus lurched to a stop in front of her apartment complex. She woke with a start and glanced out the window to see Jackie sitting at the foot of the stairs with a large slow cooker at her feet.

"You know, I could have just called you when I got home," Mary said as she stepped off the bus.

"Nonsense, girl. Nobody wants to come home to an empty house when you can come home to this."

Mary's stomach rumbled at the delicious aroma pouring from the slow cooker. With the nausea taking a temporary leave of absence, Mary was famished. "It smells amazing."

"It tastes even better. My momma used to make it when I was growin' up, and my daddy said it'd put hair on my chest. I spent more nights than I care to admit thinkin' I was gonna wake up one mornin' with a fur rug sproutin' out of my nightshirt." Jackie chuckled at the nostalgic memory. "Now, it might not really put hair on your chest, but it'll sure warm you right up and cure whatever's ailin' you."

Mary led her upstairs into the apartment. Jackie heaved the slow cooker onto the kitchen counter with a grunt and shooed Mary toward the couch. "You sit yourself over there and let me take care of this. I'll bring it to you in a jiffy."

Mary didn't argue. She sank into the couch and watched Jackie ladle two steaming helpings of soup into a bowl. Then she grabbed a folded quilt from the bed and placed it over Mary's legs before handing her a TV tray with the bowl sitting on top.

"You spoil me, Jackie."

"And I'm happy to do it." She leaned down and kissed Mary on top of the head. "I'm gonna get out of your hair so you can eat and relax. I won't waste my breath tellin' you to stay home tomorrow because I know it won't do no good, but try to get some rest."

There was a knock at the door, and Jackie peered through the peephole. "Well, look who we have here!" Jackie threw open the door and smiled.

Joseph stood in the doorway with a wide grin, his broad shoulders taking up most of the doorframe. His white t-shirt was damp with sweat, accentuating the muscular physique underneath. His wavy black hair clung to his glistening forehead.

"Get your handsome self in here and give me a hug."

"I don't think you want one from me. I've been in the workshop all day, and I stink."

"Don't make me ask you twice, Joseph. You'll go and hurt ole Miss Jackie's feelings." "If you insist." Joseph laughed and pulled her into his arms.

"I'll take a sweaty hug from you over a normal hug from any other man, and that's the truth!" Jackie hugged him like a drowning victim clinging to a life raft.

Joseph slid out of Jackie's grip and knelt in front of Mary. "How are you feeling?" He caressed her cheek with a dry and calloused hand from years of carpentry work.

"Better now that I'm home. I'm just tired."

"We're getting you to a doctor first thing in the morning," he said.

"I'll be fine. It's just a bug."

"You've been saying that for a week. I'm worried about you."

"Joseph, we can't afford a doctor right now." Mary loved that he was always looking out for her, but a hospital bill was the last thing they needed.

"Don't worry about that. I've got a few orders in the pipeline that will bring in some good money."

Mary squeezed his hand. "That needs to go toward our future."

"There is no future if something happens to you. I'm taking you to the doctor tomorrow, and that's final."

Jackie cleared her throat. "Well, it looks like I turned myself into a bit of a third wheel here. I'll just see myself out and let you two have your little chat. For what it's worth, and it ain't much, I think you should see a doctor, Mary."

Jackie said goodbye and closed the door behind her. Seconds later, they heard her shouting from the bottom of the stairs.

"You kids get away from my car! I might be old, but I'm strong. Don't make me take a whoopin' to you!"

They both laughed, and Joseph shook his head. "I don't want to fight about this. Let's just go to the doctor to be safe. It'll make me feel better."

Mary sighed. "Okay, I'll go. Thanks for taking care of me."

"Always." He kissed her cheek. "I better make sure Jackie doesn't kill those kids. I'll come by tomorrow morning, and we'll take the bus over to First Medical. Tell your boss you'll be late."

"They've fired people for less, you know." Mary thought of her boss's regular tirades.

"You're one of their best workers. They won't let you go." Joseph kissed her again and stood up. "I love you."

"I love you too."

Mary watched him go as she took a sip of Jackie's soup. It was even better than it smelled. She devoured the rest while watching an episode of *Family Ties*. The lighthearted comedy was a welcome distraction from the harsh realities of her life. Mary wrapped the quilt around herself and stretched out on the couch. She was asleep in seconds.

CHAPTER 3

"Wake up, Mary."

Mary stirred under the quilt.

"Mary!"

"Joseph?" Mary said as she rubbed her eyes.

She opened them to see a man standing in front of her wearing a white button-down shirt and tan linen pants. His blonde hair and fair skin looked nothing like Joseph. Mary screamed. She reached for the empty soup bowl and hurled it at the stranger. It sailed to his left, shattering against the wall.

"Get out of here!" she yelled at him.

The man smiled. "Mary, there is nothing to be afraid of. I will not hurt you."

Mary leapt off the couch and raced to the kitchen counter, grabbing a steak knife from the drawer. "Somebody help me!" The knife shook in her trembling hands.

Someone downstairs banged on the wall. "Shut up, lady! It's two in the morning!"

"Mary, listen to me. I am here to bring you good news," the man said.

Mary waved the knife in front of her. "What do you want? If you're here for money, you've picked the wrong place."

"My name is Gabriel, and I have been sent by God."

"By God? You're insane." Mary stomped on the floor. "Somebody down there call the police!"

Gabriel closed his eyes and lifted his hands. "Lord, show her the things that I cannot."

Mary watched as white light pulsed from his fingers and spun its way around his hands. The bright aura worked its way down his entire body, making him glow like a human candle. Mary could sense a presence inside the room that shook her to her core. She felt an overwhelming peace unlike anything she'd ever experienced. The knife slipped from her hands, and Mary fell to her knees.

"I don't believe it. You really are from God."

He approached her with a smile. "Yes, Mary. I am an angel sent from God." He held out his hand. "Come sit down. We have a lot to discuss."

The guilt was too much for Mary to handle, and she began to sob. "Lord, forgive me for doubting the man you sent to me. I've failed you."

"Far from it." Gabriel helped her to the couch and sat next to her. "You have found favor with the Lord, and he has something very special in store for you."

Mary wiped the tears from her face. "What would God want with someone like me? I have nothing to offer him."

Gabriel placed a hand on her shoulder. "Oh, Mary. You have no idea just how much you have to offer. What I am about to tell you will come as quite a shock, but I promise you it is the truth. You are pregnant with a baby boy."

"No!" Mary backed away from him. "I'm still a virgin. Surely the Lord knows that."

"Your child is not from a man, but from the Holy Spirit. He is the Son of God. He will become a great man, and he will reign forever."

Mary felt faint. It was like her brain had short-circuited, and she couldn't process what this man was saying. No, not a man. An angel. "This is all too much," she whispered.

"I know it is a shock, but God chose you for a reason. He has planned this since the beginning."

"The beginning of what? My birth?"

"The beginning of time."

"So, I'm pregnant with God's child even though I'm a virgin, and it will be a boy that will rule forever? Is that all?" Mary felt like she was teetering on the edge of hysteria.

Gabriel chuckled. "That's it. Oh, and you should name him Jesus."

Mary bolted upright, her eyes wide. "How am I going to explain this to Joseph? There's no way he's going to believe me. He'll think I cheated on him!"

"Your future will not be an easy one, but God will see you through it. That includes any issues with Joseph. God never promises the road will be easy. He only promises it will lead to him. You can do this, Mary. God uses normal people to do extraordinary things all the time, and you are about to do something *very* extraordinary."

"If it's God's will, then I'm ready to do what he asks. I'm the Lord's willing servant." Mary swallowed hard. She meant what she said with all her heart, even if she didn't know how she could do it.

Gabriel smiled as he stood. "Just remember that God is always with you. Seek him, and he will guide you."

"What should I do next?"

"Go visit your cousin, Elizabeth. She is also pregnant and will be receptive to your news. She will support you through the struggles to come."

The white aura surrounding Gabriel became brighter. Mary shielded her eyes and turned away. In the next instant, the light vanished along with Gabriel. She sat in stunned silence while her mind tried to process what had just happened. Was it a dream? She looked behind her and saw the knife lying on the floor. Definitely not a dream.

She thought back to the overwhelming presence she had felt. A feeling so unique she couldn't describe it. A feeling so powerful it had brought her to her knees. She was certain it had been God revealing himself to her.

She felt alone now that Gabriel was gone, and the magnitude of everything weighed her down like an anchor. Sleep was out of the question, so Mary walked to the 24-hour mini mart down the street.

The hollow silence of the early morning was unnerving. The sodium lights in the mini mart's parking lot beckoned to her like a lighthouse in a storm. She relaxed a little as she walked into the welcoming light.

Inside, a middle-aged man with long hair and a coarse beard stood behind the counter. He hummed along to the song on the radio as Mary approached the counter.

"A pretty little thing like you shouldn't be out at this hour. You're just asking for trouble," the man said.

"I know, but I have a bit of an emergency."

"What kind of emergency are we talking about here? Bandages, stomach medicine, cigarettes?"

"I need a pregnancy test," Mary mumbled. She had never felt so embarrassed.

"A what?"

Mary cleared her throat. "A pregnancy test."

"Ohhh. That kind of emergency."

"It's not what you think—"

The man held up a hand decorated with three gold rings and a matching bracelet. "You don't have to explain anything to me, darling. I see and hear all kinds of things working the night shift, and none of it's any of my business." He pulled a pregnancy test from the shelf behind him. "This one here's the cheapest. They're all basically the same. They either say yes or no. Don't need to get too fancy with them unless you prefer the bells and whistles, and I'm guessing you don't really care."

13

"The cheapest will be fine. Thank you."

The man rang her up and walked her to the door. "You really shouldn't be out there by yourself. The least I can do is keep an eye on you until you're out of sight."

She glanced at his nametag. "Thank you, Bruce. I appreciate it."

"Don't mention it." He nodded toward the bag. "And good luck with your emergency. I hope everything works out the way you want it to."

"It will."

Halfway home, she looked back and saw Bruce standing in the doorway, watching her. He waved, and she gave a silent prayer of thanks. Bruce had been exactly what she needed at that moment: a friendly face who was there to help and not judge.

Mary tore open the pregnancy test as soon as she got home. She followed the instructions and sat on the edge of the bathtub to wait for the results. It was like taking a test when you already had the answers ahead of time. There was no doubt in her mind that she was pregnant, but she needed the ultimate confirmation to prove she wasn't going crazy.

Mary stood and hovered over the pregnancy test. A pink plus sign stared back at her. "I'm pregnant," she said to herself. "With God's son. I'm going to sound like a nut. Who in their right mind is going to believe me?"

Her thoughts turned to what Gabriel had said about Elizabeth's pregnancy. Was that even possible? She hadn't seen Elizabeth in a few months, but they had spoken over the phone on multiple occasions. Elizabeth had said nothing about being pregnant or even thinking about having a baby.

There was only one way to know for sure. Mary threw on a clean set of clothes and ate an apple with a piece of toast. Her stomach felt okay, but there was no sense in testing its limits. Next, she called the laundry plant to tell them she needed the day off. The supervisor on duty hit her with a barrage of profanities, but Mary stood her ground. In the end, he relented, but not before threatening to fire her if she wasn't back first thing the following morning.

Her next call was to Elizabeth. Mary worried she would still be asleep, but the cheery voice on the other end suggested Elizabeth had been awake for a while.

"That would be wonderful! Zach and I can't wait to see you," Elizabeth said. "I've actually been meaning to talk to you anyway. I have some exciting news to share when you get here."

Goosebumps crawled across Mary's arms.

Her last call was the one she had been dreading the most. She dialed Joseph's number and waited, her throat tightening like a vise. Mary gulped the rest of her water and cleared her throat when Joseph answered.

"Hey, babe. I wanted to catch you before you left the house," Mary said, doing her best to sound normal.

"Everything okay?"

"That's actually why I'm calling. I'm feeling a lot better this morning. Whatever bug I had must have worked its way out of my system."

"I still think you need to see a doctor just to be safe."

"I honestly feel great. I might as well go to work today."

The bald-faced lie ate at her like acid. What was wrong with her? The Lord's son was growing inside of her, and she was defiling it with her own sin. She wanted to tell the truth, but she didn't know how. She couldn't tell Joseph about seeing Elizabeth. That would raise all kinds of questions she didn't want to answer right now.

"If you say you're better, then I'll stop bothering you about it. I trust you." Joseph's words dug into Mary's heart like a dagger. "Just promise me you'll tell me if you start feeling sick again."

"I promise."

"Okay, I'll swing by after work to check on you. I love you."

"I love you too." Mary hung up the phone and cried.

CHAPTER 4

Elizabeth was waiting at the bus stop when Mary arrived. She wore a simple, faded house dress, and her graying hair was wrapped in a bun.

"My beautiful, sweet cousin. It's so good to see you!" Elizabeth said. She hugged Mary and immediately jerked away like she'd been shocked.

"What's wrong?" Mary said.

Elizabeth leaned in and whispered, "Are . . . Mary, are you pregnant?"

Mary gasped. "How could you possibly know that?"

"You'll think I'm crazy, but a voice inside me just said you were pregnant. Not really a voice. More like the Holy Spirit was showing me. I don't know. I can't really explain it, but I swear it's true. And you know what else? I was going to wait until we got home to tell you, but I'm pregnant too. Going on five months now." Elizabeth pulled her house dress tight to reveal a slight bump.

Mary took her hands. "You want to hear something that will make you think *I'm* the one who's crazy? I already knew you were pregnant."

Elizabeth leaned against a pole and took a steadying breath. "Why don't you save that story until we get to the house? Zach will want to hear this too."

Zechariah, Zach to anyone who knew him, was sitting on the porch with a cup of coffee when they arrived. A pair of rimless glasses rested halfway down his nose, his brown eyes scanning the newspaper in front of him.

The house behind him was old and worn. The paint was peeling in most places, and the roof was past its prime. There were missing planks along the porch, and the ones that remained were splintered. Although most American citizens would consider the house to be subpar, the average immigrant would see it as luxurious. Even the most basic home was unaffordable for most immigrants, including Mary.

Zach and Elizabeth were the exception when it came to immigrant home ownership. Zach held a prominent position as a Jewish priest. With Judaism being the predominant religion among Middle Eastern immigrants, the job came with a lot of responsibility, but it also provided enough income to afford a decent life for the priest and his family. The government viewed Jewish priests as a necessity to keep the immigrants happy and under control. Jewish temples were a sacred haven for Jewish immigrants, and priests were the lynchpin that kept things running smoothly. The government was happy to subsidize their salaries as long as the priests played their part in keeping the immigrants happy.

The Jews also had their own legal system overseen by a group of Jewish priests known as the Sanhedrin. The United States government allowed it to exist because they saw it as a way for the Jews to keep themselves in check while lessoning the strain on the government's already overburdened court system. The Jewish legal system could handle any issue as long as it only impacted the Jewish community, would be a misdemeanor under U.S. law, and didn't interfere with existing cases or laws of the United States. Since priests played such a huge role in every facet of the Jewish community, it was easy to justify their higher salaries.

Zach looked up from his paper as the two women walked across the front lawn. With a wide grin on his face, he met Mary at the top of the steps with a bear hug that took her by surprise.

"Easy, Zach. You don't want to hurt the baby," Elizabeth said.

Zach looked from Mary to Elizabeth, and then back to Mary.

"It's true," Mary confirmed. "I'm having a baby boy."

Zach turned to Elizabeth and pointed at her stomach.

"Yes, dear. She knows about our baby too."

"Have I stunned you speechless?" Mary asked Zach.

"That's actually part of the story I haven't told you yet," Elizabeth said. "Let's go inside. We have a lot of catching up to do."

Zach brought a tray of pastries and coffee into the living room. The women took the couch, and Zach sat in a nearby recliner.

"I don't really know the best place to start," Elizabeth said. She bit into a warm pastry while contemplating her next words. "You already know I'm pregnant, but what you don't know is that Zach knew about it before I did."

"How?" Mary said, already enthralled.

"You're going to think I've spiked my coffee with a little brandy when you hear this, but God as my witness, it's the truth."

Elizabeth reached for her coffee as Mary leaned in. She glanced at her husband, who gave a consenting nod.

"Zach was alone at the temple about six months ago when a man called out to him. The man said . . . well, there's just no way to tell you this without sounding crazy, Mary. The man said he was an angel."

Mary slumped against the back of the couch with a hand over her mouth. "It was Gabriel, wasn't it?"

Elizabeth's cup rattled as she placed it on the tray. "How did you know that?"

"Because he visited me too." Mary's hands rested on her belly as she spoke.

"When?"

"Why don't you finish your story first? I think it'll help make sense of what happened to me," Mary said.

Elizabeth nodded. "The man said his name was Gabriel. He said God had sent him with a message that I was going to have a baby boy and should name him John. As you can imagine, Zach was pretty freaked out." She smiled at Mary. "I guess you probably were too."

"Something like that," Mary said, recalling the knife she'd pulled on Gabriel.

"Zach couldn't help laughing at the man because doctors told me I was barren years ago. Can you believe he laughed at an angel, Mary? Praise God Gabriel didn't strike him dead right there on the spot."

"So what happened?"

"Gabriel said he was going to take away Zach's voice until the baby was born to prove that God can do anything." Mary looked over at Zach, who nodded and pointed at his throat. "Gabriel told him John is going to be a great man filled with the Holy Spirit, and he'll bring many people to the Lord. Can you imagine? My son is going to be a great man of God!"

Mary felt like someone had lifted a weight off her shoulders. "You have no idea how wonderful it is to hear your story. I felt so alone after what happened to me last night. I didn't think anyone would believe me, much less understand."

Elizabeth reached over and took Mary's hand in both of hers. "And yet, here you are with maybe the only two people in the world who can relate to what you're going through. Now, why don't you tell us what happened last night?"

Mary poured out her heart, revealing every detail of her encounter with Gabriel. "And when I looked back, he was gone," Mary finished. "I tried to tell myself it was just a dream, but I knew it was all true when I saw the pregnancy test."

"Oh, Mary. This is the most amazing news! You're going to have God's son! We have to celebrate. Right, Zach?"

Zach stood from the recliner and plopped down next to Mary, giving her another one of his furious bear hugs.

"I think that's a yes," Mary said.

***

They decided on an upscale restaurant in the nicer part of town. Elizabeth insisted they do something fancy for such a special occasion.

Elizabeth loaned Mary a sleeveless black dress that fell just above her knees. Mary admired herself in the mirror and spun from side to side like an actress showing off for the paparazzi. She cupped the hem of the dress in her hand and let the cool fabric slip between her fingers.

"It looks like it was made for you," Elizabeth said.

Mary gave another twirl in front of the mirror. "It's lovely. And you look beautiful too."

Elizabeth looked down at her full-length blue dress. "I'm amazed I can still fit into this thing."

Zach came up behind Elizabeth and kissed her on the cheek. He walked in front of her while adjusting his tie in an exaggerated fashion.

"Yes, dear. You look very handsome. Now, stop showing off for Mary."

Mary giggled and grabbed his arm. "You look dashing, Zach."

With a slight bow, he offered an elbow to each lady and escorted them to the car.

***

The restaurant was dimly lit. The acoustics allowed one to hear the piano playing in the corner, the soft tinkle of silverware, and the murmur of subdued conversation. Mary felt out of place.

The hostess took them to a table near a giant picture window overlooking a pond with a fountain in the middle. A waiter took their drink orders and returned with three iced teas while they looked over their menus.

The conversation was light and jovial until the main course arrived. The filets, steamed vegetables, and baked potatoes were served alongside a more serious conversation.

"We haven't really talked about Joseph," Elizabeth said, cutting into her steak. "When are you going to tell him?"

Mary stared out the window and plucked at the edge of the tablecloth with her fingers. Just the thought of Joseph racked her with worry and guilt.

"I know it's going to be difficult, Mary, but the sooner you tell him the better. You shouldn't keep this from him."

Mary continued to look out the window in silence. Elizabeth reached across the table and touched her hand.

"Mary."

"I can't do it. He'll break off the engagement, and who can blame him? Nobody in their right mind will believe me. Other than you, of course, but that's only because you have your own little miracle going on." Mary pushed her vegetables around the plate with her fork.

"I think you're selling God a little short, don't you? He put a baby inside of you. Do you really think his plan stops there? Don't you think he has a plan for Joseph too?"

"You're right. Less than twelve hours ago I had an angel in my living room, and now I'm sitting here doubting God. I'm awful."

"No, dear. You're human."

Mary took a bite of her steak. It seemed to melt in her mouth. "Oh my goodness. This is delicious! Here we are having an incredible meal, and I'm ruining it with my pity party. I'm sorry, guys."

"Don't be sorry. Besides, it's not hurting Zach's appetite any."

Mary looked at his plate and saw it was half empty. He gave her a playful smirk before devouring another bite.

Mary let out a deep sigh. "Joseph is coming over tonight. I guess I can tell him then. Would you come with me? He might believe me if you tell him your story too."

"Mary, you know I'd do anything for you, but I really think you should tell him by yourself. I could always call him later if you need me to."

"Okay. Everything is just happening so fast." Mary felt like her life was spinning out of control.

"God doesn't always work at our pace. Sometimes we have to keep up with his."

"How do you always come up with the perfect thing to say?"

Elizabeth smiled. "You get more than just gray hair with old age. You get a little bit of wisdom too. What do you say we get back to enjoying our celebration?"

"I think that's a wonderful idea." Mary raised her glass. "How about a toast? To our sons, and to the Lord who blessed us with them." The three of them brought their glasses together over the middle of the table.

Eating her first big meal in days, Mary stuffed herself full of steak and baked potato, finishing it with a molten chocolate souffle. By the time they got home, Mary was struggling to keep her eyes open. The lack of sleep coupled with a heavy meal had her fighting to stay awake. Elizabeth insisted she get some rest before seeing Joseph later that afternoon. She showed Mary to the guest room, and Mary slipped out of her dress and into the cool sheets.

Despite the day's excitement, Mary fell into a deep and restful sleep. She awoke three hours later to see it was almost four o'clock. Joseph would be at her apartment soon. The thought made her sick to her stomach.

Mary walked into the living room and saw Elizabeth watching the TV with a scowl on her face. The news was covering the most controversial, yet charismatic presidential candidate of the 1984 election. The young and handsome Alexander Herod stood behind a podium in front of thousands of his supporters. His piercing blue eyes and wavy blonde hair played well on the television. The crowd was cheering and chanting his name.

"It makes me want to puke," Elizabeth said when she noticed Mary standing there. "God help us if that man becomes president."

"I think he'll win. His poll numbers keep going up."

"A campaign run on hate, and these people eat it up. I don't get it."

They watched as Herod spoke of the struggling economy, high unemployment, and increasing crime rate. He painted a desolate picture like Vincent Van Gogh creating a masterpiece. He then turned the conversation toward the supposed cause of all these problems: the immigrants were taking jobs from the American people, creating a burden on the average taxpayer, and murdering and raping citizens all over the country.

Herod grabbed the microphone from the podium and walked the stage, owning every square inch of it. He pleaded for a crackdown on immigration while promising to pass new regulations if he became president. One of his more popular campaign promises was a mandatory immigrant census that would require all immigrants to report to a census station once a year. Anyone who failed to show up would either be thrown in jail or deported.

Herod was adamant that immigrants lose access to necessities like jobs and healthcare in the United States unless they had a valid green card. Without the ability to provide for themselves, they would have no choice but to leave the country. He vowed to capture and deport illegal immigrants by any means necessary.

The crowd was electric. Chills ran down Mary's spine.

"Any means necessary. Did you hear that, Mary? That's a slippery slope."

"His fans love it, though."

Elizabeth scoffed. "Like rats eating poison. They don't know it's bad for them until it's too late." She turned off the television.

"Immigrants aren't the problem, and anyone with half a brain knows it. Herod's just deflecting the issue onto us because he knows it's easier to get voters to point the finger at someone besides themselves."

The grandfather clock in the entryway announced the top of the hour. "I should go," Mary said.

"I'll drive you home. I need an excuse to get off this couch anyway. Old and pregnant can be a lazy combination."

The ride to the apartment was a quiet one. Nervousness ate away at Mary like a flesh-eating virus. Elizabeth broke the silence as they pulled into the parking lot.

"I know this is going to be tough, but you can do it."

"I still don't know what I'm going to say to him."

"Just tell him the truth, and let God do the rest." Elizabeth dug in her purse and brought out a bus card. "Zach got this while you were sleeping. It's enough for you to ride the bus to work and come visit us whenever you want. I want you to know you have options, Mary. You're more than welcome to stay with us if things get bad."

Her cousin's generosity overwhelmed Mary. She lunged across the console and hugged Elizabeth tight. "I love you."

"I love you too. Now go on up and get ready. Remember to be strong."

Mary felt all alone as she closed the apartment door behind her. The afternoon with Elizabeth and Zach seemed like memories from a pleasant dream.

As the minutes crawled by, she kept playing out scenarios in her head of how Joseph would react to the news, each one more dreadful than the last. Her heart pounded against her chest like a SWAT team kicking through the front door.

Lost in her own thoughts, a knock at the door startled her. She wiped her sweaty palms against the front of her jeans and opened it. Joseph greeted her with his all too familiar smile. Mary sank into his arms for what she prayed wouldn't be the last time.

"I've been worried about you all day. How are you feeling?"

"Joseph, we need to talk." It was blunt, but Mary needed to get to the point before she lost her nerve.

Joseph searched her face. "Nothing good ever comes from 'we need to talk.'"

She led him over to the couch and pulled him down next to her. "I need to tell you something, but promise me you'll let me finish before you say anything."

"You're scaring me, Mary. What's going on?"

"I woke up last night and saw a man in my apartment—"

"What!"

"The guy said he was an angel named Gabriel. He started glowing and then I could feel the presence of God. He said I'm—"

"Mary."

Mary pushed on. "He said I'm pregnant and going to have a baby that's God's son. After the angel disappeared, I bought a pregnancy test, and he was right. I'm pregnant. This morning I visited my cousin Elizabeth, and she's pregnant too. She said the same angel visited Zach a few months ago. I know this sounds ridiculous, but I swear it's true."

Joseph sat in silence for what seemed like an eternity.

"Joseph, please say something. Please believe me."

"You slut."

The vile words took her breath away, and she felt her heart shatter.

"You lying slut."

"Stop saying that." Mary began to sob.

"Who is he? What's his name?"

"What? There is no he. I told you the baby is from God."

"From God? How stupid do you think I am?" Joseph looked around the room. "If God took the time to send you an angel, then he won't mind sending me one too, right? I could use some divine intervention right about now. Call him down for me. I'll wait."

"It wasn't like that."

"Oh, I'm sure it wasn't. Does this angel happen to work with you at the laundry plant instead of the pearly gates?"

"You can call Elizabeth! Call her right now! She'll tell you it's true!" Mary's worst fears were materializing right before her eyes.

"The Elizabeth you lied about seeing today?"

"I lied because I thought you'd be angry!"

"And you were right!" Joseph snatched an empty glass off the coffee table and hurled it against the wall. His body was shaking. "I should go," he said through clenched teeth.

"Don't go! Not like this."

"How could you do this to me? I gave you everything, Mary. I even saved myself for you. We had something special, and you threw it away for what? A one-night stand? Or was it more like a month? I hope it was worth it."

Mary grabbed his arm as he stood up, but he shook her off. Ignoring Mary's tearful pleas, Joseph threw open the front door and slammed it behind him without another word.

CHAPTER 5

"I believe you," Jackie said between mouthfuls of apple cobbler.

"Really? You're not just saying that to humor me?"

Jackie shook her head. "I wouldn't lie to you, honey." She used her thumb to wipe a spot of caramel sauce from her chin, studied it for a moment, then stuck it in her mouth. "The way I see it, your story's so crazy it has to be true. Surely you'd come up with somethin' more believable if you were tryin' to pull one over on me."

Mary breathed a sigh of relief. She looked around the break room to make sure no one was listening. The last thing she needed was a coworker, or worse, a supervisor hearing her crazy story. Jackie seemed to read her mind.

"Don't you worry about no one else in here. Miss Jackie will give them a piece of her mind if they go buttin' into business that ain't theirs." Jackie turned to the young man sitting at the next table and raised her voice. "Isn't that right, Carl?"

Carl glanced up from his magazine with a puzzled look. "What?"

"Take yourself over to the other side of the room. We don't need you droppin' an ear over here."

"I'm not even listening to you."

"Don't sass me, Carl. You better get movin' before my foot does, if you catch my drift." She kicked the air in his direction and gave a playful smile. "You can help yourself to some of the cobbler in the fridge if you do."

That was all the motivation Carl needed. He scooted back from the table and trotted over to the refrigerator.

"Now where were we?" Jackie said.

"You were telling me why you believe my story."

Jackie snapped her fingers. "That's right! Well, another reason that story don't sound too crazy is because I've seen an angel myself."

"Really?"

"It's been more than thirty years ago, back when I was pregnant with my baby girl, but I remember it like it was yesterday. I was comin' out of the grocery store with my hands full of bags, and it was rainin' like you wouldn't believe. I didn't have an umbrella, and just before I start runnin' across the parkin' lot, a man with an umbrella walks up to me and says, 'Ma'am can I escort you to your car?' He says it just like that. All prim and proper like.

"I told him that would be real nice, and so he walks me to my car with the umbrella over my head the whole way. By the time we get to my car, he's wetter than a drowned cat, and I'm bone-dry. I felt bad for him, but he was smilin' like he hadn't a care in the world.

"Then he looks at my belly and says, 'Congratulations on the baby girl.' I asked him how he knew it was a girl, and he just stood there with that same smile. He held the umbrella while I got in the car. Then when I turned around, he was gone. Poof! Just like that."

"And what makes you think he was an angel?"

Jackie leaned across the table, her arms crossed in front of her. "Because he disappeared, Mary. And what was he doin' leavin' a grocery store when he didn't have no groceries?" She tapped the side of her head with her index finger. "Angels don't need no groceries."

"That's incredible." Mary wondered if Jackie's memory had blurred some details over the years to make her encounter seem more supernatural than it really was, but who was she to question someone's story when she was sitting on a doozy of her own?

Jackie beamed. "Isn't it? It's like we both have our own little guardian angels. So the question is, what are you gonna do now?"

"The first thing I need to do is get Joseph back, but how am I going to do that when he won't even talk to me?"

Jackie shook her head. "You've got it all wrong. It's not how are *you* gonna do it? It's how is *he* gonna do it?"

"I don't think he's going to do anything except find another girl and forget all about me."

"Wrong he, sweetie." She pointed toward the ceiling. "I'm talkin' about the man upstairs. It's all his plan, not yours. And there ain't nobody that can change Joseph's mind but God. I'll admit I'm not the best when it comes to sayin' my prayers at night, but one thing I know is God is the man with the plan. Sometimes it's best to just leave it up to him."

"That sounds like something my cousin would say."

"She sounds like a smart lady."

Mary moved to Jackie's side of the table and kissed her on the cheek. Jackie stood up and gave her a hug.

"Break it up, ladies. Time to get back to work," Carl said on his way out the door.

"Carl, I'm gonna whoop you like your momma should have."

"The cobbler was delicious!" he called over his shoulder.

Jackie shrugged at Mary. "Well, how can I whoop a man who just complimented my cobbler?"

Mary collected her things and returned to work. She spent the rest of the day doing her best to take Jackie's advice and leave her problems to God. It was easier said than done.

CHAPTER 6

Joseph picked up speed as he finished the last leg of his morning jog. Sweat poured from his body, and his lungs burned like someone had dropped a match down his throat. Putting his head down, he sprinted up the driveway and into the front yard, where he dropped to his knees and drank from the hose watering the flowerbed.

Joseph's father stood on the front porch watching his son. The two looked so much alike that Joseph thought looking at his dad was like seeing himself twenty years in the future.

"Did you get it all out of you, son?"

"What?" Joseph took another drink from the hose.

"Everything that's eating you up inside. You looked like a man trying to outrun his problems."

"Something like that," Joseph said as he dropped the hose back into the flowerbed.

"Well, you can't outrun these problems. You have to confront them like a man."

"It's not that easy." It had been four weeks since he'd walked out of Mary's apartment, but the pain of her unfaithfulness still stung like a fresh wound.

His dad shook his head and sighed. "Mary is a sweet girl, and we all loved her very much. But she slept around behind your back and got pregnant. It doesn't take a genius to see what needs to be done here. You need to move on with your life."

"I just need some time to think."

"Think about what? She calls here every day, but you won't even talk to her. Frankly, I'm tired of playing the middle man on the phone. Why don't you just end things? I see your face when she calls, and each time it's like she hurts you all over again."

"We were about to get married, Dad. I can't just act like all those good times never happened. Why can't you get that through your head?"

His dad shoved a finger into Joseph's chest, his face reddening. "You listen to me closely, because I'm only going to say this once. I know you're going through a tough time. I get it. I really do. But disrespect me like that again, and I'll knock you upside the head. I don't care how old you are. We clear?"

"Got it." There was more Joseph wanted to say, but he bit his tongue.

"I want you to cut things off with her for good. I'm done enabling this mess. We clear on that too?" Joseph nodded, and his dad put an arm around him. "Good. Now come inside and get something to eat. Your mother has a stack of pancakes waiting for you."

***

That night Joseph returned to an empty house. He turned on the television and helped himself to some leftover pizza. He thought about Mary while he ate. His dad had been right about ending things with her. It was obvious he couldn't marry her now, but that didn't make it any easier. She had been the love of his life, his perfect soulmate. He kept trying to rationalize the idea of getting back together with her. It was ludicrous, but the more he tried to push the thought from his mind, the harder it dug in.

The phone rang, pulling him out of his thoughts. He didn't have to answer it to know who it was. It was Mary. She had called every night for the past month. Joseph's parents had been more than patient with her, but he had an idea that was about to end based on the conversation he'd had with his dad.

The phone rang until Joseph couldn't take it anymore. He picked up the receiver and slammed it back into its cradle. Then he picked it up again, listened for a dial tone, and dropped it on the floor. There would be no more phone calls tonight.

Joseph turned off the television and took a long, hot shower. By the time he slipped into his favorite pair of gym shorts, all he wanted to do was jump into bed and let his problems fade away until morning. Joseph was asleep almost as soon as his head hit the pillow.

He woke to a breathtaking sunrise pouring in through the bedroom window. The colors were more vibrant than usual. He felt refreshed; his mind was tingling with clarity. He knew what he needed to do. First, he'd apologize to his dad, and then he'd end things with Mary once and for all.

He jumped out of bed and hurried to the living room, where his parents always drank coffee and read the morning paper as the sun came up. It was a morning ritual they had followed religiously since he was a kid, but this morning was different. They weren't there.

Joseph walked to the front window. He noticed the texture of the carpet on his bare feet. It was like his senses were in overdrive. He peered through the blinds and saw his parents' car sitting in the driveway. So they had come home last night, but where were they?

He turned around to see a man standing in the living room with a smile on his face. His blonde hair glowed in the morning light, and his white shirt and linen pants were immaculate.

"Do not be afraid," the man said. "My name is Gabriel, and I have been sent here by God."

"You . . . you can't be him. There's . . . I mean . . . it's not possible." The natural and supernatural had collided in Joseph's living room. His mind struggled to process what he was seeing.

"Joseph, I have some very exciting news for you."

"It's all true, isn't it? Mary was telling the truth." Joseph remembered how he had treated Mary on that fateful night. The angry, hurtful words he'd said to her. Guilt flooded his body like water in a sinking ship. He grabbed the back of the couch for support.

"Yes. Everything she told you is correct."

"I didn't know. I swear I didn't know." He backed against the wall and slid to the floor, burying his face in his hands. "What have I done?"

Gabriel approached Joseph. "It is not about what you've done. It is about what you're going to do."

Joseph looked up at him. "And what's that?"

"Great things, Joseph. Very great things." Gabriel sat next to him and put an arm around his shoulders. A sensation surged through Joseph's body that filled him with a peace strong enough to wash away the guilt he was feeling. "Mary is carrying the Lord's son. The boy will become a great man that will save people all over the world from their sins. Mary needs you right now, Joseph. The Lord needs you. Go back and marry her. Raise the boy to become the man the Lord has willed, and name him Jesus."

"You know everyone's going to think I'm crazy when I tell them about this."

Gabriel smiled. "I hear that a lot. It will be difficult, but that's why the Lord has brought you and Mary together. You will hold each other up when the rest of the world tries to tear you down."

Gabriel removed his arm from Joseph's shoulders, and a bright light exploded across the room, blinding him. When the light faded, he looked around and saw that he was back in bed. The sun was still rising, but the colors had dulled. He sat up and dangled his feet over the side of the bed, letting them brush across the carpet. The texture was no longer intense.

He ran down the hall toward the living room, bumping against the wall and knocking a family portrait to the ground. His parents stared at him over their respective sections of the newspaper.

"Dear, are you okay?" his mom asked.

"I don't know what just broke, but you're paying for it," his dad said.

Joseph searched the room. "Did you guys see a man in here?"

"Yes, son. A man broke into the house, but I fought him off with my coffee mug. We would have called the police, but we didn't want to wake you. How'd you know?"

"Stop it, David," his mom said.

"Stupid questions get stupid answers, Carrie."

"And this is the first time you've seen me this morning, right?" Joseph said.

His dad shook his head and returned to his paper, muttering to himself.

"Of course it is. What's wrong? Did you have a bad dream?" his mom asked.

"It couldn't have been a dream. It was so real. Actually, it was more than real."

"What was?" his mom pressed.

"It was more like a vision." Joseph laughed. "This is crazy."

"That's the first sane thing you've said since you came in here," his dad said.

His mom got up from the recliner. "Why don't you sit down and let me make you some breakfast?"

"No time for breakfast. I've got a lot to do today." He lowered his dad's newspaper and looked him in the eye. "Dad, I'm really sorry about yesterday. I had no right to talk to you like that. Do you forgive me?"

His dad's face softened. "Thank you, son. Of course I forgive you. Is that what's causing all this craziness this morning?"

"Not exactly." Joseph started back down the hall.

"Where are you going?" his mom said.

Joseph turned and smiled. "I've got to get dressed. I need to go see Mary."

CHAPTER 7

Mary dropped her toothbrush into the plastic cup next to the faucet. She checked herself in the mirror and wiped a streak of toothpaste from the corner of her lip. She frowned at the face staring back at her. The bags under her eyes were dark and heavy. Her eyes were bloodshot from crying.

She felt like she was clinging to the edge of sanity. Joseph ignoring her had been horrible, but her father disowning her had made things even worse.

When her mother passed away years ago, her father became a shell of his former self. He turned to alcohol and isolated himself from the rest of the world, including his family. Mary loved her father fiercely, and watching him fall apart had been devastating.

He had erupted into an alcoholic rage when Mary told him about the pregnancy. He demanded she get an abortion and became even more enraged when she refused. The conversation ended with her father saying he never wanted to see her again, and that her mother would be ashamed of the woman she had become.

Feeling more alone than ever, Mary had temporarily moved in with Elizabeth and Zach. They didn't judge her or try to tell her what to do. They just loved her, and that was exactly what she needed.

A loud knock at the front door startled her. She heard Elizabeth whispering to the person on the other side. Mary stuck her head around the corner and locked eyes with the man standing on the porch. Her jaw dropped.

"Mary! Mary, I saw him! Gabriel! I saw him this morning!"

Mary hardly even heard his words as she ran down the hall and into Joseph's arms. He embraced her and looked at her belly like a child seeing snow for the first time.

"It's all true." He looked at her with tears in his eyes. "We're going to have God's son!"

Mary's emotions turned from joy to anger at everything she'd already been through on her own, and she balled up her fists and beat them against his chest. "I already told you that, you big dummy! Then you ran off and left me. Remember?"

Joseph pressed his forehead against hers. "I was an idiot. I don't know what else to say except I'm sorry, and I love you with all my heart." He dropped to one knee. "I know you already said yes, but I want a fresh start from the beginning. Mary, will you marry me?"

Mary's anger vanished like a fine mist. She nodded with tears running down her face. "Yes, you big jerk. Of course I'll marry you."

Joseph sat with her on the porch swing and told her about his encounter with Gabriel. Then he suggested they get married right away so he could be there for her and the baby. He said they could live in Mary's apartment for now and move to something bigger once the baby was born. With all the money he'd saved from living with his parents, he thought they could make it work.

Mary marveled at how God had taken an impossible situation and worked it out in an instant. Yesterday their relationship had been all but over, and today they were moving up the wedding date. Jackie's words played in the back of her mind. *God is the man with the plan. Sometimes it's best to just leave it up to him.* Once again, God had shown that he was faithful. Always.

***

With a kiss goodbye, Joseph left so that Mary could get ready for work. On the bus ride home, the thought of confronting his parents with the news about Mary caused his body to ache with dread. He prayed that his parents would somehow believe him, or at least try to understand. They didn't.

"You have lost your mind," his dad said.

"I know how it sounds, but I swear on my life it's true."

"What a load of crap. It was just a dream!"

"You don't understand. It was too real to be a dream." Joseph had been trying to explain it to them, but they didn't get it. He *suddenly* understood how Mary had felt on the night he left her.

"This is absurd," his dad said. "Do you even hear what you're saying? You're just trying to rationalize getting back together with Mary."

"It's not like that, Dad."

His dad slammed his hand on the table. "Don't tell me what it's like!"

"David, calm down." His mom placed a trembling hand on his arm.

"Calm down? I can't calm down! Our son is talking about marrying a woman who's pregnant with another man's child!" He pointed at Joseph. "You will not embarrass our family like this. Do you have any idea what people will say when you tell them angels are talking to you, and Mary is carrying God's son? We'll be the laughingstock of the Jewish community. Heck, we'll be shunned from the temple! You call Mary right now and tell her it's over."

"No."

His dad's eyes narrowed. "What did you just say to me?"

"We're getting married with or without your consent. I know what I saw this morning. Just because you don't believe me doesn't mean it's not true."

"Get out of my house." His dad's voice shook like a volcano preparing to erupt.

"David, don't," his mom said.

His dad ignored her. "Pack up your stuff and get out!"

Joseph ran to his room and slammed the door. Fear, anger, and love battled inside him like emotional gladiators. He yanked a suitcase from the closet and threw it on the bed. He would take what he could carry and come back for the rest when his parents weren't home.

There was a knock on the bedroom door. His mom stood in the doorway, her eyes full of tears.

"Your father doesn't mean what he said. He's just angry. This will all blow over in a few days."

"Do you really believe that?"

His mom looked away. "Are you sure you won't change your mind about Mary?"

"No." Even though it seemed pointless, Joseph decided to give it one last try. "Will you at least come to the wedding?"

"I'll talk to your father about it."

Joseph shut his suitcase and kissed his mom goodbye. He walked past his dad without a word, opened the front door, and stepped into the new life that awaited him.

CHAPTER 8

The wedding took place in Zach and Elizabeth's backyard. Joseph wore the only suit he owned, a dark blue ensemble with a brilliant red tie and a white button-up shirt. Mary wore Elizabeth's wedding dress, which looked just as stunning as it had when Elizabeth wore it over ten years ago. Mary's ring was a simple gold band purchased from a local pawn shop. Joseph promised to buy her something nicer once his carpentry business took off, but she scoffed at the idea. Joseph had bought the ring with love. Mary thought it was perfect.

Jackie and Carrie were the only other guests besides Zach and Elizabeth. Although Carrie had ultimately attended the wedding, David had refused to be her plus one. Even though his mother didn't seem excited to be there, Mary knew it meant the world to Joseph that she had come.

Jackie had insisted on doing the catering for free. She provided a wide assortment of dishes she referred to as "down home cookin'." Fried chicken, mashed potatoes, sweet potato casserole, fried okra, and homemade biscuits sat on a folding table alongside a generous bowl of gravy. A red velvet cake, topped with a miniature bride and groom, was off to the side on a separate table.

It wasn't the fancy wedding Mary had dreamed about when she was a little girl, but it was beautiful nonetheless. They were surrounded by the people who loved them unconditionally, and the Lord had blessed their marriage. What more could she want?

Everyone celebrated late into the night. As midnight approached, Jackie escorted the newlyweds to her car as the other wedding guests tossed rice in the air. Jackie opened the back door and ushered them inside with a dramatic bow. She climbed into the driver's seat and pulled a chauffeur's hat from the floorboard. Pieces of rice fell from her hair like dandruff as she smashed the hat on top of her head.

"Where to, young lovebirds?"

Mary giggled. "We're only going back to my . . . I mean, *our* apartment. Is this really necessary?"

"Of course! It might only be a trip to your apartment, but it's gonna be the fanciest darn trip you've ever had. Now sit back and enjoy the ride."

Jackie pulled a cassette from the middle console and inserted it into the radio. *Endless Love* poured from the speakers.

"Jackie, did you make us a mixed tape?" Joseph said.

"Comes standard with the wedding night package here at Miss Jackie's Fancy Fleet."

"Jackie!" Mary could feel her ears burning.

"Oh, sweetie. Don't go gettin' all embarrassed. I'm no spring chicken, you know. I learned about the birds and the bees long before you were even born."

Several songs later, they pulled in front of the apartment. Joseph helped Mary out of the car and then swept her off her feet. He carried her up the stairs, pausing at the front door to wave goodbye to Jackie.

Slamming the door behind him, Joseph carried Mary over to the bed and sat beside her. Mary's heart raced as she stared into his eyes.

"My wife," Joseph whispered.

"My husband."

Joseph kissed her. She relished the softness of his lips. Mary locked her hands around his back and pulled him close. Her passion burned like a raging forest fire.

Mary loosened Joseph's tie and tore the blazer off his shoulders. Joseph suddenly pulled away.

"I can't do this," he said.

"What do you mean?"

"I want to, but I just can't."

Mary frowned. "Did I do something?"

"No, of course not."

"Then what?" Mary felt self-conscious. Was he not attracted to her?

Joseph pointed at her stomach.

"The baby?" Mary still didn't understand.

"Not just any baby. *The* baby. A part of God is growing inside of you. That makes all of this feel . . . wrong somehow. Is that weird?"

The tightness in Mary's chest relaxed, and she smiled and held his hand. "After everything that's happened the last couple of months, this is far from weird."

"So you won't be upset if we wait until after the baby's born?"

"Of course not, silly. We have the rest of our lives together. I don't care how long we wait." Her heart overflowed with love for this wonderful man that was finally hers.

Joseph brushed a lock of hair out of her eyes and kissed the tip of her nose. "I love you, Mary."

"I love you too."

They spent the next several hours talking about their future and what God had in store for them. By the time they drifted off to sleep, the sun was already peeking its head over the horizon.

***

Several hundred miles away, Alexander Herod was preparing for a long day of speeches, interviews, and hopefully a victory party. Today was Election Day.

CHAPTER 9

The election was over before polling stations had even closed. Exit polls showed Herod winning by a landslide in almost every state. Immigrants across the nation watched with dismay as a Herod presidency became a reality. Big changes were coming, and they spelled disaster for immigrants.

Things became even more bleak when most of the open House and Senate seats went to Herod's party. With Congress now on his side, there would be no stopping his agenda.

Herod's first order of business was to create an immigrant census. Going forward, green cards would only be good for one year, and they would have to be renewed at a designated census station prior to their expiration date. Failure to renew your green card would put you on a national registry that would keep you from being legally employed, applying for any type of federal aid, enrolling your children in school, or receiving treatment at a hospital. Any business or individual caught assisting an undocumented immigrant would face severe penalties, including prison. The message was clear: renew your green card every year, or be forced to leave the country.

Herod argued the census and registry would crack down on illegal immigration and rampant crime. Anyone convicted of a crime would lose their green card and immediately be deported.

A green card renewal tax would fund the plan, which meant American citizens wouldn't have to pay a dime. This made the initiative even more popular.

Anti-immigrant sentiment was at an all-time high, and anyone speaking out against the bill was met with instant backlash. Few members of Congress were willing to criticize it out of fear of losing their seat in the next election.

By the time Herod was sworn in as President of the United States, the bill was all but a done deal. They presented the Herod Reformation Act to Congress during Herod's first week in office, and it was approved two weeks later. He ordered the first official census to occur within the next few months. Although it was a daunting task, Herod was adamant it could be done. The government already had a list of legal immigrants. The first census would simply require them to report to their local census station to receive a new green card that expired in one year. This would be the first stepping stone to enforcing restrictions on things like employment and federal aid to illegal immigrants.

President Herod's reign of terror had officially begun.

CHAPTER 10

Mary looked up the flight of stairs like she was standing at the base of Mt. Everest. Entering her eight month of pregnancy, things she used to do with ease now required an inordinate amount of effort. With a groan, she started up the stairs, one hand gripping the metal railing and the other holding the day's mail.

Once inside the apartment, she eased herself onto the couch and propped her feet on the coffee table with a great sigh. Moments later someone knocked on the door.

"You've got to be kidding me."

She struggled off the couch and looked through the peephole to see a delivery man standing on the other side of the door. She slid back the lock and opened it.

"I'm sorry to bother you, ma'am, but I have a letter I need you to sign for."

She took the clipboard and scribbled her name along the dotted line. Closing the door behind her, Mary noticed the bright red *URGENT* stamped underneath the return address. It was from the United States Immigration and Naturalization Service. Mary didn't have to open it to know what it was. It had been all over the news the past couple of weeks.

She tore open the envelope and read through the papers. The first was a standard letter informing her and Joseph of the new green card regulations. The rest of the pages were registration forms and instructions on what to do on the day of the census. Mary thought the entire process was ridiculous and shook her head.

Joseph came home a couple of hours later. He danced over to the couch and presented Mary with a handful of wildflowers.

"Flowers for me?" Mary asked.

"The best money can't buy. I saw them in the field behind the workshop and thought you'd like them." He bent down and kissed her.

"I love them." She pulled the bouquet to her face and breathed in the sweet fragrance.

Joseph dropped to his knees and placed his cheek against her stomach. "How's my little man doing?"

"Moving and kicking nonstop."

"I can feel him. God's son is kicking my face." Joseph laughed. "How many people can say that?"

He sat next to Mary and began massaging her shoulders. She closed her eyes, relishing the relief to her aching muscles.

"What's this?" He reached over and grabbed the census papers.

Mary opened her eyes. "Oh, that's our census information. Exciting stuff."

Joseph leafed through the pages. "Bethlehem? We have to go all the way to Bethlehem to register? That's like a two-hour bus ride!"

"The news said they're spreading everyone out to reduce overcrowding. I guess we drew the short straw."

"What a bureaucratic nightmare. They couldn't send us somewhere a little closer like Philadelphia?"

"Apparently not."

Joseph threw the papers on the table and returned his attention to Mary's shoulders. "Whatever. I'll get our bus tickets tomorrow. I just hate that you have to make that long trip. You're going to be miserable."

"Let's stay positive. Besides, all you have to do is rub my back all day, and I'll be fine."

Joseph wrapped his arms around her and kissed the back of her neck. "It's a deal."

CHAPTER 11

Dawn was still a couple of hours away when Mary and Joseph left for Bethlehem. The wind outside howled, and frost covered the apartment's windows. Mary listened to the weather forecast on the radio as Joseph filled a backpack with food, water, and their census paperwork. The weatherman was calling for an ice storm sometime between late afternoon and early evening. Mary and Joseph wanted to get to the census station early so they could make it home before the storm hit.

Mary's throat burned as she breathed the frigid air. She pulled a scarf over her face so that only her eyes were showing. She lowered her head and took Joseph's gloved hand as they walked down the stairs.

The walk to the bus stop was brutal, and the flimsy partition surrounding the bench was useless against the cold. When the bus arrived, the door creaked open, and warm air rushed out to greet them. The driver was an elderly man whose smile was as warm as the interior of the bus. Tufts of white hair peeked out from underneath his hat.

"Good morning, folks. Where you headed?"

"Bethlehem," Joseph said.

"Bethlehem, huh? For the census?"

"Yes sir."

"Couldn't have picked a worse day to be having this. They're saying one heck of an ice storm is headed this way."

"That's what we heard. We're hoping to get there early enough to beat the storm," Joseph said.

"You and about a thousand other people. I've got a buddy down there who says the line is already wrapped around the building."

Mary gripped Joseph's arm. "We're going to get stuck down there. I just know it!"

"We'll be fine. I'm sure the line will move fast once it opens."

"Come on up and have a seat. I'll get you there as fast as I can," the driver said.

Mary and Joseph found a pair of empty seats behind the driver. Mary fell into a restless sleep while Joseph watched the world race by out the window.

When they arrived in Bethlehem, the sun was hiding behind a blanket of thick, gray clouds. It gave the morning a dreary and ominous look. Mary thought she could almost feel the storm working its way toward the city.

The high school gymnasium serving as the census station bloomed into view as the bus rounded a corner. Mary looked at the swarm of people surrounding the building. Any attempt at an orderly line had disintegrated into a ball of chaos.

Mary and Joseph exited the bus and joined the mayhem. People of all races and ages were crammed into the parking lot like toys in a claw machine. There were police officers scattered along the outskirts of the crowd, but not enough to provide any real sense of protection.

"What do we do now?" Mary said.

"The only thing we can do. Wait for our turn."

"I'm freezing."

Joseph took her into his arms. Mary buried her face in his jacket. Her cheeks and the tip of her nose were numb.

An hour later a wave of cheers rippled across the parking lot. Mary saw movement at the front of the building; the doors had opened.

They inched their way toward the building as the hours went by. Mary was still miserable, but the body heat from the compacted crowd made the cold a little more tolerable.

At lunchtime, Mary sat on the ground eating a peanut butter sandwich. She noticed a little girl watching her from the safety of her mother's legs. The girl stared at her lunch with a longing that tugged at Mary's heart. She held out the rest of her sandwich to the girl, but her mother smiled and shook her head.

"It's okay," Mary said. "I want her to have it."

"No English," the mother said.

"Please, take it." Mary offered the sandwich to the mother while nodding.

The woman hesitated, then took it from Mary's hands. "Gracias," she said, bowing her head.

She gave the sandwich to her daughter, who devoured it in an instant. The little girl smiled at Mary with lips caked in peanut butter. It gave Mary a maternal longing for the days when her own son would smile at her in the same way. Her hands drifted to her stomach at the thought of her future little family.

Four hours later, they made it to the front door of the gymnasium. Once inside, they discovered another long line leading to a row of tables manned by government officials. As they neared the front of the line, they heard a soft pinging against the metal roof. Mary looked out the nearest window and saw what she had been fearing all day—ice.

CHAPTER 12

"Next!"

Mary and Joseph approached the table. A plump, middle-aged woman looked up from her computer.

"Registration and ID," she said.

Joseph handed her a stack of forms with their identification on top.

"And your payment?"

Joseph pulled several crumpled bills from his pocket and laid them on the table. The woman counted the money and dropped it into a bank bag. She keyed their information into the computer, stamped their registration, and pointed to another line of people standing in front of a camera.

"Take your registration over to the gentlemen working the camera, and he'll take care of your green cards. You'll have one year to register your child after it's born. A birth certificate will be sufficient until then. Just be sure to bring the little one with you next year, or they'll deport all of you."

"Thank you very much. Have a nice day," Mary said.

"Next!" the woman hollered over their shoulders.

***

Ice pellets rained from the sky as they left the high school. Joseph helped Mary across a parking lot that had turned into an ice skating rink. They passed hundreds of people still waiting in line. Children clung to their parents for warmth and husbands consoled their wives.

It was already dark by the time they reached the bus stop. The street lamp towering over them cast a deceivingly warm glow. Mary's teeth chattered, and her body shivered underneath multiple layers of clothing.

"The bus will be here any minute," Joseph said.

"I su-su-sure h-hope s-s-so. I'm about t-t-to freeze."

A family of four approached the bus stop. The husband and wife guided their children across the slippery sidewalk.

"No more buses tonight," the husband said.

"Seriously?" Joseph said.

"The city's shutting down all public transportation until the storm blows over. They said it's going to be worse than they thought. You guys better find someplace warm."

Joseph shook his head. "You've got to be kidding me."

Mary sunk into Joseph as the family continued down the sidewalk. She was too exhausted to cry.

Joseph nudged her and pointed across the street at a gas station with a bank of pay phones. "Look over there. I can call around and find a hotel room while you go inside and warm up. Sound good?"

Mary thought anything would be better than waiting in an ice storm for a bus that would never come. She nodded her head, and they navigated their way across the treacherous road.

Mary and Joseph walked through the sliding doors of the gas station and into the welcoming warmth. The inside of the building was buzzing with activity.

They looked for a place where Mary could rest, but there weren't any chairs or benches to be found. Joseph led Mary over to a coin-operated donkey ride to the left of the front doors. The paint was chipped in several places, and one of its legs was missing. The dilapidated donkey told a story of hundreds of children begging their parents for a ride over the years.

"Here. Sit on this until I get back."

"Are you out of your mind? I'll break that thing!"

"No you won't. Look how sturdy it is." Joseph rocked the donkey back and forth. "See? It's perfect."

"I don't think so," Mary said, horrified.

"We don't have the luxury of being picky. It's this or nothing. Now, let's get you up there."

Mary glanced around the store. "I can't believe I'm doing this."

Joseph helped her onto the donkey. She sat sideways with her back resting against the window.

"How do you feel?" Joseph asked.

"Ridiculous."

"Perfect. Do you want a quarter in case you get bored?"

"Why don't you zip it and find us a hotel?"

Joseph laughed and patted her leg. He walked out of the building and back into the icy night. The wind rattled the doors as they closed behind him.

***

Joseph found an open pay phone and dug a quarter out of his pocket. He dialed the operator and asked to be connected to the hotel closest to the gas station.

"Thank you for calling Bethlehem Inn. How can I help you?"

"Yes, I'd like to book a room for the night, please."

"I'm sorry, sir, but there's no room at our inn. We're all booked up."

"Then can you give me the number to another hotel nearby?"

"I'd be happy to, but I don't know that you'll have much luck. Every hotel is full because of the storm."

"I don't have anywhere else to go, so let's hope luck is on my side. What's the number?"

Joseph called the next hotel, but they were full as well. The cycle repeated itself until he had worked his way through every hotel in Bethlehem.

He looked at Mary through the window. Her hair was a mess, and her makeup was streaked. She had never looked more beautiful.

Joseph marveled at how lucky he was to have such an amazing woman in his life, and he was forever thankful that God had brought them back together. At the same time, he felt like such an incredible failure. His job was to take care of his family, but all he'd done was strand his pregnant wife in the middle of an ice storm with nowhere to go. He'd failed her, and he'd failed God.

Mary glanced outside and saw Joseph watching her. She slapped the rear of the donkey and pulled on the reins like she was about to take off. Joseph laughed despite their dire situation. He put aside his pity party and donned the look of confidence he needed to make Mary feel safe.

***

"Well?" she said when he came back inside.

Joseph pulled off his gloves and blew into his hands. "Every hotel is booked. There's not a single room in this whole town."

Mary felt disheartened. "So now what?"

"I think we should find the nearest shelter."

"Are you crazy? I don't want to spend the night with hundreds of strangers."

Joseph eased her off the donkey. "It's either that, or we sleep outside. We don't really have a choice."

"I think I can help." A man who looked old enough to be their father approached them, wearing a flannel lumberjack shirt and faded denim jeans. His black beard and work boots completed the rustic ensemble. "The name's Ray Wilmington."

Joseph shook his hand. "I'm Joseph, and this is my wife Mary."

"Pleasure to meet you. I couldn't help but overhear your conversation. I own a car dealership that's only a couple of miles from here. The waiting room's big and has some comfortable couches. Much better than anything you'll get over at the shelter. The room is yours for the night if you want it. Free, of course."

"I . . . I don't know what to say." Mary felt ashamed of herself. The thought of having to share a room with a bunch of strangers had appalled her, and here was Ray, selflessly offering his own place to people he'd never met.

"I don't mean to sound ungrateful, but why are you doing this for us?" Joseph asked.

"Just helping a young couple in need. I don't blame you for being skeptical. I probably would be too." Ray pulled a business card from his wallet. "Here's my card to prove I own a dealership. Jason over at the counter can vouch for me too."

Joseph studied the card. "Ray, what you're offering is more than generous. I don't know how to thank you."

"Buy me a cup of coffee on your way out of town, and we'll call it even."

Joseph looked over at Mary, who nodded. "It's a deal," Joseph said.

The three of them crammed into Ray's Ford pickup truck, with Joseph tucked in the middle. The engine roared to life, and Ray eased the truck into the empty street.

A few minutes later, they pulled into the dealership. The high beams illuminated countless rows of ice-covered vehicles. Ray parked in front of a building lined with floor to ceiling windows. The only light came from somewhere in the back.

Ray unlocked the front door and stuck his head inside. "Darin! You in there? It's me, Ray!" He looked at Mary and Joseph. "Darin's one of my security guys. It's best to let him know you're here before you go inside. Good way to catch a bullet if you don't." He chuckled when he saw their reaction. "I'm only joking. Kind of."

Footsteps echoed from the other side of the room. A beam of light danced along the wall before settling on their faces. Mary squinted against the glare.

"Darin, put that thing down before you blind me," Ray said.

"Sorry, boss. Just making sure."

Darin flipped several switches along the nearest wall, and the room lit up like a roman candle. Darin was much less intimidating in the light. His face looked like he was in his early twenties, but he had the lanky body of a teenager working his way through puberty.

"Darin, I'd like you to meet Mary and Joseph. They need a place to stay for the night, so I'm putting them up in here."

"Sounds good, boss. I could use the company for a change."

"I've got some blankets in the storage closet, and there's plenty of food in the break room. Make them feel at home."

"You got it," Darin said.

Ray turned his attention to Mary and Joseph. "Darin will be here all night if you need anything, and we've got a backup generator in case the power goes out. I'll swing by at dawn to get things squared away before we open." Ray looked outside and shrugged. "*If* we open."

Ray's incredible generosity humbled Mary. She hugged him when he turned away from the window. "You're a good man, Ray. You'll never know how big this is. It goes way beyond just helping me and Joseph."

Ray smiled. "I'm not sure what that means, but I'm sure you'd tell me if I was supposed to know. I'm just glad I could help."

"Go on home, boss. The storm's getting worse. I'll take it from here."

The ice was changing over to snow. Ray got in his truck, and the three of them watched him pull out of the dealership. Once the taillights disappeared into the white abyss, Darin led Mary and Joseph into the break room. He took two frozen dinners from the freezer.

"You guys hungry?"

"Starving," Mary said.

Darin threw the dinners in the microwave. "We'll let these cook while I show you around. Follow me."

They crossed the showroom floor, where a Jaguar, Mustang, Ram, and Bronco stood like giant trophies. Next to the showroom was a waiting room with several chairs, two couches, a table covered with magazines, and a wooden console television.

"You guys are going to love these couches. I've caught a wink or two on them myself, but shhhhhh." Darin placed a finger against his lips and winked. "Don't tell the boss."

Mary ran her hand along the plush cushions. "Joseph, feel this. It's softer than our bed."

"You guys make yourselves comfortable. I'll be back with your dinner and some blankets."

Darin disappeared between the Ram and Mustang as they seemed to watch over the waiting room and its new occupants.

CHAPTER 13

A sharp pain jolted Mary from a deep sleep. She winced while cradling her belly. The meatloaf and mashed potatoes seemed to have come back with a vengeance.

The pain subsided after a couple of minutes. Mary closed her eyes and settled back into the couch. She had almost fallen asleep when the cramps returned with a suddenness that made her gasp. The pain rolled through her stomach like an angry wave, and a dull ache throbbed in her lower back. A few minutes later, the pain disappeared once again.

Mary rose from the couch and wandered over to the frosted windows facing the parking lot. She drew a heart through the frost like she had as a child and put her and Joseph's initials inside of it while smiling at the nostalgia. Wiping it away with the sleeve of her shirt, Mary peered out the window. The parking lot had turned into a winter wonderland. Several inches of snow covered the vehicles.

The cramps hit her again with a viciousness that caused her to double over. Panic set in. *Surely not,* she thought to herself. *The due date is still three weeks away.*

Although she tried to deny the unthinkable situation playing out before her, Mary was forced to accept her worst fear when the cramps continued to grow stronger. She was about to have a baby.

Mary shook Joseph's shoulder. He snorted and mumbled something unintelligible.

"Joseph, wake up. I think it's time."

He looked up at her through half-lidded eyes. "Ray's here? It's still dark out."

"Not that kind of time. I mean it's *time*. I think I'm having contractions. The baby's coming."

"What!" Joseph rolled off the couch and leapt to his feet. "Okay, okay. Don't panic. Everything's fine. We're going to be just fine. Darin! We're having a baby over here!" Joseph ran both hands through his hair.

Mary heard Darin's feet pounding against the tile. The room exploded in florescent light as he hit the switches.

"A baby? Right now?" Darin's eyes were wide.

Mary rubbed her belly. "I think so."

"How far apart are the contractions?" Joseph said.

"I don't know. How far apart should they be?" Mary tried to remember what she'd read in the birthing book Jackie had given her, but she was drawing a blank.

Joseph shrugged. "I have no idea."

"I'll call an ambulance," Darin said.

"No ambulance," Mary said. "We don't have insurance. We have a midwife back home, but a lot of good that does me right now."

"You want me to call Ray and see if he'll drive you home?" Darin said.

"Um, no. I'm not getting stuck in the snow and having this baby on the side of the road."

"Let's just go to the hospital," Joseph said.

"Absolutely not. We'd be in debt for the rest of our lives." Mary glanced around the room. "We'll have to do it here."

"Uh, I'm going to have to go with a big fat no on that one," Darin said. "People don't have babies in a car dealership."

"First time for everything, Darin. Our midwife showed us what to do. We'll be fine. Can you grab us some towels and warm water?" Mary said.

Joseph shook his head. "How are you being so calm?"

"Shock most likely. Do you realize things will never be normal again after tonight?"

Joseph smiled and kissed her lips. "I think things quit being normal months ago."

Darin returned with several shop towels and a yellow mop bucket with a squeaky wheel. Water sloshed over the sides as he maneuvered it around the furniture. He stopped in front of the couches and used one towel to wipe the sweat from his forehead.

"Okay guys, what's next?"

***

Bethlehem was a ghost town. The storm had dumped inches of ice and snow. Businesses, temples, and schools were all closed.

When Ray heard the news about Mary, he had followed a snow plow all the way to the dealership. The drive had been treacherous, and he had been fortunate not to end up on the side of the road like all the other vehicles he passed along the way.

Now, he sat on the floor next to Mary, dabbing her forehead with a wet towel. She rested on a row of couch cushions with a blanket covering her from the waist down. Joseph sat at her feet while Darin paced the building like a caged animal.

"I see the head!" Joseph said. "Push, Mary!"

"I am pushing," Mary said between clenched teeth.

"Push harder!"

She glared at him over the blanket. "If I could push harder, I would."

"Okay, okay. I'm sorry. It's just that we're so close."

Mary pushed with every ounce of strength she had left. She grabbed Ray's arm, her fingernails digging into his flesh. Just when she thought she couldn't take the pain any longer, an intense wave of relief coursed through her body.

"You did it!" Joseph cried.

A tiny wail floated out from underneath the blanket, and Mary burst into tears. She had never heard a more beautiful sound. Joseph wrapped him in one of Ray's sweatshirts, and Mary laid eyes on her son for the first time. His skin was a blotchy mixture of purples and reds. His black hair was a wet and tangled mess.

"He's perfect," Mary said.

"Congratulations," Ray said. "You kids did great."

Ray and Darin excused themselves to the back of the building to give the new parents some time alone. Joseph helped Mary into a sitting position and handed Jesus to her. They sat on the floor and prayed over their newborn baby.

Mary didn't argue when Joseph suggested she get some sleep. He took Jesus from her arms and left her to rest while he wandered the building with his son.

***

Ray smiled when he saw Joseph standing in the doorway of his office and motioned for Joseph to join him. "There's nothing more special than when a father holds his child for the first time. It seems like only yesterday I was holding my own little girl."

Joseph took a seat across from Ray's desk. "How many children do you have?"

"Just the one. She's been grown and gone for a while now. She's married and has a family of her own." Ray grabbed a picture of them from his desk and showed it to Joseph. "They live in Arizona, so I don't get to see them much."

"You have a beautiful family, Ray."

Ray leaned back in his chair while admiring the photograph. "I can't help but think of them when I look at your family. I try to imagine them in your situation, and it breaks my heart. It makes me want to do everything I can to help you because that's what I'd want someone to do for my little girl." He sat the picture back on the desk. "I called a doctor buddy of mine and told him what's going on. He's agreed to check on your baby for free once the roads are clear."

"That's incredibly generous. Thank you."

Ray waved a hand at him. "It's no trouble. He owes me a favor anyway. But I have another offer for you to consider. The buses are down until tomorrow, and even then you don't want a newborn baby on a long road trip. My place has an upstairs that's not being used. It's got a bedroom and a bathroom. Basically its own little apartment. I've got way more space than one man needs, and I'd like for your family to stay with me until you feel like traveling."

Joseph shook his head at Ray's endless generosity. "We couldn't possibly accept that. It's way too much."

Ray gave a warm smile. "Please, I insist. If you say no, you're going to hurt my feelings."

Joseph looked at Jesus. He felt tears in his eyes. "Thank you, Ray. I don't know how I can ever repay you for this."

"I don't expect you to. Accepting my offer is thanks enough." Ray stood and arched his back. "There's no sense in risking the roads right now. They should thaw some by this afternoon, and then we can head over to my place." Ray nodded toward Jesus. "You want me to watch your boy so you can rest?"

"No thanks. I'm fine."

Ray chuckled and patted him on the shoulder. "You might as well get used to being tired. You've got a lot of sleepless nights in your future."

CHAPTER 14

Ray pulled up to a colonial style home with a decorative front door flanked by a pair of towering pillars. Once inside, the entryway opened into a spacious dining room. Beyond that was a living room and then a kitchen. Long halls to the left and right led to a myriad of other rooms.

"It's gorgeous," Mary said. She had never been inside a more beautiful home.

"Thank you. Like I said, it's a bit much for one person. It'll be nice having company for a change." Ray led them upstairs to a mini living room with a bathroom and bedroom on opposite sides. "I've still got Amy's bassinet somewhere up in the attic. If you give me a minute, I'll bring it down and clean it up for you."

Ray left to search the attic while Joseph and Mary sat on the edge of the bed admiring their son. Joseph placed a finger in the palm of Jesus's hand. His tiny fingers closed around it.

"Look at that grip," Joseph said.

"He's got strong hands like his daddy."

"You know what's funny? I think he looks like me. I know that sounds crazy, but I swear he does."

"It's not crazy. He can't look like God, so why wouldn't God make him look like you?"

Ray returned to the room, pushing a bassinet in front of him. It had seen better days, but it still looked serviceable.

"I wiped it down and got all the dust off. Just need to grab some sheets, and it'll be good to go."

The doorbell rang. Ray disappeared down the stairs and returned carrying a box of diapers with a plastic sack on top. A short man in glasses trailed behind him. The light from the ceiling fan reflected off his bald head.

"Mary, Joseph, I'd like you to meet Dr. Mathis. This is the guy I was telling you about."

"Please, call me Edward. I hear congratulations are in order. How is Mom feeling this evening?"

"Pretty good. Just tired and sore," Mary said.

"All perfectly normal. Your body has gone through a lot over the last twenty-four hours."

Edward placed his medical bag on the bed and pulled out a blood pressure instrument. He wrapped the cuff around Mary's arm and inflated it. He looked at the gauge and nodded as the cuff deflated with a sharp hiss.

"We appreciate you taking the time to come out here," Joseph said.

Edward examined Mary's stomach. "My pleasure. When Ray told me about your situation, I didn't give it a second thought. Besides, I've been stuck at the hospital since yesterday and needed a change of scenery."

"And he's come bearing gifts," Ray said as he kicked at the box of diapers on the floor.

"Oh, that's nothing really. Just some diapers and a couple of hospital onesies from the supply closet. I thought you might need them with you being so far from home."

"You're a lifesaver," Mary said.

"No trouble at all." Edward shined a penlight into her eyes. "Well, everything looks perfectly normal. All you need is rest and fluids. Take some ibuprofen for any pain, and a warm bath will do you some good once you feel up to it. Now, let's have a look at the little one."

Joseph placed Jesus on the bed. Edward unwound the blankets swaddled around him and removed the makeshift cotton diaper held in place with a safety pin. Edward placed a stethoscope against his bare chest, and Jesus flinched against the cold metal. A stream of pee splashed the doctor's outstretched arm. Edward quickly covered the boy's waist with a blanket while laughing.

"Oh my goodness! I'm so sorry," Mary said, mortified.

"Don't worry. Happens all the time. Something about removing a boy's diaper sets him off like a ticking time bomb."

"So how is he?" Mary asked after the doctor had finished looking over Jesus.

"A strong, healthy boy. Nothing out of the ordinary."

"Praise God," Mary said.

"You'll need to get an official checkup in the next few days. Blood tests and all that fun stuff. Do you have a pediatrician back home?"

"Not officially, but my cousin has one she really likes."

"Perfect. Make sure you get in touch with them as soon as you can. I know doctors are expensive without healthcare, but skipping checkups with a baby is a dangerous game you don't want to lose."

Although his voice was gentle and kind, Mary noticed the seriousness in his eyes. "We'll be sure and call the hospital first thing tomorrow."

Edward put a diaper on Jesus, swaddled him, and handed him back to Joseph. Then he wished them good night and followed Ray downstairs.

Mary marveled at the way God had provided for her family during this difficult time. God had put the right people in their life at just the right time. First Ray, and now Edward. She closed her eyes and gave a fervent prayer of thanks.

Ray returned thirty minutes later with a tray of cornbread and three bowls of chicken and dumplings. They ate in silence, seemingly too famished to speak, but once the bowls were empty, the conversation flowed.

"So what do you two do for a living?" Ray asked.

"I own a carpentry business, and Mary works at a laundry plant."

"Do you enjoy it?"

"I love it. I have a passion for taking regular pieces of wood and turning them into something beautiful."

"And what about you, Mary?"

"Sorting other people's laundry isn't what I'd call my dream job, but it provides a paycheck that I'm grateful for."

"That doesn't sound very glamourous," Ray said.

"It's not, but I believe God has a plan and purpose for everything. I know there's a reason he has me working there."

"And what do you think that reason is?"

Mary shrugged. "Who knows? Maybe it's keeping me humble, or maybe I'm there to show someone God's love. I think we're all a tiny piece of God's puzzle, but only he knows how we fit into the finished picture. I just go where he moves me."

Ray stared at the wall behind her while swirling the ice in his empty glass.

"I'm sorry, did I say something wrong?" Mary said, noticing the sudden change in his demeanor.

Ray blinked and turned his gaze back to her. "What? No, of course not."

"Does religion make you uncomfortable? I shouldn't have brought it up, but it's such a big part of my life."

"It's not that."

Ray paused, stroking his beard with his thumb and index finger. He stood up and walked into the bedroom. Mary looked at Joseph, who shrugged, looking just as confused as she was. Ray returned with a framed picture of three people sitting on a dock with their feet dangling in the water. The one on the right was a younger and slimmer version of himself. There was a teenage girl in the middle, and another woman on the left. Ray handed the picture to Mary.

"This is me with my wife and daughter almost ten years ago. We used to go to the lake every summer and rent a cabin for two weeks. We made some wonderful memories there."

"I didn't know you were married," Joseph said.

"Used to be. Laura was diagnosed with a brain tumor not too long after this picture. She passed away a few months later."

Mary gasped. "Ray, I'm so sorry."

"Our faith was strong before Laura died. We went to temple every week and prayed multiple times a day. We were good people, just like the two of you.

"The brain tumor took us by surprise, but I knew in my heart God would heal her. We prayed for a miracle, but she went through a kind of pain and torment I wouldn't wish on my worst enemy. Watching her slowly wilt away was the hardest thing I've ever had to do, and I can't imagine how hard it was on her. It took a huge toll on our daughter too.

"After my wife passed, Amy became a totally different person. My bright and bubbly daughter turned into a withdrawn, depressed shell of her former self. I couldn't help but wonder where God was through all of that, because he sure wasn't with us. It was around that time I decided either God didn't care about my family, or he didn't exist. Either way, I was done. I washed my hands of him and never looked back.

"You think we're all pieces of some big galactic puzzle, and maybe you're right. I used to think the same thing. But any puzzle that needs my family to go through what they did is a puzzle I have no interest in being a part of."

Ray cleared his throat and looked away. Tears rolled down Mary's cheeks. Her heart broke for the man standing in front of her. She tried to imagine losing Joseph in the same way Ray had lost his wife, but she couldn't. The pain was too unimaginable.

"You have no reason to believe me, but God is closer to us now than ever before," Joseph said as he wiped his eyes with a napkin. "I don't always understand his ways either, but they're good, Ray. That much I know."

"I'm glad you find comfort in that. I really am. Maybe I'll find comfort again myself someday, but not today."

"I'll pray that you do," Mary said.

"If you'll both excuse me, I think I'll call it a night. I have to be at the dealership early in the morning, but you two make yourselves at home while I'm gone. What's mine is yours, and I really mean that." Ray gave them a smile, but Mary saw the sadness behind it.

"I'll make some calls this evening to see if we can arrange for someone to pick us up, but I'm not sure when they'll be able to make it out here," Joseph said.

"I hope you'll stay at least another couple of nights, but if you decide to leave tomorrow, be sure to swing by the dealership on your way out. You mind if I peek in the bedroom and say goodnight to Jesus?"

"Of course not," Mary said.

Ray walked to the bedroom with Mary and Joseph trailing behind him. The way he smiled at Jesus broke Mary's heart. She could see him remembering the days when his daughter was the same age, back to a time full of happiness and innocence. Mary didn't know when Jesus would change the world, but she prayed he would start by changing Ray's heart.

CHAPTER 15

Joseph called his parents to tell them about Jesus, but he didn't bother asking for a ride home. His mom seemed somewhat excited about the news, but his dad only muttered a brief congratulations before handing the phone back to his mom. It wasn't much, but at least he was talking to him again. One step at a time.

His next call was to Jackie. She offered to bring them home before he could even ask. Since the side roads were still dangerous, Joseph thought it would be best for Jackie to wait a couple of days before making the trip to Bethlehem.

Mary and Joseph felt right at home with Ray. Every night after work, Ray's first stop was always the bassinet to check on Jesus. Then the adults would spend the evening talking and playing cards around a folding table in front of the fireplace.

After a game of Crazy Eights on their last night together, Ray got up from the table and stood in front of the fireplace. "I need to talk to you guys."

"Everything okay?" Joseph said, concerned.

"There's something I've been wrestling with that I can't get out of my mind. I want you to stay here in Bethlehem. I know you have a hard life back home."

"What's that have to do with staying in Bethlehem?" Mary asked.

"I want to offer you a job, Mary. There's a secretary position at the dealership that's been open for a while. I don't know what you make at the laundry plant, but I'm sure you'll make more working for me."

"But I don't have any experience doing that kind of work." Mary looked to Joseph. He could see the uncertainty in her eyes, but Joseph felt God's hand at work in what was transpiring.

"You don't need any. You'll be perfect for it. And Joseph, your business will thrive in a city like this. I've got all kinds of leads to help you get started here."

Ray's unexpected offer stunned Joseph. "I honestly don't know what to say."

"Before you say anything, there's something else," Ray continued. "I want your family to live here with me. You pay for food and part of the bills, and we'll call it even. That'll let you save up for a place of your own someday. What do you think?"

"But . . . why?" Joseph said as Mary's mouth dropped open.

Ray laughed and threw up his hands. "I have no idea. I know it sounds crazy, especially coming from someone you've only known for a few days. I can hardly believe I'm saying it myself."

"Ray, that's an amazing offer, and I hope you don't take this the wrong way, but what's the catch?" Mary said.

A log in the fire broke apart, sending a mist of sparks up the chimney with a crackle. Ray sat down at the table and held each of their hands.

"I shared a lot with you the other night. Do you remember?"

Mary squeezed his hand. "Of course we do."

"When I went to bed that night, my heart stirred like nothing I've ever felt before. For the first time since Laura died, I felt completely at peace. Before I knew what I was doing, I was on my knees praying to a God I wasn't even sure existed."

"What did you pray for?" Mary asked.

"I asked God to give me a sign if he was real and to let Laura know that I love her, just in case he was listening." A tear spilled from the corner of his eye. He let go of Mary's hand and wiped it away with his sleeve.

"Did God answer you?" Joseph said.

"No. It felt like I was talking to myself, but the next morning I kept thinking I needed to do more to help you guys. The longer the day went on, the more I thought about it. I couldn't focus on anything else because it kept beating against my brain like a sledgehammer. Finally, I couldn't lie to myself anymore. I wasn't the one telling myself to help you." Ray pointed at the ceiling. "It was him."

Mary hugged Ray, and Joseph put an arm around his shoulder. They held each other in silence, not like people who'd just met, but like family.

"This house is full of painful memories. For years I've told myself I need to sell it, but I've never been able to go through with it. The other night you told me we're all a tiny piece of God's puzzle, and we're all here for a reason." Ray spread his arms wide and looked around the room. "Mary, this is my piece. This is why I'm here. Let me help you."

"We could never come close to repaying you for this," Joseph said. He was grateful for what Ray was offering them, but he felt guilty for the one-sidedness of it all.

"That's where you're wrong. You already have." Ray dabbed at his eyes again with the back of his sleeve. "I've spent years running away from God, but you've helped me find him again. No, Joseph, I'd say *I'm* the one that could never repay *you.*"

"Our friend is coming to pick us up tomorrow. Can we go home and take some time to think about it?" Joseph said.

"I've got all the time in the world. Take as long as you need. I know it's a big decision."

Tiny cries drifted into the living room from upstairs. Mary left to check on Jesus while the two men stayed at the table, staring into the fire like they'd been hypnotized. Mary sang a soothing lullaby, and Ray hummed along to himself until she closed the bedroom door. A single tear rolled down his left cheek.

"My piece of the puzzle," Ray said.

CHAPTER 16

Jackie arrived Sunday afternoon before lunch. Joseph led her upstairs, where Mary was changing Jesus.

"Oh, would you look at that sweet, precious child! I've been dyin' to get my hands on him ever since you called me."

Mary buttoned the onesie and placed Jesus into Jackie's outstretched arms. Jackie pulled him against her breast and kissed his forehead.

"Well, aren't you the cutest baby in the whole wide world? Yes you are. Miss Jackie thinks you're just about the most beautiful thing she's ever seen."

"Thank you for coming all the way out here on your day off," Mary said.

"Are you kiddin' me? I'm not about to let you take this bundle of joy on a germ-infested bus. There's no tellin' what he might come down with."

"Would you like to meet Ray?" Mary asked.

"You mean the man who rescued you from the storm? Don't mind if I do."

Jackie clung to Jesus as she followed Mary and Joseph into the kitchen. Ray was in the backyard, standing over the grill with a spatula in one hand and a can of Crystal Pepsi in the other. He looked over the top of the grill and saw them watching him through the bay window. He gave the hamburger patties a final inspection before going inside.

"There's nothing like the smell of meat on a grill," Ray said as he pulled a towel from his back pocket and wiped his hands.

"Ray, we'd like you to meet our friend, Jackie. Jackie, this is Ray," Joseph said.

Ray's eyes settled on Jackie, and his face brightened. "It's a pleasure to meet you, Jackie."

"Oh, the pleasure's all mine. And might I say, you smell delicious." Jackie blushed. "I didn't mean *you* smell delicious. I meant the food smells delicious. I could smell it on your body. Not that I was smellin' your body." Jackie fanned her face with her hand. "Good Lord, I think I'm havin' a hot flash. I'm just gonna shut up."

Everyone roared with laughter. Mary noticed Ray's neck was red, and she thought his cheeks were probably burning behind his beard as well.

"Would you like to join me outside while I finish up these burgers? It's not too cold as long as you stand next to the grill."

Jackie looked at Mary with wide eyes. Mary nodded and took Jesus from Jackie's arms.

"I think that sounds like a lovely idea. Can we start our introductions all over again and forget that first one?"

"What first one?" Ray gave her a sly wink.

"Oh, you are just a hoot!" Jackie laughed and slapped Ray on the arm, letting her hand linger on his bicep. She looked over her shoulder on the way out the door and gave Mary a thumbs up.

"I didn't see that coming," Joseph said.

Mary smiled. "Jackie is always full of surprises."

***

"I think it's a wonderful idea!" Jackie said.

The four of them had finished lunch and were discussing Ray's proposal from the night before.

"It's definitely a great opportunity, but there's a lot to think about. Leaving your home is never easy. Plus, we'd be leaving behind a lot of friends," Mary said.

"Well, don't stay on account of me. You know I'd be comin' down here all the time to visit." Jackie smiled at Ray. "If you'd have me, of course."

"You'd be welcome anytime," Ray said.

"We just want to take some time to think it over and make sure we do the right thing," Joseph said.

"Of course. You don't want to go rushin' a decision like this. You should take a couple days to think it over."

"I actually meant more like weeks, not—"

"So Ray," Jackie interrupted. "How'd you like for me to whip up one of my famous homemade pies?"

Ray leaned back and patted his belly. "I've never been one to turn down dessert, especially a good pie."

"Wonderful! I'll just run to the store real quick and pick up a few things."

"Would you like some company?" Ray said.

Jackie beamed. "I'd like that very much."

The afternoon was filled with baking and laughter. They all helped themselves to generous slices of peach pie, bursting with gooey filling. A scoop of vanilla ice cream and a steaming cup of coffee put the finishing touches on a dessert they all agreed was worth the wait.

Mary felt a tug at her heart when it was time to leave. As she hugged Ray goodbye, she reflected on the special bond that had formed between them over the last few days. A bond that seemed almost supernatural. *This feels right*, she thought to herself as Jackie backed the car out of the driveway. *This feels like home.*

When Mary returned to the laundry plant the following day, her supervisor berated her for missing so much work. He assigned her the worst shifts for the upcoming month and told her to be thankful she still had a job.

Joseph visited his parents and brought Jesus along with him. Carrie enjoyed getting to meet her grandson, even though she still believed he was illegitimate. The only time David showed any interest was when he told Joseph the kid looked nothing like him.

After only being home for one day, God had made it clear this wasn't where he wanted them to be. They needed a fresh start. They needed to return to Bethlehem.

CHAPTER 17

Summer had arrived in the town of Bethlehem. Mary sat at her desk, relishing the cool air blowing from the vent above her head. She thought about Joseph, working in that heat box he called a workshop. Instead of purchasing an air conditioner, Joseph had insisted the money go toward their savings and had settled for a box fan instead.

Saving money used to be something they only dreamed about, but now they were actually doing it. Joseph's business had taken off since moving to Bethlehem. Ray had referred several customers to Joseph, and word of his excellent craftsmanship had traveled fast.

Mary's new job was also contributing to their savings. She was making twice what she had made at the laundry plant, and the working conditions were infinitely better. For the first time in her life, Mary looked forward to coming to work each day.

With the money they were saving on rent, they could afford a nice daycare only two blocks from the dealership. It made dropping Jesus off and picking him up a breeze, and she could visit him on her lunch break. Jesus loved the place. He always smiled and giggled when they pulled into the parking lot each morning. Leaving Jesus with someone else was hard, but it was easier knowing he was happy to be there.

Mary stared at the family picture on her desk. Jesus was sitting in Mary's lap, and Joseph was kissing him on the cheek. The picture served as a constant reminder of how blessed they were and how God had kept his promise to watch over them. To go from where they had been to where they were now was nothing short of a miracle.

"So how do I look?"

Mary looked up and saw Jackie standing in the doorway in a red dress and high heels. Her hair was curled and bounced on the top of her shoulders like coiled springs. Jackie had always been a pants and cotton shirt kind of woman. Mary hardly recognized her.

"Jackie! You look amazing!"

"Do you think Ray will like it?"

"I think you'll have to beat him off with a stick when he sees you."

"Now why would I want to go and do a thing like that? I *want* him comin' after me. I even put on some of that perfume with the half-naked people on the box. Lord knows I was embarrassed standin' in line with that smut." She shook her head. "The things I'll do for my man."

"I wish you'd told me you were coming. I would have taken off work early."

"I didn't want Ray to know I was comin'. Today's our six-month datin' anniversary, and I want to surprise him."

"Oh, he's definitely going to be surprised. Come with me. He's in his office looking over some contracts."

One of Jackie's high heels buckled underneath her when she stepped into the hall. She steadied herself against the doorframe.

"These dang high heels are gonna be the death of me. If I fall and break a leg, then I pity the poor man that's gotta carry me out of here. I'm sure Ray would try, God bless him, but his back ain't made to hold ole Miss Jackie."

Mary laughed. "Why don't you take them off?"

"Are you kiddin' me? And let Ray miss out on how amazin' these make my butt look? I don't think so." She turned with a flip of her curls and walked toward Ray's office, leaving her hand on the wall for support.

Ray was hunched over his desk with a pile of papers on either side of him. A knock at the door grabbed his attention.

"Jackie?" Ray dropped his pen and stood up. "Jackie! Wow! You look beautiful."

"Oh, this old thing? It's nothin' really." Jackie turned sideways and batted her eyes.

Ray hurried to the door and kissed her lips. "I thought you had to work today."

"I wanted to surprise you for our anniversary."

"Best gift I could have asked for. Tell you what, let me finish up here, and then we'll have a night on the town. I have to show you off."

"Sounds good, baby. I'll be waiting." Jackie blew him a kiss and shut the office door behind her. "And *that's* why I wore the heels," she said to Mary.

***

That night Mary was buried in her latest mystery novel while Joseph flipped through a *Sports Illustrated* magazine next to her. Mary was in the middle of the latest plot twist when Joseph knocked the book out of her hands, laughing as it tumbled to the floor.

"Joseph, you big dork! I don't know what page I was on."

He gave her a mischievous grin. Mary rolled her eyes as she picked the book off the floor and settled back into the couch. Moments later, Joseph reached over and knocked it out of her hands again.

"You're dead," Mary said.

She pounced on top of him. Joseph tickled underneath her arms, and Mary shrieked with laughter. A sudden noise from the other room made them stop.

"Great. Now look what you've done. You woke up Jesus," Mary said.

"Worth it," Joseph said with a grin.

Mary gave his arm a playful slap. Joseph pushed himself off the couch and went to the bedroom door. He put a hand on the doorknob and froze.

"Mary, come here. Listen to this."

Mary crept up behind him and leaned her head next to his. "Is he talking?"

"It sounds like he's saying 'dada.'"

Mary listened again. "It does!"

Joseph opened the door. "Dada's right here, buddy."

"Dada, dada, dada, dada," Jesus repeated.

Mary peered into the crib. Jesus wiggled back and forth, holding his arms in the air. His eyes were fixed on the ceiling.

Joseph pulled him from the crib. Jesus turned around and reached toward the ceiling again. "Dada, dada, dada." Jesus giggled while opening and closing his hands.

Chills ran down Mary's spine. She felt something she had only felt once before, on the night of Gabriel's visit. It was an overwhelming presence almost too much to bear. She dropped to her knees and buried her face in the carpet.

"You feel it too?" Joseph whispered.

Mary couldn't answer. Her throat felt like she had swallowed a handful of sawdust. Joseph put Jesus in the crib and knelt beside her. They bowed before God's presence in complete silence.

Jesus continued to babble and squeal with delight. Mary felt a sudden change around her as the weight of the Lord's presence lifted as quickly as it had arrived. They pulled themselves to their feet, Mary gripping the crib's railing for support.

Neither of them understood what had happened. Was God sending them a message, or was he just checking on his son? While they contemplated the supernatural events that had just unfolded, Jesus drifted off to sleep as if nothing had happened.

CHAPTER 18

Immigrants were fighting back. The first census had been a disaster. There had been multiple deaths, riots, and arrests at many of the census stations. Thousands of immigrants had either been deported or thrown in jail during the first week.

The violent outbursts attracted the wrong kind of attention to President Herod's administration. Emboldened by its failure, critics began to show their faces. News stations ran stories sympathetic to immigrants, and some of them even called for the Herod Reformation Act to be repealed. The media coverage inspired immigrants to stage protests across the country.

The critics enraged Herod, and he fought back with a vengeance. He claimed the news stations were spreading propaganda to further their own interests and divide the country. He even accused the protestors of being paid actors, funded by the billionaires that opposed him. The critics were loud, but they were the minority. Herod used his popularity to sway the public, and soon they turned on the media. With the people's support, he pushed a bill through Congress to fund a government-owned television station. The Unified Nation Network promised to deliver timely and accurate news to everyone in the United States. The bill also funded a government newspaper called *True American News*. They undercut the cost of every other major newspaper, choking out their competition.

At the same time, Herod's cabinet members worked behind the scenes to file various lawsuits against the media for what they considered slanderous hate speech. The networks became tied up in legal issues and lost millions in ad revenue from the fallout. No longer able to distinguish which media outlets were telling the truth, people flocked to the Unified Nation Network and *True American News*.

Herod's critics retreated into the shadows. With momentum on his side, he became even more brazen in his push for control. He expanded the role of the Immigration and Naturalization Service (INS). They were now responsible for all security related matters involving immigrants, both legal and illegal. The definition was intentionally vague in order to allow Herod to use the agency however he wished. The Senate confirmed one of Herod's closest friends as the new INS Director. President Herod had created his own personal army.

CHAPTER 19

"Jesus, sit still so Mommy can button your shirt." Jesus stopped playing with his Teddy Ruxpin bear long enough for Mary to finish getting him dressed. "That's better. Now, look how handsome you are." She held Jesus in front of the mirror.

"I hasom Mommy!"

"Yes you are. All the ladies are going to want to kiss that sweet little face."

"Ewww!"

"What about me?" Joseph walked into the room, buttoning the sleeves of his white dress shirt.

Mary grabbed his tie and pulled him close. The smell of his cologne made her heart skip a beat. "There better only be one pair of lips kissing your face tonight, mister." She leaned in and kissed his lips.

"Yes, ma'am! You look fantastic by the way."

"Thank you, love. We clean up pretty nice if I do say so myself."

"Shall we go?"

They went downstairs, Jesus hopping down each step while clinging to Joseph's hand. The backyard was full of guests who had already arrived. Mary, Joseph, and Jesus walked to their reserved seats along the front row. Jackie's daughter sat with Amy and her family down at the other end.

"Doc!" Jesus climbed into the empty chair next to Edward and hugged his arm.

Edward was now Jesus's primary physician. Between doctor visits and Edward coming by the house to visit Ray, the two had become close.

"How you doing, big guy?" Edward held his hand up high.

"Good." Jesus slapped his hand.

Edward winced. "Ow! You're getting so strong."

Jesus fell back against his chair, laughing. Mary hushed him as music began to play from the speakers. Ray came around the side of the house, wearing a black tuxedo and bowtie. He took his place under a wooden arch decorated with white lace and colorful flowers. He was gripping his hands so tight that his fingers had turned bone white. Beads of sweat settled along his forehead.

"Hi Papa!" Jesus yelled.

The crowd laughed and Jesus laughed along with them. Ray gave a sheepish wave and dabbed his forehead with a handkerchief.

Ray wasn't a blood relative, but he was more of a grandpa than anyone else in Jesus's life. Jesus had always called him, "Papa," which Ray accepted with great pride.

Everyone stood as Jackie, known as "Gammy" to Jesus, walked out the back door, wearing a flowing white gown. Her hair was braided and pinned up in the back, her hands hidden behind a bouquet of red and white roses. Expecting another outburst from Jesus, Mary placed a finger against his lips before he could even think about calling out to her.

Jackie walked down the aisle alone. They had kept things simple by only including the priest and the bride and groom in the ceremony.

Ray beamed and took Jackie's hands as she reached the altar. "I don't know if I can wait until the end to kiss you," he said.

"Who says you have to?"

Jackie grabbed his face with both hands and smashed her lips against his. She pulled back with an audible smack that had everyone laughing and whistling. The priest chuckled.

"Sorry about that, Rabbi. Couldn't help myself. The floor is yours." Jackie winked at Ray.

They held the reception in the backyard under strands of decorative lighting. Caterers provided a wide assortment of fancy dishes and wine. A band played throughout the night while guests danced on a wooden floor constructed in the middle of the lawn. At the end of the evening, Ray and Jackie ran through a cloud of rice toward a waiting limousine that whisked them away to a nearby hotel. The following morning they would be on their way to a Hawaiian paradise.

With the crowd thinning, Joseph took Jesus from Mary's lap. He was half-asleep, his face covered in icing and cookie crumbs.

"Come on, buddy. Let's get you to bed," Joseph said.

Jesus nestled his head into Joseph's shoulder and wrapped his arms around his father's neck. Mary smiled at her two favorite guys. Staring at her son, she marveled at how it seemed like only yesterday she was holding him for the first time, and now he was already two years old. A lot had happened to their family in those first two years, and she couldn't help but wonder what was in store for them in the years to come.

CHAPTER 20

Anthony beat two sticks of red licorice against the desk in rhythm to the Queen song blasting through the headphones of his Walkman. He rocked his head back and forth, his sandy hair flying in every direction.

Kevin pulled away from the telescope lens and glared at him. After living with Anthony in the observatory for almost a week, Kevin's nerves were wearing thin. Both of them were brilliant astronomers, but that's where the similarities ended. Kevin was the stereotypical scientist with round glasses, short hair parted to one side, and slacks pleated down the middle. Anthony's tie dye shirt and long hair made him look more like a hippie than an astronomer. His go-with-the-flow, carefree attitude was at constant odds with Kevin's Type A personality.

"Could you stop that?" Kevin snapped.

Ignoring him, Anthony hit a pair of imaginary cymbals and twirled the licorice between his fingers like drumsticks. After a moment of silence, he sang along with Freddy Mercury in a voice that sounded like an alley cat in heat. Kevin shook his head and returned to the telescope.

Logan, the unspoken leader of their group, came into the room pulling a t-shirt over his head. He slapped Anthony on the back of the head, knocking the headphones onto the floor.

"Hey, what'd you do that for?" Anthony said.

"Because you're being obnoxious. I can hear your screeching from the bedroom."

Anthony muttered something under his breath, turned off the Walkman, and rummaged through the stack of charts in front of him. They were preparing for their final night at the observatory. Their goal was to chart various stars throughout the galaxy, and enter the data into a computer system scientists could access all over the globe.

"How's it looking out there?" Logan said.

"Not a cloud in the sky." Kevin adjusted the knobs on the telescope.

"Perfect." Logan poured himself a cup of coffee from the machine in the corner. "Hopefully we can wrap this up in the next few hours and be out of here before dawn."

"What in the world?" Kevin couldn't make sense of what he was seeing. He shook his head and looked over his shoulder. "You guys come take a look at this."

Anthony shoved himself in front of Kevin and peered through the lens. "I see a star. A bright one, but so what?"

"It wasn't there last night," Kevin said.

"What do you mean it wasn't there?" Anthony said.

"I charted this area last night, and it wasn't there. Now it is."

"Maybe you're looking at the wrong spot," Logan suggested.

Kevin grabbed a long sheet of paper off the top of the desk and held it in front of Logan. "Look at this and tell me it's not the same area minus that one star."

Logan studied the chart, looked through the telescope, and then returned to the chart. "You're right. It's the same area," he said slowly.

Anthony whistled. "Discovering a star that big? Holy cow, Kevin. I bet they'll let you name it."

"Something's not right. This isn't a normal star," Logan said, looking through the telescope again.

"Is it a UFO?" Anthony wiggled his index fingers behind his head like antennas.

"Shut up and take another look at this thing. The size and brightness keep changing."

Anthony swapped places with Logan, and Logan started toward the door.

"Where are you going?" Kevin called after him.

"To have a look at this thing with my own eyes."

Kevin grabbed his sheet of paper and chased after him. Outside, the night was alive with the sounds of insects in the tall grass. Logan worked his way down the steps and onto a rocky path that wove in front of the observatory. He stopped just below the dome and looked up, pointing toward a spot in front of them.

"There. Do you see it?" Logan's voice was little more than a whisper.

Kevin stared at the sky like he'd been hypnotized. "Unbelievable."

It was the brightest star in the sky, but the most intriguing thing to Logan was its shape. It had a pointed edge descending toward the earth like a giant icicle.

"That can't be a star, can it? I mean, I don't know what the heck it is, but I've never seen a star that looks anything like that," Kevin said.

"I think it's a sign."

"A sign? Like someone trying to communicate with Earth?"

"The one who hears the words of God, who has knowledge of the Most High, who sees a vision from the Almighty, who fall prostrate, and whose eyes are opened. I see him, but not now. I behold him, but not near. A star will come out of Jacob; a scepter will rise out of Israel."

"Logan reciting his Torah verses again?" Anthony shuffled up behind them.

"It's part of the prophecy of the coming Messiah," Logan said. "I've always believed those verses referenced a literal star. It's what made me want to become an astronomer."

"Those verses sound pretty vague. They could mean anything," Kevin said.

Logan shook his head. "Vague to you, maybe, but not to me. I think it's a sign the Messiah is here."

"Then where is he?" Anthony spun around with his arms out wide.

Logan wished he knew the answer to that million dollar question. "The prophecies say he'll come from Bethlehem, but I'm not sure how to find him. If I had to guess, I'd say the star is announcing his birth."

"So what do you suggest we do? Call up all the hospitals and ask if anyone's seen a baby Messiah?" Anthony said.

"We do what any scientist would do. We report our findings up the chain and get it in the hands of NASA. See what they think."

Kevin nudged Logan in the arm. "You're a wise man, Logan."

Anthony threw his arms around the other two. "Excuse me? I think you mean wise *men*."

***

NASA was fascinated with the new discovery. They agreed most of the properties followed that of a star, but some things, such as the constant fluctuation in size and brightness, had them perplexed.

NASA invited Logan, Kevin, and Anthony to present their findings at NASA's headquarters in Washington, D.C.. Logan offered his opinion about the star being a sign of the Messiah, but it was met with little fanfare.

The transcript from the meeting found its way to the desk of the NASA administrator. Being a devout Jew himself, he was intrigued by Logan's theory. After doing his own research into the Torah, he determined there was enough correlation to justify including the theory in his report to the White House. He was well aware of President Herod's reputation, and he knew what happened to people that withheld information from him. It was better to provide too much information than not enough.

The NASA administrator filed his report the following morning. Two days later, the mysterious object in the sky disappeared.

CHAPTER 21

Herod sipped a glass of Jack and Coke, his favorite afternoon beverage. He leafed through the report sitting in front of him with little interest.

"So what?" he said.

The Chief of Staff, Ethan Whinegart, stared out the window facing the immaculate South Lawn. "Mr. President, I think this could become a bigger problem if we don't do something about it."

"What exactly am I supposed to do? A light shows up in the sky for a couple of days and then disappears. Sounds more like something that belongs in the tabloids instead of on my desk. I've got a budget crisis and an immigrant uprising to deal with. So explain to me why I'm wasting my time on this crap."

Herod loved Ethan's unwavering loyalty. Ethan wouldn't hesitate to take a bullet for him, both figuratively and literally, but Herod couldn't stand his incessant worrying over every little thing. It grated on his nerves like nails on a chalkboard.

Herod threw the papers at Ethan, where they smacked against his chest and fluttered to the ground. Ethan picked them up while Herod returned to his drink.

"Sir, now that NASA has admitted they don't know what it is, rumors are running wild. People are panicking."

"So let them panic. There's always some new conspiracy theory out there. It's better to keep them distracted with silly things like this than real problems anyway."

Ethan stood and pushed his glasses back into place. "Well, that's the thing. This one's making a real problem even worse."

Herod put down his drink and leaned forward. "Go on."

"A lot of Jews believe a theory from one of the scientists that discovered the light. They think it's a sign their Messiah is here. The idea is spreading like wildfire through the Jewish immigrant community."

Herod roared with laughter. "You had me worried there for a minute, Ethan. A bunch of religious nuts think their God is talking to them through signs in the sky? That's the big news? Are you worried they'll start rioting or something? I'll send INS in there to kill every last one of them."

"It's more than that, Mr. President. I'm not worried about there actually being a Messiah. I'm worried about what might happen if they find someone they *think* is the Messiah. I have some people outside I'd like you to meet."

"Oh, what the heck. Bring them in. You've already taken me this far down the rabbit hole. I might as well see where it goes."

Ethan ushered in two men wearing sleeveless blue robes adorned with tassels and golden bells. Each wore a colorful breastplate and a white headdress.

"Is it Halloween already, gentlemen?" Herod said with a smirk.

"Mr. President, I'd like to introduce you to two of the Jewish priests from the local immigrant community."

"Of course, of course. I'm only kidding. My apologies if the joke was in poor taste. Please, have a seat over there." Herod rose from his desk and pointed to the couches in the center of the room. He thought all religious people were out of their minds, but these two wackos in clown costumes took it to a whole new level. "And what brings you highly esteemed men of God to my office this afternoon?"

"These men are well-versed in the Jewish prophecies, and I asked them to come share their thoughts with you," Ethan said.

"I'd love to hear them." Herod could hardly suppress the laughter bubbling up inside of him.

The older of the two priests leaned forward. "Mr. President, let me start by saying what an honor it is to speak to you today. As it relates to the Messiah, we aren't sure if the light signals his coming or not, but given the mysterious nature of its arrival and departure, it's certainly possible."

"I was thinking the same thing. I told Ethan the light seemed like a sign from God, but I'm admittedly ignorant in the study of prophecy." Herod smiled graciously while trying to decide if he should thank Ethan for bringing these entertaining nut jobs into his office, or fire him. Did Ethan really think he needed to listen to this?

"Why don't you tell the president a little bit about the Messiah?" Ethan said.

"Oh Ethan, is that really necessary? I already know all about him. He's going to be a great man. A man as great as the two sitting here in front of me."

"No!" The younger priest cried. "We are lower than dirt when compared to the Messiah. He will be far greater than any mortal man."

"Yes, of course. That's what I was trying to say," Herod said.

"The Messiah will rule all nations," the younger priest continued. "He will bring Jews to the center of the world government and reestablish Jewish law. He will be the one true king!"

The smile on Herod's face vanished. "One true king?"

"The entire world will pay tribute to him and bow at his feet," the younger priest said.

Herod was seething inside. How dare these men come into his office and tell him about some mythical Jew that was going to overthrow him? He thought their heads would look better on the end of a stick instead of on top of those ridiculous robes.

"And if the Messiah *has* come, any idea where he might be?" Herod asked.

"The prophecies suggest he'll come from a place called Bethlehem," the older priest replied.

Herod slapped his knees and stood up. "Outstanding! Gentlemen, I can't thank you enough for coming to see me on such short notice. I really appreciate your time, but I'm afraid I have other business I need to attend to."

"It was an honor, Mr. President. Perhaps we can meet again to dive further into the Torah," the older priest said.

"That's a fantastic idea! I'm always interested in learning more about God." His only real interest in God was learning how to get people to shut up about him.

After the priests left, Herod jammed a finger into Ethan's chest. "Bring me the crazy scientist that started this rumor. I want to talk to him and whoever else discovered the light. You were right to bring this to my attention. If these people find someone they think is the Messiah, we'll have a real problem on our hands."

CHAPTER 22

Logan, Anthony, and Kevin sat across from President Herod in the center of the Oval Office. Logan knew their discovery would get a lot of attention from the scientific community, but he'd never imagined it would lead to a meeting with the most powerful man in the world.

"You men have done some fantastic work. Your discovery has caused quite the commotion," President Herod said.

"To be honest, we were pretty surprised by it. We thought we had just discovered a new star with abnormal qualities. We were as dumbfounded as everyone else when it disappeared," Kevin said.

"So what do you think it was? There's all kinds of theories being thrown around, but men with your intellect hold more weight in my mind than the general public."

Logan couldn't keep from smiling. Being valued outside the scientific community was a rarity, and to be recognized by the President of the United States made his chest swell with pride.

"We think the most likely explanation is that it was some sort of hibernating neutron star that had a brief explosion of activity before going dark again," Anthony said.

"Most likely, but still not *very* likely," Kevin said. "Many of the light's characteristics don't follow that of any known stars. Also, its brightness suggests it was closer to us than other stars. If that were the case, we would expect to be able to locate its mass even if it had gone dark."

"Very interesting. So that's the scientific theory, but what about explanations that are, shall we say, less science-y?"

"Those would be outside our area of expertise," Kevin said.

"Oh, come on," Herod coaxed. "I appreciate the cookie cutter response, but we're all human, right? Surely you have your own personal theories."

Logan weighed the pros and cons of what he was about to say. He determined the potential benefits of Herod believing him far outweighed the risk of being laughed out of the Oval Office. "I have a theory, Mr. President."

"Logan, don't do this," Anthony groaned.

"No, no. This is good. If science can't explain it, then we must look elsewhere. Go ahead, Logan," Herod said.

"I don't know how religious you are, but I think the answer might lie in the Torah," Logan said.

Herod's eyes lit up. "Wait. Do you think this has something to do with the prophecies?"

"You're familiar with them?" Logan's heart leapt. He'd made the right decision.

"Of course! When I first saw the star, I remembered that one verse in . . . what was that book again?"

"Numbers, chapter twenty-four?" Logan provided.

Herod snapped his fingers. "That's the one! At first I told myself I was crazy, but the more they struggle to come up with a logical explanation, the more I'm convinced it's a sign of the coming Messiah. Is that what you think as well?"

Logan looked at his two friends. Neither of them met his gaze. He thought they looked embarrassed, but he didn't care. President Herod's interest emboldened him. "Yes, that's my opinion."

Herod leaned in toward the three men. "This wasn't my initial intention for bringing you here today, but now that I know you're interested in the prophecy angle, I'd like for you to lead an expedition on my behalf to find the Messiah."

"An expedition?" Anthony said.

"You'd report directly to me, and all of your expenses would be covered. Along with a substantial salary, of course. You can pretty much name your price for something of this magnitude."

"But why us? Surely there are plenty of other people that could do this for you," Kevin said.

"But you were the ones who discovered the light, and you're clearly well-versed in the Torah. I can't think of anyone more capable of finding the Messiah quickly. It's important that I be one of the first to bow at his feet."

The three scientists looked at one another and nodded in agreement. Having the president on their side was like having an enormous weight lifted off Logan's shoulders. It was the highest form of validation he could have hoped for. Herod seemed as excited about the Messiah as he was. This was incredible.

"Mr. President, we'd be honored to look for the Messiah on your behalf," Logan said.

Herod crossed the room and shook their hands. "Wonderful news! You can start immediately. Take some time to come up with a game plan, and then off you go. Ethan will get you anything you need. This mission is top priority for me, and frankly, for the world. No request is too large. Literally anything you need is yours."

"Thank you, Mr. President," all three said in unison.

"Oh, and one more thing. Let's keep this between us and Ethan. The last thing we need is a bunch of people interfering with your search."

The scientists agreed and discussed a few other details before leaving the office.

***

Herod chuckled after he closed the door closed behind them. "Shmucks."

He grabbed the phone on his desk, fell into his chair, and swiveled ninety degrees to face the giant window behind him.

"Mr. President," the voice on the other end said.

"Ethan, they bought the whole thing! They were more than happy to be our little pawns. Make sure they have everything they need. Give them a ridiculous advance while you're at it. I want to keep them fat and happy until they find someone the Jews think is the Messiah."

"And then?"

"We kill them all."

CHAPTER 23

"This is unbelievable!" Anthony shouted in front of the limousine waiting for them outside the airport terminal. "We're working on a top secret mission for the President of the United States!"

"You make it sound like we're spies," Kevin said.

"Well, we kind of are. Sneaking around, looking for the greatest man ever born. Hiding our true intentions and reporting directly to President Herod. We should have code names," Anthony said, his eyes growing wide at the idea.

Logan rolled his eyes. Left unchecked, Anthony would have them using walkie-talkies while hiding in bushes outside the local hospital. "Nobody is getting a code name." They dropped their luggage next to the chauffeur and piled into the backseat. "Look, I know you guys aren't sold on this whole Messiah thing, but I'm convinced. I really believe God's put us here for a reason."

"Just to be clear, we believe the Messiah will come someday. We're just not convinced this light has anything to do with it," Kevin said.

"Or that we even have the right Bethlehem," Anthony said. "I still think the Messiah is more likely to come from the Bethlehem in Israel than the one in Pennsylvania."

Logan knew the prophecies alluded to the Messiah coming from Israel, but they could also be referring to his family lineage rather than the Messiah himself. Heck, there were no guarantees he would even be born in a place called Bethlehem. Logan was going with his gut on this one and praying God would lead him in the right direction.

"You might be right, but Pennsylvania is as good a place to start as any. Plus, the United States is the most powerful country in the world. It makes sense that a future global leader would come from here. If we hit a dead end, we can always go to Israel next," Logan said.

Twenty minutes later, the limousine pulled in front of the largest hotel in Bethlehem. A bellhop escorted them to the Presidential Suite on the top floor. The spacious living room had a glass wall overlooking downtown Bethlehem, and a chandelier dangled above several pieces of luxurious furniture. Each bedroom had a king-size bed with fluffy pillows and a down comforter.

Kevin took in the view while Logan ran his hand along the back of a plush sofa. He was sure it cost more than all the furniture in his apartment combined.

Anthony grabbed two packages from the dining room table and held them above his head. "Got my licorice!"

"You seriously asked Ethan to get you candy? What are you, five?" Kevin rolled his eyes.

"Hey, they said to ask for whatever we need, and I need licorice." He tore open a package and stuck a piece in his mouth. "Look at all this stuff over here. Tab, Cheez Balls, Hubba Bubba. Man, we're set! I'm gonna check out the bedrooms."

Anthony disappeared through one of the bedroom doors. Logan heard a soft thump as he launched himself onto the bed.

"Ready to get started?" Kevin said.

Logan grabbed a phone book off the desk and leafed through it. He tore out a page near the front, folded it, and stuffed it in his back pocket. "Let's go."

***

They spent the rest of the day scrolling through rolls of microfilm in a stuffy, dark room at the Bethlehem Public Library. They were looking for any unusual stories in local publications that might hint at the Messiah being in Bethlehem. It seemed like a longshot, but the odds were better than walking the streets asking if anyone had seen a miraculous birth.

A few hours later, Anthony glanced at the clock on the far wall and rubbed his eyes with both fists. "Guys, there's nothing here. I think this is a dead end. I say we call it a day and get something to eat."

"You can't say it's a dead end when we don't even know what we're looking for," Logan snapped.

He'd grown increasingly frustrated as the hours ticked by without any leads. As a scientist, he was used to putting in countless hours of research with nothing to show for it. However, deep down he'd believed they would find something right away that would lead them closer to the Messiah.

"All I'm saying is we've gone through every newspaper in this town for the last couple of years and haven't found a thing. If something was here, I think we would have stumbled across it by now. Either way, I'm hungry and tired."

"I'm with Anthony on this one," Kevin said. "I think we could all use a big meal and a good night's sleep. Let's pick it back up in the morning."

Logan clicked off his machine and sighed. "I guess you're right. Let's take this stuff back to the front desk and get out of here."

The librarian recommended a quaint Italian restaurant a few blocks away. After gorging themselves on mountains of home-made pasta, meatballs, and breadsticks, the men called for a taxi and returned to the hotel.

Three hot showers later, they all lounged around the living room, watching a basketball game. Logan stared at the television without seeing it. His mind was engrossed with the task at hand.

How were they ever going to find the Messiah? All the resources in the world wouldn't help them if they didn't know where to look.

Having no interest in the game, Logan wandered over to the window. "Where are you?" he said to himself. "God, please show me where he is." He watched a trail of taillights wind their way along the interstate and disappear behind a hill. A bright mass above the traffic caught his attention. "Guys, the light is back!"

Anthony and Kevin ran to the window. The mysterious light was hanging low in the sky, which made it look much larger than last time. The spear of light protruding from the bottom appeared to be almost touching the rooftops.

"I knew it!" Logan screamed. "The Messiah is here!" He pumped his fists in the air like a kid who just scored the winning goal.

Kevin pressed his nose against the glass, creating a small ring of fog on the window. "I don't believe it, but you're right. I mean, what else could it be? Merciful God, our Savior is here."

"But where?" Anthony said. "Assuming you're right, how in the world are we going to find one person in a city this big?"

"We follow the star . . . or whatever it really is." Logan was shaking with excitement. "Look how close it is to the ground. It's basically hovering over the city. I think that beam of light will lead us to him."

"It's really true, isn't it? As crazy as it sounds, it's really true," Anthony said.

Logan watched the light with tears in his eyes. God had heard his prayers and come through in a big way. "Let's go find the Messiah."

**

After studying a map of the city, the three men piled into a taxi and drove to a shopping center that appeared to be near the light. A crowd was already stargazing by the time they arrived in the parking lot. One man was taking pictures with his Polaroid camera while telling his wife they'd make a fortune selling them to the media. A young couple sat on the hood of their car and discussed the possibility of aliens being involved.

The light hovered almost directly over them, and the protruding beam seemed to hang over an area just north of the shopping center. The scientists walked in the direction of the light and came to a thicket of trees bordering a nearby park. After hiking through the dense brush, they came to the edge of an open field.

"We're here," Logan said.

The beam of light hung directly over a house surrounded by acres of untouched land, leaving little doubt as to where they should go.

"What do we do? Just knock on the door and ask to see the Messiah?" Anthony asked.

"I think that's exactly what we do," Logan said.

They walked to the front door, where bugs darted around the porch light in dizzying patterns. Logan swatted at a moth near his forehead and rang the doorbell. His heart pounded inside his chest. All his life he had dreamed of the Messiah's arrival, but never in a million years did he think he'd be the one to discover him.

A shadow floated past the front window. The door opened halfway, and a man's face appeared in the gap.

He looked them over and frowned. "Can I help you?"

"Good evening, sir. I'm sorry to bother you so late, but we have an urgent issue I think you might be able to help us with. My name is Logan Witherspoon, and these are my colleagues Kevin Bloom and Anthony Vaughan. Are you the owner of this house?"

"No, that would be Ray, but I live here too. My name's Joseph. What's going on?"

"We're scientists researching the strange light that appeared in the sky a few nights ago," Logan said.

"You mean the star that's been all over the news? I'm afraid I can't help you with that one. It disappeared before I could see it for myself."

"Well, that's the thing. It's back." Logan pointed at the sky. "And it's right over your house. And you want to hear something really strange? It led us to you."

"What are you talking about?"

"Come see for yourself." Logan stepped back and motioned toward the front yard.

"Hang on a second." Joseph closed the door.

"Let's get out of here. He's either calling the cops or getting a gun," Anthony said.

"Calm down. He's not getting a gun," Logan said, praying his assumption was correct.

The door reopened, and Joseph stepped outside, unarmed. Logan breathed a sigh of relief. An older man had taken Joseph's place behind the door.

"Let's go have a look." Joseph marched into the front yard, looked up at the sky, and froze. "You were serious. It literally looks like it's pointing at our house."

"Like I said, it led us right to you," Logan said.

"But what made you think to follow it here?

"How familiar are you with the Torah prophecies?"

Joseph looked away from the light and met Logan's gaze. "I think I know where this is going."

Logan smiled. "Then I think we came to the right place. Is there a child inside your home? Perhaps a young boy?"

Joseph nodded.

Logan couldn't believe it. They'd found him. "I can see on your face that I don't need to tell you just how special your boy is. He's the one I've been waiting for my entire life. The one the whole world has been waiting for. He's the Messiah, isn't he?"

"How—" Joseph cleared his throat and tried again. "How could you know that?"

"I've had a passion for prophecy my whole life, and I knew that light was a sign from God the moment I saw it. Most people think I'm crazy, but maybe God put it on my heart all those years ago so I would show up right here at this exact moment."

"Everything okay, Joseph?" The older man had come out from behind the door and now stood with Kevin and Anthony.

"Everything's fine, Ray. Go inside and tell everyone to come out here. They won't believe this," Joseph said.

"Even Jesus?" Ray asked.

"Especially Jesus."

Everyone gathered on the front lawn and exchanged introductions. Mary, Joseph, Jackie, and Ray gazed with wonder at the star hanging over their house while Jesus clung to Mary's leg, half-asleep. Logan, Anthony, and Kevin fell at his feet and prayed.

Afterward, the scientists shared their story, beginning with the discovery of the light, and ending with President Herod sending them to find the Messiah. Everyone's eyes turned to Jesus. He shied away from their gaze, burying his face in his mother's leg.

Mary picked him up and nuzzled his cheek. "Don't be shy, Jesus. These men came a long way to see you."

"How old are you, Jesus?" Anthony asked.

Jesus extended two pudgy fingers without looking at him.

"Two? Wow! You're a big boy. I bet you like presents, don't you?"

That got Jesus's attention. He looked at Anthony with wide eyes and nodded his head like a bobblehead doll.

"What if me and my friends come back tomorrow and bring you some presents? Would you like that?"

"Yeah!" Jesus screamed, now wide awake.

Anthony looked at Mary and Joseph. "If it's okay with your mom and dad, of course."

Logan admired the way Anthony had connected with the kid. His childlike mentality, while often annoying, had proven to be a tremendous asset in this situation. Logan reminded himself that God can use anything for his good, even immaturity.

Joseph smiled and ruffled Jesus's hair. "You guys don't have to do that."

"It'd be an honor," Logan said.

"Well, I'm sure Jesus would love that. Thank you," Joseph said.

"Woo-hoo!" Jesus bounced up and down while clapping his hands.

Mary shifted Jesus into her other arm. "Can I ask for one small favor?"

"Of course," Logan said.

"Could you please not tell anyone about this? At least not yet. We thought it would be years before other people learned about Jesus, and we don't want his childhood to be a crazy media circus."

Logan considered the request. "We won't tell the press if that's what you're worried about, but I'm afraid we'll have to tell President Herod. He's just as excited as we are and will want to pay his respects. But I'm sure he'll honor your wishes to stay anonymous."

"It'd be fine by me if he kept his respects all to himself," Jackie grumbled.

"Jackie!" Mary scolded.

"He ain't done nothin' for immigrants since he took office, but now he wants to be your best friend because of Jesus? To that I say no thank you."

Logan gave Mary a reassuring smile. "Don't worry. We won't share any of that with the president. Our orders are to tell him where the Messiah is, and that's all we plan to do. But I do think you'll like him once you meet him."

Jackie grunted her disapproval. Logan glanced at his watch and decided they had bothered Jesus and his family enough for one night. Anthony coaxed a high five out of Jesus before they left, the promise of future gifts cementing his status as Jesus's new best friend.

***

The next morning Logan and Kevin sat at the dining room table in silence, feasting on scrambled eggs, fresh fruit, and pancakes. Anthony's bedroom door flung open, and he plopped himself into the dining room chair next to them.

"Man, I had the strangest dream last night," Anthony said, pouring a generous amount of syrup across the top of his pancakes. "There was this guy. Well, he looked like a guy, but he was really an angel. Anyway, he told me we shouldn't tell President Herod about Jesus, and we should leave Bethlehem. He said—"

"The president is lying to us," Logan finished.

Anthony looked puzzled. "Yeah. How'd you know that?"

"Because I had the same dream." Logan dropped his napkin over the remaining food on his plate. He'd lost his appetite.

Kevin's fork slipped from his hand and rattled against his plate. "It didn't feel like a dream though, did it? It was like real life."

"You had the dream too?" Anthony said.

Kevin nodded slowly. "Yeah. What'd the angel look like?"

"White dude with blonde hair. Had a bright white shirt and brown pants," Anthony said.

Logan rubbed the goosebumps crawling across his arms. "I *knew* it had to be more than a dream."

Kevin looked at both of them intently. "All three of us having the same dream is more than a coincidence. That was obviously God. We can't tell the president about finding Jesus now, right?"

Anthony threw up his hands. "He's not stupid. He's going to find out we're hiding something, and then he'll throw us in jail for insubordination."

"Or worse," Logan said. "Anthony's right. We can't lie to him forever. At some point he'll figure it out." He took a deep breath. "We've got to go into hiding."

Anthony stood up and paced in front of the window. "Whoa, whoa, whoa. Hang on a second. Hide from the president? That's a suicide mission."

"We call Ethan this morning and tell him we're going to spend the day scouting the town. He'll think everything's normal as long as we don't check out of the hotel," Logan said.

"And what if we're being followed?" Kevin said.

Logan shook his head. "I doubt it. They'd know we already found Jesus if they were, and they'd have called by now. I think we're safe."

"I'm sorry, but I'm not running. I've got a life back home, and I can't just give it all up," Anthony said.

Logan thought of his own friends and family he would be leaving behind. It was a tremendous sacrifice, but a necessary one. "You can stay behind if you want. Tell them we ran off and left you. But I know what that dream meant, and I can't ignore it, even if it means my life."

"Kevin?" Anthony pleaded.

"Sorry, Anthony. I'm with Logan on this one. Those dreams came from God. They had to."

Anthony ran his fingers through his hair and grimaced. "I can't give up the kid," he said after a prolonged silence. "I guess I'm in, no matter how much I hate the idea. Any volunteers to call Ethan?"

"I'll do it," Logan said. "Then we'll go see Jesus."

***

They arrived at the house after lunch, carrying two large shopping bags and a backpack bulging at the seams. They sat everything on the floor next to Jesus, who was entertaining himself with a pile of building blocks. He saw the bags and looked at Anthony with a huge smile.

"That's right, buddy. They're all yours. Go ahead and open them," Anthony said.

Jesus looked at Mary, who nodded her approval. He tore into the first bag and pulled out several boxes of action figures.

"Batman! I wuv Batman!" Jesus hugged the first box. "And He-Man! I wuv He-Man too!"

"Go on and open the other one," Kevin said.

Jesus dropped the box he was holding and ripped into the second bag. He pulled out a giant red firetruck with an extendable ladder. Logan leaned over and pushed the buttons along the top of the hood. An array of lights and sounds filled the room. Jesus squealed with delight and began pushing the buttons repeatedly.

Joseph rolled his eyes as the siren wailed. "Thanks a lot, guys."

With the help of his father, Jesus opened the boxes of superheroes and lined them around the truck in a battle scene only a two-year-old's imagination could create.

Logan gripped the handle of the backpack and dragged it in front of Joseph. "This one's for Jesus too, but you should open it."

Joseph tugged on the zipper. The flap peeled back, and a pile of cash spilled onto the floor.

"Lord have mercy," Jackie said, her hand going to her chest.

"We took it out of our account this morning," Logan said. "We want you to have it."

Mary's heart leapt into her throat as she sifted through the bag. "There's thousands of dollars in here."

"A hundred of them to be exact," Kevin said.

"A hundred thousand dollars!" Joseph exclaimed.

"Use it to give Jesus a good life. School, clothes, whatever he needs." Kevin said.

"I won't go into details, but we won't tell the president that we found you. That's why the gift is in cash. They'll know we withdrew the money, but they'll have no way of finding out what we did with it. Your secret will be safe," Logan said.

"Why would you get rid of all this money? What are you not telling us?" Ray asked, worry lining his brow.

"The less you know the better, but I promise this is on the up and up. We want to honor Jesus with this gift. We insist you take it," Logan said.

Mary burst into tears and fell to her knees. God had miraculously provided for them once again, and in an unimaginable way. Every time she thought she'd seen it all, God found a way to outdo himself. Jesus wrapped his tiny arms around Mary's neck.

"Don't cry, Mommy."

Mary smiled and kissed his cheek. "Mommy's fine. These are happy tears."

Joseph asked the scientists to leave the room so the family could discuss their options. They all agreed the gift was incomprehensible, and God's divine intervention was the only thing that made sense. To refuse the money would not only be an insult to the scientists, but it would be an insult to God's generosity as well. He had brought these men here for a reason, and the only logical thing in this illogical situation was to accept what God was providing them. They took the money.

CHAPTER 24

Rain pelted the window panes of the Oval Office as Herod signed an executive order approving the execution of six immigrants responsible for an uprising in Washington, D.C.. A peaceful protest had turned deadly when a group known as The New America had instigated a riot leading to the deaths of over 100 people.

The New America was a group of activists who believed all immigrants, both legal and illegal, deserved the same rights as those born in the United States. Their vision was an America without borders, a melting pot of citizens who were all equal. The movement was gaining serious momentum, and it concerned Herod. There was strength in numbers, and the group had the potential to cause serious problems if left unchecked. So far the movement was mostly immigrants, but their ideology was beginning to infect the minds of citizens as well. If enough people with voting power sympathized with the immigrants, Herod's administration would be in trouble.

Herod's attempts to squash the movement had been unsuccessful. They had made arrests, placed spies within The New America's leadership, and issued serious threats; none of it worked. Whenever they successfully disbanded one chapter, two more popped up in its place. The group was like a den of breeding cockroaches.

The latest protest had been the final straw. Herod declared animals deserved to be treated like animals. Even lethal injection was too good for these barbarians. He ordered them to be lined up along a wall and shot. A firing squad was technically legal, but no longer used because of its brutality. The entire event would air live on the Unified Nation Network. He wanted everyone to see what happened to those who refused to fall in line. The kid gloves were off. Now he was ruling with an iron fist.

He smiled as he handed the executive order to the general standing next to him. The families of the guilty parties were doing everything they could to get Congress to stop the executions, but Herod knew better. Congress valued their power just as much as he did, and they understood that drastic measures needed to be taken in order to protect their livelihood.

Ethan entered the room as the general and the rest of the signing party left. His troubled look contrasted the satisfied grin on Herod's face.

"Ethan, where were you? You missed all the excitement."

"Mr. President, we have a serious problem."

Herod's face clouded. "I'm having a great day, Ethan. Do *not* crap all over it."

"Sir, it's about the scientists looking for the Messiah."

"Did they find him?"

"I'm not sure. They've disappeared."

"They *what?*"

Ethan tugged on his tie and cleared his throat. "They skipped town without checking out of the hotel. We haven't heard from them in three days. I sent someone over to the hotel, and their stuff is gone. I also had the FBI check the bank accounts we wired the money to. They were emptied shortly before their last call with me."

Herod's face burned with fury. He'd been fooled by fools. He was livid. "This better be some sort of sick joke, Ethan, or so help me God I'll have you lined up on the wall and shot with the rest of those lowlifes."

"I'm sorry, Mr. President, but they've taken the money and ran."

Herod snatched a crystal paperweight off his desk and hurled it across the room. The paperweight struck the wall and broke in half, leaving a tennis ball-sized hole in its wake. He slammed his hands against the desk and released a barrage of obscenities. A young woman knocked on the door and peeked inside.

"Is everything alright, Mr. President?"

"Get out!" he barked.

Herod marched toward her, and she scampered out of the room. He slammed the door behind her and kicked it for good measure. A line of sweat broke out across his upper lip. Why had he put such a hapless moron in charge of something so important? He turned on Ethan.

"They've found the Messiah. Or at least they *think* they have. Why else would they run unless they're trying to hide something from me? And do you know why they're hiding it?"

Ethan took a step back while avoiding eye contact. "No, Mr. President."

"Of course you don't, you worthless idiot. It's because they think this Messiah is the start of a revolution. A king, isn't that what they called him? Someone that will overthrow the government and put the Jews back in power? I'm sure they're telling everyone about their little discovery as we speak. That'll really get these fanatics going. They'll make the New America look like child's play if we don't squash this."

"It's possible they didn't tell anyone. Maybe they just found out what you were planning to do and got scared."

Herod sneered. "Did you tell them, Ethan? Because you're the only other person who knows about that."

"Of course not, Mr. President."

"Then your theory is garbage."

"Should we send out a search team to find them?"

"No. This has become much bigger than those three. We'll deal with them eventually, but right now I want to find and kill whoever they found in Bethlehem. I want all INS leaders in the briefing room immediately. Call me when they're ready."

***

Herod sat in the briefing room with five of the highest ranking members of the Immigration and Naturalization Service. An agency that had once detected and deterred illegal immigration had now become an army that intimidated, defeated, and destroyed. The INS engaged in clandestine missions that circumvented the military's normal chain of command in order to respond quickly to any threats posed by immigrants.

Herod patted himself on the back for how well it had all come together. His meticulous planning had paid off in a big way. Through manipulation and superior intellect, he'd created an army that reported to him and no one else.

Herod had appointed Jarod McMillan head of the INS shortly after becoming president, and he still wasn't sure how he'd pulled that one off. Their friendship went back more than fifteen years, and they saw eye to eye on just about everything, including immigrants. Having Jarod at the helm made his agenda that much easier.

"Thoughts?" Herod said after laying out his orders.

"I think the plan is outrageous, ruthless, and borderline psychotic. I love it!" Jarod said.

Brandon Sealy, Jarod's number two in command, spoke up. "With all due respect, Mr. President, you're talking about taking the lives of innocent children."

Jarod grinned, exposing yellow teeth stained from years of smoking. "You going soft on me, Sealy?"

"Innocent lives are always an unfortunate casualty of war, and this time is no different. The body count will be high, but the number of lives lost will pale in comparison to what will happen if we do nothing," Herod said.

Jarod nodded. "It's tough but necessary. Can you imagine if the Jews rally around some baby they think is their Savior? They'll be lining up to martyr themselves. It'll be the start of a religious war right here on American soil."

"But we don't even know if it's a child. They could have found an adult," Brandon said.

Herod shook his head. "No, it's a kid. They told Ethan they thought the star meant the Messiah was born. Their confirmation bias would lead them to a baby. I'm sure of it."

"That's good enough for me," Jarod said.

"What about you, Brandon? Can I count on you?" Herod asked. He'd expected a lot pushback from such an egregious order, and the fact that Brandon appeared to be the only one with a moral conscience surprised him.

"Yes, Mr. President. If you say go, then we go," Brandon said.

"Excellent! I'll leave the details up to you gentlemen, but anything you need is at your disposal. If you need more men, more weapons, just ask. And I'm sure this goes without saying, but discretion is key. No one outside this room can know what's coming. Understood?"

The INS leaders nodded as Herod got up from his chair. The planning was underway before he had left the room.

CHAPTER 25

Joseph woke up from his nap on the living room couch, screaming and covered in a cold sweat. He looked around the room with wild eyes.

"Mary! Mary!"

Hurried footsteps echoed down the stairs. Mary came around the corner with a finger pressed against her lips.

"Would you keep it down? Jesus is taking a nap," Mary said.

"We've got to get out of here right now! They're coming for Jesus!"

"Who's coming?"

Joseph brushed past her and ran up the stairs. Mary chased after him. "Horrible dream. Just like the one with Gabriel. Only a different angel this time." He turned in a frantic circle. "Where's the suitcase?"

"Calm down, Joseph. You're scaring me. What's going on?"

Joseph burst into the bedroom. "The angel told me we have to leave Bethlehem right now because President Herod is coming to kill Jesus." He hurried to the closet and tossed handfuls of clothes onto the bed. "The dream started in a wheat field, and then the angel brought me back here. I could see myself running through the house with you and Jesus. There were soldiers with guns, and I saw you—" Joseph couldn't bring himself to finish. The end of the dream had been too horrible for words.

"Play with me Daddy?" Jesus bounced up and down in his crib.

"Not now, buddy. We'll play later, okay?"

"This is real? You're sure?" Mary clutched her hands against her chest.

Joseph gripped her shoulders. "As real as Gabriel. We have to hurry."

***

The Black Hawk screamed through the air toward Bethlehem. Jarod watched the two dozen helicopters flying in formation around him. Countless other vehicles were already positioned outside the city, waiting on their arrival.

The plan had come together with surprising ease. If the Jews believed the star signaled the birth of the Messiah, then killing every male child two years and under would ensure they got the right kid. Anyone who interfered with the mission would be eliminated as well.

Ground troops would block access into and out of the city. They had identified every road running through Bethlehem, including the back roads, and troops were waiting at the city limits of each of them.

Many reporters from the Unified Nation Network had traveled with the military convoy to Bethlehem. Senior members of the network had been briefed on how to spin the story. The official narrative would be that hundreds of well-armed members of The New America had stormed the streets and began slaughtering children, killing thousands of people before INS could arrive.

With President Herod's influence over the Unified Nation Network, the story would be easy to control. They would keep all other news outlets outside the city limits to prevent them from witnessing the event. Eyewitnesses brave enough to come forward with conflicting stories would be countered with the Unified Nation Network's own paid eyewitnesses. The network would also release doctored footage of the day's events that would corroborate their version of the story. Anyone with a different opinion would be labeled a conspiracy theorist.

Once the barricades were in place, helicopters would enter the city, dropping hundreds of troops on the ground. Their job was to create as much chaos as possible while additional troops arrived via transport vehicles.

Each squad had a designated zone within the city, and a list with the names and addresses of all known children within their zone, guaranteeing every child in Bethlehem would be accounted for. They created the list using information from birth records and immigrant census data, and anyone they couldn't find today would be eliminated with smaller, clandestine missions at a later date.

As the Black Hawks began their descent into Bethlehem, several of them hovered over the downtown plaza.

"You boys ready?" Jarod cried over the sound of the propellers. "First confirmed kill gets a three-day furlough."

The rest of the men responded with a chorus of grunts that would have made their caveman ancestors proud. Jarod pulled a Beretta M9 from his holster and released the safety. It was go time.

***

Ray and Jackie walked along the crowded streets of downtown Bethlehem. The suffocating heat of summer had given way to a beautiful Sunday afternoon. People sat on benches near the downtown fountain, eating ice cream and tossing pennies into the water. The city park was filled with giggling children on the playground and families tossing bread crumbs to a flock of ducks near the pond's edge.

The doors to the town's bakery stood wide open. Ray took a deep breath as he walked past, staring into the windows with a longing normally reserved for Jackie. His stomach growled with anticipation.

"Now, don't you give those pastries another look, mister," Jackie said.

"Just one, babe? I promise we'll go back on our diet first thing tomorrow."

"We? What do you mean we? Don't you go draggin' me down with you."

Ray slipped his hand into hers and kissed her cheek. "How about we split one?"

Jackie waved a finger in his face. "Shame on you, Ray Wilmington. Trying to seduce an innocent old woman who's just tryin' to lose some weight for her husband. You should be ashamed of yourself."

Ray smiled. "Is that a yes?"

"Let's make it one of those giant cinnamon rolls. If we're gonna cheat, then let's do it right."

"That's my girl!" Ray pulled her into the store before she could reconsider.

The young woman behind the counter opened the glass warmer and grabbed a cinnamon roll lathered in white icing. Ray watched it like a tiger stalking its prey. A low rumble from outside caught his attention. He looked out the window to see several helicopters soaring past the bakery, the roar of their rotor blades causing his eardrums to pulse. A Black Hawk broke formation and lowered itself into a nearby parking lot. Gunshots rang out from somewhere in the distance.

"Stay here," he told Jackie. Whatever was happening couldn't be good, and he didn't want his wife anywhere near it.

Ray was out the door before she could respond. Armed soldiers were spreading out around the town square. A few people ran, but most stood like statues in a wax museum, frozen with uncertainty.

A father near the fountain grabbed his son and sprinted across the square. One soldier raised his rifle and fired a three-round burst. The shots went high, spitting concrete off the side of a nearby building. The soldier fired again, this time hitting his target. Two bullets slammed into the man's back, and a third hit the top of the child's head.

Ray's blood ran cold as his mind worked to process what he was seeing: a young boy with his head blown open, crushed under his father's lifeless body. It was like a scene from a war-torn Third World country, only it was happening in Ray's hometown.

A wave of panic rushed through the crowd. People ran in every direction, bloodcurdling screams filling the air. The rest of the soldiers opened fire.

Ray spotted a young boy lying next to his dead parents. Blood oozed from his hip, and tears were running down his pale face. Ray sprinted over to him.

"It's going to be okay, son. I'm going to get you out of here."

Ray scooped up the kid and raced toward the bakery, ignoring the surrounding gunfire. A powerful hand grabbed him from behind and spun him around. A soldier stood before him with a Beretta M9 pointed at the boy's chest. He pulled the trigger. The boy jerked as the bullet tore through his body. Ray stumbled, clinging to the lifeless child. He looked at the soldier in numb shock.

"Why?" Ray said.

"Stupid old man."

He kicked Ray's legs out from underneath him. Ray fell to the ground, dropping the boy and exposing a blossoming red stain on his own shirt.

"Two with one shot! Not bad, McMillan. Not bad at all," the soldier said to himself.

A bloodthirsty scream erupted from behind him. The soldier turned to see Jackie barreling toward him like a raging bull. The man pistol-whipped her across the shoulder, sending her face-first into the asphalt.

"I should kill you," the beast growled at Jackie. "But I'd rather make you watch him die instead."

"No!" Jackie screamed.

He fired two shots into Ray's body and left to search for his next target.

Jackie ran to Ray, sobbing uncontrollably. Ray's eyes were half-closed. His breathing was shallow. Jackie took his hand and pressed it against her blood-streaked face, kissing it repeatedly.

"Hang on, sweetie. I'm gonna get you some help. Just hang on."

Ray fought for another breath. "Save Jesus." He closed his eyes.

"Ray!" Jackie slapped his face. "Ray, wake up! Don't you dare leave me!"

Ray opened his eyes, but everything was hazy.

"I love you, Ray. You hear me? I love you." Jackie put his head in her lap and wept, rocking back and forth amidst the chaos.

He gave her hand an almost imperceptible squeeze. He tried to tell her how much he loved her, but all he could manage was a final wheezing breath.

CHAPTER 26

Joseph watched the unfolding carnage from the living room window while Mary finished packing.

"Helicopters are landing all over the city! We've got to go!" Joseph called to Mary.

He raced up the stairs to see Mary closing the suitcase with a backpack thrown over her shoulder. He could see there was more to pack, but they were out of time.

"Pow pow! Hewicopters go pow pow!" Jesus said.

Joseph pulled him out of the crib and handed him to Mary. He picked up the suitcase and led his family down the stairs and out the front door. Joseph threw everything into the trunk of the car while Mary buckled Jesus into his car seat.

"Joseph, look!" Mary shouted.

He turned to see two military trucks pulling into the neighborhood down the hill from their house. Soldiers piled out of the vehicles and began going door to door. He watched in horror as a soldier yanked a screaming boy from the arms of his mother. The woman clawed at the soldier in a frantic rage. A second soldier came up behind her and crushed the back of her skull with the butt of his gun. She dropped to the ground in a lifeless heap.

"Run, Mary!"

She yanked Jesus out of his car seat. Shielding his eyes from the madness, Mary sprinted back to the house with Joseph hot on her heels. He slammed the door behind them and turned the deadbolt.

"Let's turn off the lights and hide. Maybe they'll think nobody's home and move on," Joseph said.

More gunshots rang out as they turned off the lights and locked the doors. Afterward, they hurried to the laundry room at the back of the house and closed the curtain over its only window. Joseph told Mary to stay there with Jesus while he returned to the living room window to stand guard.

Joseph's stomach churned at the massacre going on down the hill. It was horrifying even from a distance. He couldn't imagine what it was like up close and personal.

Joseph watched a jeep pull into the neighborhood. The passenger hopped out and approached a man who was barking orders at the other soldiers. After exchanging a few words, the one barking orders pointed at Ray's house. The other soldier nodded, offered a salute, and jumped back into the jeep. It sped out of the neighborhood and onto a side road leading up the hill.

Joseph raced to the laundry room. "They're here." He closed the door and sat on the floor next to his family. "We have to be really quiet, Jesus. Can you do that for Daddy? Can you be quiet?" Joseph put a hand over his own mouth to demonstrate.

Jesus gave an exaggerated nod and slapped both hands over his mouth, giggling at what he thought was a game.

"That's good, buddy, but no laughing either. If you're really quiet, then Mommy and Daddy will get you pizza."

"Pizza!" Jesus said.

"Shh! Yes, pizza. But only if you're quiet the whole time. Starting now."

"I'm worried about Ray and Jackie. Do you think they're okay?" Mary asked, her face filled with worry.

"I'm sure they hid when they saw the helicopters. Let's pray that God is watching over them like he's watching over us."

They heard the jeep approach the house. Joseph put his arm around Mary while she clutched their son.

***

Outside, Brian stood on the front porch with his battle buddy, Chris, studying the piece of paper they'd been given. "Looks like there's two families here, but only one of them has a kid. We're looking for a boy named Jesus." Brian banged on the door and tried the doorknob. "It's locked."

"I'll check around back. Stay here in case anyone makes a run for it," Chris said.

A chatter of gunfire went off behind them followed by several screams. Brian looked down the hill and groaned. "Hurry, Chris. We're missing all the fun down there."

Chris raised his assault rifle and disappeared around the side of the house.

"Anything?" Brian said when he returned.

Chris shook his head. "Doors and windows are locked, and the blinds are all pulled shut. I bet they're hiding in there. Let's flush them out."

Brian sighed and readied his assault rifle. He just wanted to get back to the real action. "Alright, let's get this over with."

***

The sound of shattering glass caused all three of them to jump. Joseph placed a hand over Jesus's mouth and pulled him into his lap. They heard the front door open.

"Knock knock!" came a deep voice from the entryway.

Mary shook with terror. Now that the men were inside the house, it was only a matter of time before they found her family. She prayed to God for yet another miracle.

Joseph leapt to his feet. He slid the window open and motioned for Mary to go. She climbed onto a folding table and lowered herself out the window. Joseph handed Jesus to her, jumped onto the table, and threw himself out the window, landing hard on his shoulder.

"Are you okay?" Mary whispered.

"Run," Joseph said.

The back door crashed open, and two soldiers came barreling through. One soldier put a boot on Joseph's neck before he could get up. The other grabbed a handful of Mary's hair and flung her sideways. She put herself between Jesus and the ground before slamming into it. The wind rushed out of her lungs, and her grip on Jesus loosened.

The soldier that had grabbed her plucked Jesus from her arms. Jesus screamed and reached out for his mother. Joseph tried to get out from underneath the other's boot but froze when he saw a pistol pressed against Jesus's skull.

"Please don't hurt my baby! Please! You can take me, but let him go! He's just a boy!" Mary said.

"Wait! We have money in the house. Tons of it. It's yours if you let us go," Joseph said.

That got their attention. "Where is it?" asked the soldier holding Jesus.

"It's in a backpack upstairs. I can take you to it, but you have to promise to let us go."

"You're in no position to neg—"

An explosion filled the air, and the man standing on Joseph's neck jerked sideways, the left side of his body ripping open. Mary's head whipped around in time to see Jackie pumping another round into the chamber of her shotgun. Jackie's sweet-natured face had transformed into a mask of rage and sorrow, making her almost unrecognizable. Her shirt was covered in blood, which Mary prayed wasn't hers, and her hair was a tangled mess. She looked like a woman possessed.

The remaining soldier turned his gun on Jackie and pulled the trigger. The gun emitted a small click. He dropped the jammed pistol and let go of Jesus. Mary reacted instantly, yanking Jesus into her arms. The soldier reached for the rifle slung over his shoulder, but Joseph smashed into him, sending the two men tumbling to the ground. There was a satisfying crunch as Joseph landed on top of him. He rolled off the soldier and scrambled away.

"Shoot him, Jackie!"

Another blast erupted from the shotgun. The top of the soldier's head disintegrated.

Jesus, who was terrified but otherwise unharmed, clung to Mary with a death grip. His high-pitched screams pierced her eardrums like a knife. It was the most beautiful sound in the world; it was the sound of life.

Joseph threw his arms around Jackie. She dropped the shotgun and leaned into him, wrapping her arms around his neck. Her body shuddered.

"Where did you come from? Where's Ray?" Joseph said.

"Ray's dead." Jackie's voice trembled. "His last words were tellin' me to save Jesus. He thought he was in danger."

Mary sobbed. Ray was dead. The man who had taken them into his home and changed their lives forever. She thought of the loving way he looked at Jesus every night before bedtime. It crushed her soul.

"Y'all have to go. Those other men will come pokin' around up here when those two don't come back," Jackie said.

"Go where?" Joseph asked. He sounded as desperate as Mary felt.

Jackie pointed over his shoulder. "The woods. There's lots of places to hide. Take the money with you and start a new life somewhere else. Don't tell no one where you go. Word gets out, and they'll come for you again. The devil wants our sweet baby Jesus dead. I can feel it."

"Aren't you coming with us?" Mary asked, already dreading the answer.

"'Fraid not. I'm too old to be goin' on the run, and I don't have much reason to go on without Ray anyway." She bent down and picked up her shotgun. "No, I think I'll stay behind and buy you kids some time. Give those boys a little surprise party when they come knockin'."

"No!" Mary said. "We're not leaving you here." Too many people had already died today, and she wasn't about to lose another one.

Jackie pointed at Jesus. "That boy's all that matters now. Don't go riskin' his life worryin' about me. You need to get out of here."

Joseph slid an arm around Mary's waist and helped her to her feet. "She's right, Mary. We have to go."

Joseph ran into the house to grab the bag of money and whatever else he could carry. Jackie held Jesus for one last time and smothered him in kisses.

After Mary and Joseph gave her a hug goodbye, Jackie looked at the two men she'd killed. "You think God will forgive me for this?"

"Of course he will. You saved his son's life," Joseph said.

"I hope you're right, because I sure do want to see y'all again in Heaven someday."

"You will." Mary's voice was a hoarse whisper. "I promise you will."

Jackie watched them go. Mary and Joseph looked behind them when they reached the edge of the woods. Jackie gave them a final wave and went inside to wait for the rest of the soldiers. Mary took Joseph's hand and stepped into the woods to begin their new life.

PART II
THE LIFE

I have come as a light to shine in this dark world,
so that all who put their trust in me
will no longer remain in the dark.

-John 12:46

CHAPTER 1

Mary hummed to herself as she poured orange juice into the four glasses sitting around the kitchen table. "Time for breakfast, Jesus! Hurry up, or you'll be late for school!"

She smiled at the sound of his footsteps racing down the hall. Jesus bolted around the corner and slammed into his mother's leg, giving her a fierce hug. Mary kissed the top of his head. Jesus plopped into his chair and patted the chubby arm of the boy sitting in the high chair next to him.

"Morning James," Jesus said.

James had been born two years after Mary and Joseph fled Bethlehem. After the horrific day known across the country as the Bloodbath in Bethlehem, Mary and Joseph had spent two nerve-wracking days trekking through the woods of Eastern Pennsylvania. Once they had put a safe distance between themselves and the military, they had taken shelter in a rundown motel that took cash and didn't ask questions.

They had hidden inside their dingy motel room and watched the aftermath of the massacre from the tiny back and white television bolted to the dresser, only venturing out late at night for food and other necessities.

President Herod's plan to spin the story had failed miserably. Not everyone had believed the Unified Nation Network's report that The New America was behind the violence. Too many eyewitnesses told stories of the military dragging children into the streets and murdering them. Herod's camp had dismissed the eyewitnesses as immigrants and immigrant sympathizers who were trying to undermine his presidency.

Initial polls had shown an overwhelming majority of the public thought the government was hiding something. Congress, who only days before had been first in line to promote Herod's anti-immigration initiatives, had backpedaled at the first sign of negative public opinion.

With the loss of support came the loss of power, and Herod's remaining days as president were filled with opposition at every turn. Herod had underestimated the public's intelligence and grossly overestimated his own abilities. His agenda was officially dead.

After weeks of hibernating in the motel, Mary and Joseph had ventured back into the real world. With all eyes on Herod, and an active investigation into what had happened in Bethlehem, the barbaric violence appeared to be over. They began a new life on the other side of the country, somewhere far away from the violence and painful memories that had wrecked their lives. They rented a modest home in the suburbs that was older but affordable. Joseph took a job with a local furniture company while he rebuilt his carpentry business, and thanks to the money from the scientists, Mary was able to stay at home with Jesus.

As time passed, Joseph's business took off, and he left the furniture company to focus on his business full time. They started talking about growing their family, and soon God had blessed them with another baby boy, this one conceived between husband and wife. Mary's heart was full. Life had returned to normal, or at least as normal as she thought it could ever be after the horrific day in Bethlehem.

"Good morning everyone." Joseph hugged Mary around the waist and kissed her lips.

"Hi Daddy!" Jesus said.

"How you doing, buddy? Are you hungry?"

"Starving."

Joseph ruffled Jesus's hair and stopped to tickle James under the arm. He plucked a grape from Jesus's plate and popped it in his mouth.

"Daddy!" Jesus said.

Joseph gave him a mischievous grin. "What? I'm just making sure it's safe for you to eat."

Mary swatted his shoulder. "You behave, or you're going to work without breakfast, mister." Sometimes she thought she was raising three children instead of two.

Joseph held up his hands in mock surrender and took his seat. Jesus laughed, and James laughed along with him.

Jesus shoved the last spoonful of cereal into his mouth and slurped the remaining milk from the bottom of the bowl. He smacked his lips and wiped at his face with the sleeve of his shirt.

"Use your napkin, please," Mary said.

"Sorry, Mom." Jesus patted his mouth with his napkin and dropped it on the table. "Hey, did you know I'm special?"

"Of course you are, kiddo. You're Mommy's special little boy."

"I mean I'm *really* special. Like special to the whole world."

"Oh?" Mary raised her eyebrows. "That sounds pretty special. Did your father tell you that?"

"No, God did last night when I was sleeping."

Joseph choked on his coffee.

"So you dreamt it?" Mary already knew the answer. She thought back to the night in Bethlehem when Jesus had been reaching up toward the ceiling.

Jesus shrugged. "Not really. I mean, I was sleeping, but he woke me up to tell me I was really special."

Joseph leaned forward with his hands folded in front of him. "Sometimes I think something is real, and then I wake up and realize it was only a dream."

"You mean like when I think a monster is chasing me, and I wake up all scared and have to sleep with you and Mommy?"

"Yep, just like that," Joseph said.

Jesus shook his head. "This was different. God really talked to me. Doesn't he talk to you?"

Joseph glanced at Mary before answering. "Well . . . yes. Sometimes God can speak to us through other people or through his word."

"But do you hear his voice?"

"No, sweetie," Mary interjected. "We've never actually heard his voice."

Jesus's face lit up. "I did, and it was awesome!"

Mary shivered against the chill running down her spine. She didn't know what to say. "Why don't you brush your teeth and get your backpack. We can talk about this after school."

Jesus slid off his chair and ran down the hall. Mary watched him go with her mouth hanging open. In the back of her mind she had always known something like this would happen, but now that it was here, she was stunned.

"What are we going to tell him?" Mary said.

"Maybe we shouldn't tell him anything."

"Seriously? Our son just had a conversation with God, and we're supposed to act like it didn't happen?"

"What else can we do? Tell a six-year-old that he's God's son?"

Mary stared into her coffee cup like a fortune teller reading tea leaves. "Well, no, but I feel like we should do *something*."

Joseph reached across the table and took her hand. "What if God's just reaching out to let him know he's there? Building a relationship like a normal father and son. Just a little check in to say hello. If that's all it is, then there's no sense rocking the boat."

"So you really think we should ignore it?"

Joseph nodded. "For now. Let's wait and see where this goes. If nothing else happens, then I think we're better off leaving it alone. Besides, I'm sure God will let us know if he wants us involved."

Joseph always knew how to put her at ease. "He does have a way of making sure everything works out, doesn't he?"

"Exactly. If angels show up telling us to talk to Jesus, I'll be the first one to tell him." Joseph raised a hand in the air with three fingers extended. "Scout's honor."

"You're such a dork. A handsome one, but still a dork."

"Can you believe the way she talks to me, James?" He kissed his son on the cheek. "You keep her in line while I'm at work, okay?"

James patted his father's face with sticky hands. "Okay."

"Let's go, Jesus! Time for school!" Joseph said.

Jesus came down the hall, dragging his backpack behind him. Mary cringed at the sound of the zipper scraping against the wall.

"Looks like I'll be doing some touch-up painting today."

Joseph grabbed his lunch and gave her a kiss. "Just leave it. The boys are always leaving scratches and stains all over the place."

"Uh-huh. And which *boy* put that stain on the wall when trying to squirt ketchup on his hotdog from across the room?"

"That was a science experiment. We were testing propulsion," Joseph said.

"Right. Why don't you propel yourself out of this house before you dig yourself an even deeper hole?"

He gave Mary a wink and held the door open for Jesus. Mary blew him a kiss. As the door closed behind them, Mary heard the inquisitive voice of her son.

"So why do you think God talked to me last night if he's never talked to you and Mom?"

CHAPTER 2

Joseph pulled into the driveway amidst the screams and tears of his children. Mary sat in the passenger seat with a dull throb pulsing at her temples, threatening to bloom into a full-blown migraine.

It had been the kind of day people joked about in casual conversations. A family fighting on their way to temple, forcing a smile on their faces as they arrive, and then resuming their family Royal Rumble once outside the holy grounds.

The morning had been a disaster. James had said he was too tired to go to temple and then claimed he was sick when his parents told him he still had to go.

Trey had decided he wanted to wear his Cookie Monster pajamas instead of dress clothes. When Mary had forced him into a button-up shirt and slacks, he rebelled in true four-year-old fashion. He hid in his room until it was time to leave and then came to the front door dressed in his pajamas, the dress clothes buried in the bottom of the hamper.

Angela, who was normally an easy-going baby, had refused to eat her breakfast, bit Trey on the arm when he tried to hug her, and had a diaper explosion that ruined her pink dress moments before it was time to leave.

On the way to temple, Joseph had been pulled over for speeding. As the officer approached the vehicle, James's rendition of *Bad Boys* had earned him a week without television.

The ride home had been just as bad. Angela cried the entire way, for reasons unknown to everyone except her. James whined because his parents wouldn't take them to the new pizza place for lunch, and Trey antagonized his siblings by continuously smacking his lips.

Now, Mary closed her eyes as Joseph turned off the car. During a morning that had been a true test of patience, Jesus had been the only saving grace. He'd done his best to cheer up his grumpy brother, James, and had offered to change Angela's dress while his parents wrestled Trey into another set of clothes. Jesus was only twelve, but Mary thought he was more mature than a lot of adults.

A sudden realization smacked her across the face. "Jesus!"

"What?" Joseph said, pulling Angela from her car seat.

"We left him at the temple!"

Joseph did a quick headcount and screamed. "Everyone back in the car!"

"Geez, Dad. I guess we know who your least favorite kid is," James said.

Joseph spun around and glared at him. "Zip it."

James shrank into his seat. "Sorry, Dad."

It was a twenty minute drive to the temple, but to Mary it seemed like an eternity. She tugged on the hem of her dress while tapping her foot against the floorboard. "Can't you go any faster?"

"I could, but I don't think a speeding ticket is going to help anything."

"*Another* speeding ticket," James corrected.

"James!" Joseph hollered.

"What kind of mother gets all the way home before she realizes her child isn't with her? What if this scars him for life?"

Joseph laughed. "It's not like we left him under the bridge downtown. I doubt he'll be talking to his therapist about it when he's thirty."

As Joseph pulled into the deserted parking lot, Mary's shaking hands released the clip of her seatbelt, and she sprung from the car like a bull released from its chute. She prayed that Jesus was still there.

Joseph gathered the children while Mary burst into the temple. She heard a murmur of voices floating out of the sanctuary, and breathed a sigh of relief when she saw Jesus sitting on the steps of the altar, surrounded by the rabbi and several members of his board.

Jesus stood when he saw her. "Hey, Mom. I was going to call you to come pick me up when I was done. Honest."

Mary hugged him tight. "I'm just glad you're okay. I'm so sorry we forgot you."

"Why were you worried? Didn't you know I was in my father's house?"

"What do you mean? We left the house—"

The realization of what he meant struck her like an anvil. He knew. Joseph's intuition had been right all those years ago. God had revealed things to Jesus when the time was right. A million questions flooded her mind, but before she could ask them, the rabbi greeted her by placing his hands over hers.

"Mary, you have an amazing son. He's been blessing us with his wisdom this afternoon."

"He has?"

"Jesus is wise beyond his years and has frankly given me things to reflect on in my own studies. It's no exaggeration to say that he's amazed us with his knowledge. You must be very proud of your son."

"Yes, of course. I just . . . well, to be completely honest I didn't realize how much Jesus knew."

Mary felt like a failure for the second time that day. How could she have been so blind to everything her son understood? She knew Jesus studied the Torah every day, but never in her wildest dreams had she sensed a level of knowledge that would rival a rabbi. Had Jesus kept it from her, or had she failed to see it?

Joseph and the kids entered the sanctuary. "Jesus! Thank goodness you're alive. Your mother thought you'd joined a gang and were out robbing banks."

Mary poked him in the side. "Come on, you big goof. Let's go home." She put her arm around Jesus and pulled him close. "All of us this time."

CHAPTER 3

"There will be no talking, no wandering eyes, and no getting up from your desk for any reason. Raise your hand when you're done, and I will come get your test. Any questions?"

The students remained silent as Mr. Shafer walked up the aisles, dropping a test on each desk as he went.

"Psst! Jesus." Jesus glanced at the boy sitting to his left. "Tilt your paper this way so I can see it, okay?"

Jesus shook his head while avoiding eye contact. Cody Meyers was everything most kids in high school wanted to be. He was a jock with good looks that kept the cheerleaders drooling and a sense of humor that kept the guys laughing. And just like a stereotypical jock, Cody had better things to do than study. So it was no surprise that he was looking to cheat on the last Chemistry test before winter break.

"I'm serious, Jesus. Let me copy your paper."

Jesus shook his head again, keeping his eyes locked on his desk. Cody reached out and kicked the leg of Jesus's chair. The sound reverberated across the otherwise silent room.

"Quiet, please!" Mr. Shafer glared in their direction.

When the test began, Jesus used his left arm to block Cody's view. Jesus hovered over his paper like a mama bird protecting her eggs. Cody's face twisted into a deeper and deeper scowl as the test progressed. By the time it was over, he looked like he was ready to kill Jesus.

During lunch, Jesus sat in the corner of the cafeteria, reading through his Torah while waiting for his friends to arrive. Today was the Torah study Jesus held once a week during their lunch hour. What started as a meeting with three of his closest friends had blossomed into a group of over twenty people in less than a month. Jesus's passion for God's word had resonated with a lot of his classmates.

He was engrossed in the Torah when Cody approached the table with two of his friends. He slapped the book out of Jesus's hands and jabbed a finger into his chest.

"I probably flunked that test because of you."

Jesus winced as the finger dug into his chest. "I'm sorry, but I wasn't going to let you cheat off my paper. We'd both fail if Mr. Shafer caught us. Besides, cheating isn't right."

"Cheating isn't right," Cody mimicked in a high-pitched voice. Cody's friends laughed. "Is that what your little book of fairy tales told you?"

Jesus sat up straight. He could tolerate a lot of things, but listening to someone mock God's word wasn't one of them. "The Torah is not a book of fairy tales." He looked at the crowd that had gathered around them. "It's full of truth that gives us insight into who God is and what he expects from us. And yes, it says cheating is wrong."

"Of course!" Cody picked up the Torah and held it above his head. "A book thousands of years old, written by a bunch of sheep herders, is the word of God. That sounds more logical than it all being a bunch of crap meant for people who can't think for themselves." He threw the book at Jesus. "You better watch your back. I'm not through with you."

Cody returned to his table, his cohorts patting him on the back and snorting with laughter. The members of the Torah study group sat down around Jesus as the crowd dispersed. A few stragglers lingered. Jesus regarded them with a smile.

"There's plenty of room at our table if you'd like to join us. Today we'll be talking about forgiveness, which is fitting given what just happened."

Cody had done a terrible thing, but Jesus had already forgiven him for it. Besides, thanks to Cody's outburst, there were new people taking an interest in what Jesus was teaching. This was just another example of how God used all things for his glory.

Two of the girls exchanged a look. One of them nodded, and they took a seat next to Jesus.

***

When the final bell rang, Jesus and his best friend, Lazarus, walked through the senior parking lot and into the field beyond it. Jesus had met Lazarus their freshman year, and they'd been best friends ever since. They bonded over common interests, both preferring to spend their weekends playing video games or basketball instead of attending drunken parties with the rest of their classmates.

"Man, I'm sorry I wasn't at lunch today. I would have had your back. That jerk doesn't scare me," Lazarus said.

Jesus hooked his thumbs through the straps of his backpack. "Don't worry about it. I feel sorry for him. Maybe he's insecure or has a bad home life. Who knows? It's better to pray for him instead of being angry about it."

Lazarus shook his head. "Dude, you're a better man than I am."

"Especially at video games. That's why I kicked your tail at Street Fighter last weekend and plan on doing it again tomorrow."

Lazarus put Jesus in a headlock and wrestled him to the ground. "Oh really? Who's better now?"

"I think my record speaks for itself. Hadouken!" Jesus twisted out of the headlock and ran away laughing.

He sprinted to the end of the field and stopped several yards short of the street. Lazarus pulled up next to him. Cody and his two friends were leaning against the trunk of a red Camaro, hurling rocks at a nearby tree. Cody noticed Jesus. An evil smile spread across his face.

"Hey there, Jesus. Long time no see. You playing tag with your boyfriend?"

"Shut up and leave us alone," Lazarus said.

Cody whispered something to his friends, and the three of them walked up to Jesus. "All you had to do was slide your paper over so I could have a peek. Why'd you have to make things so difficult?"

"Like I told you, it wasn't the right thing to do." Jesus had already forgiven Cody once today. He thought he was about to have to do it again.

"The right thing to do? If I flunked that test, then I can't play ball. You know what that does to our team?"

"It probably makes them better. I've seen you play. You're awful," Lazarus said.

Cody's friends grabbed Lazarus and forced him to his knees. Lazarus struggled against their grip, but he was outnumbered and out-muscled.

Cody returned his gaze to Jesus. "The thing is, I can't have people thinking you got away with standing up to me. I have a certain reputation to uphold."

"As a piece of crap? Mission accomplished," Lazarus said.

Cody laughed. "Your friend's got some fight in him, Jesus. I'd almost respect him if he didn't hang around a religious freak like you."

Cody swung a right hook and connected with Jesus's face. Stars exploded in front of his eyes, and he dropped to the ground like a sack of potatoes. Lazarus fought to break free, but Cody's friends tightened their grip on him.

Cody knelt beside Jesus. "I need people to understand what happens when you cross me." He turned Jesus's face to expose a red mark blossoming around his left eye. "This should do nicely."

He shoved Jesus's face into the dirt. Lazarus spat a wad of phlegm that landed on Cody's arm. Cody stared at him with hatred in his eyes.

"Pick him up," Cody said.

His friends pulled Lazarus to his feet. Cody stood and drove a knee straight into his gut. Lazarus doubled over, his mouth opening and closing like a fish out of water as he fought for air.

"Let him go," Cody said.

Lazarus fell to the ground, his hands cradling his stomach. Cody leaned over and spat into his face.

"You boys have a nice day," Cody said.

The boys returned to the Camaro. The car roared to life, leaving behind a trail of smoke and the smell of burning rubber as it raced away.

"You okay, Jesus?" Lazarus said, sitting up and wiping the spit from his face.

Jesus winced as his fingers prodded his swollen eye. "I'll be fine."

"Those guys are dead. When I tell my cousins what happened, they'll pay Cody a little visit. I bet they'll jack up his stupid car, and probably jack up his face while they're at it." Lazarus pounded his fist into the palm of his hand.

Jesus loved Lazarus, but his temper often ran a little hot. "More violence will only make things worse. We should forgive them and move on."

"Forgive them? Are you nuts?"

Jesus stood and helped Lazarus to his feet. "As God's ambassadors, we're called to be different from the rest of the world. If we retaliate, then we're no better than they are."

"You know, having you as a friend is like having my own personal Jiminy Cricket telling me right from wrong."

Jesus smiled. "I'll take that as a compliment. So you'll forgive them?"

"I'll try."

***

Jesus could hear the whine of his dad's belt sander as he skirted around the side of the house and walked through the backyard gate. Joseph's workshop sat in the far corner of the half-acre lot. The metal frame's unassuming brown matched the dormant vegetation surrounding it.

Joseph owned a shop downtown where he did most of his business, but he liked to work from home a couple of afternoons a week so he could be there when his kids got home from school. *Family first* was one of Joseph's core values, and you could see it in the way he lived his life.

The workshop door hung open. Joseph's face hid behind a dust mask and a pair of safety glasses. His head was bent over a rough piece of wood that would soon become a beautiful hutch. Dust particles floated in the beams of sunlight like dancing fairies.

Joseph saw Jesus standing in the doorway. He turned off the belt sander and pulled down his mask to reveal a warm smile.

"Hey, son! How was school?"

Jesus stepped from the shadows and pointed to his eye. The smile on Joseph's face disappeared.

"Has your mother seen this?" Jesus shook his head. "She's going to freak out."

"That's why I'm out here. I was hoping you could calm her down for me."

"I don't know about that. Remember when James came home with lice? I thought she was going to burn the house down." Joseph pulled a can of soda from the mini fridge and tossed it to Jesus. "Put that on your eye. It'll help the swelling go down some before we go inside."

141

The cold can was soothing against his stinging eye. Jesus sank to the floor and rested his head against the wall. Joseph grabbed a folding chair and sat across from him.

"Want to tell me what happened? Fighting's not like you."

"It wasn't a fight. This guy from school slugged me because I wouldn't let him cheat off my test."

Joseph relaxed. "That's good. Not that you got beat up, but that you weren't doing anything wrong. Did you tell the teacher?"

Jesus shook his head. "It happened on the way home from school."

"Who's the kid? You want me to talk to his father?" Jesus shook his head again. "Right. Sometimes I forget what it was like to be a teenager. Having your daddy fight your battles doesn't exactly make you the cool kid."

"I'm not the cool kid anyway. Most people think I'm weird."

"Does that bother you?"

Jesus shrugged. "Sometimes. Like when they make fun of me for studying the Torah at school."

"I know it's tough, but God needs people like you. People that aren't afraid to share their faith and stand up for what's right. The world is full of people trying to be like everyone else. They need someone who's different to show them the light."

Jesus pointed to his face. "I tried to show Cody the light, but I don't think he was very receptive."

Joseph shifted in his chair. "I'm going to share something with you that might make you feel a little better. I got in a fight over a girl when I was about your age."

Jesus couldn't believe it. His dad was one of the gentlest people he knew. He couldn't imagine him getting in a fight. "You fought over a girl? Was it Mom?"

"No. Just some girl from high school I barely remember now, but at the time I thought she was my soulmate. I worked up the courage to ask her to the school dance, and she said yes. I was on top of the world. At least until she changed her mind the next day because another guy she liked better asked her out."

"Ouch."

"Ouch is right. She broke my heart, and I was furious. Not at her, but at the poor guy that asked her to the dance. I confronted him and said some things I shouldn't have. One thing led to another, and I hit him."

"Dad!" Jesus said, shocked at this other side of his father.

"I know, I know. Nothing to be proud of, but I did it. And everyone thought I was this big alpha male. Well, everyone except the guy I sucker-punched and my ex-soulmate."

"I've got to be honest. If this is supposed to make me feel better, then you're doing a terrible job."

"Stay with me, son. A couple of days later the guy came up to me, and do you know what he did?"

"Hit you back?"

"Nope. He shook my hand and said he was sorry. Said he wished things would have turned out differently, and maybe we could have lunch together to bury the hatchet. After that, I felt bad about what I did to him."

"Did you have lunch with him?"

"Well, that would be a good ending to the story, but no. I never talked to him again, and I stayed the alpha male."

"Not exactly the feel-good ending I was expecting."

"The point of the story is that even though I never let it show that he got to me, he did. Most of my high school days are nothing more than fuzzy memories, but that one moment is crystal clear even to this day. What he did played a part in the man I've become. He made a lasting impression on my life, and he'll never know it."

"So Cody might be like that too?"

"Maybe, but it might be someone else. Someone watching you from the sidelines that's too scared to join you at lunch. Your actions could change someone's life for the better, and you'll never know it. How's that for a story?"

Jesus smiled. "I retract my previous statement. You make a good point."

Joseph stood from his chair and sat next to Jesus. He slung an arm around his son. "Do you remember when you were younger, and you told us you were really special?"

"No."

"But you know that you are, right? You're more special than the rest of us." He patted Jesus's chest. "Can you feel it inside of you?" Jesus looked at his father's hands and nodded. "The things you're doing at school are only the beginning. You're destined to do great things for God. Your mom and I are so proud of the man you've become. So proud."

Jesus leaned into his father, and Joseph hugged him tight. They sat on the dusty floor and held each other without saying a word.

His dad was right. Jesus knew he would do great things, but he was struggling to come to terms with what that meant. God had been talking to him a lot lately. Well, talking wasn't exactly the right word for it. More like showing him things, giving him glimpses of his potential.

People referred to God as their father, but those words had a different meaning for Jesus. Defining that relationship was still a work in progress, but he knew he was somehow different from everyone else. It was difficult to understand and even more difficult to explain to his parents. But at least his dad seemed to know some of what he was going through. Perhaps God was showing him some things too.

CHAPTER 4

Jesus stepped inside the hospital elevator and pressed the button for the seventh floor. The elevator seemed to taunt him with its slow ascent.

His day had been turned upside down in an instant. He'd been sitting in the University Library, putting the finishing touches on his theology paper, when his mom had called with the unexpected news. After hanging up, Jesus had made the two hour drive to the hospital, every minute crawling by like someone had pressed the slow-motion button on life.

Jesus had plenty of time to assume the worst. All he'd been told was that his mom had found his dad unconscious in the bathroom, and the doctors had found some internal bleeding. Jesus wasn't a doctor, but you didn't have to be one to know that internal bleeding was bad, very bad.

James was waiting for Jesus on the other side of the elevator doors. He updated his brother on the latest while leading him through a maze of hallways.

"Bottom line is nobody knows anything yet. It doesn't look good, but right now we're staying positive for Dad," James said.

James stopped in front of the hospital room and knocked before entering. Mary jumped from her chair and wrapped her arms around Jesus.

"Come on now. Break it up so I can see my boy." Joseph's face was a shade of white that seemed impossible for someone with such a dark complexion.

"How you feeling, Dad?" Jesus wasn't used to seeing him look so weak. The sight of his dad in a flimsy hospital gown with wires and tubes coming out of him was soul-crushing.

"I've been better. They're going to give me a colonoscopy. They want to jam a camera up my backside and have a look around. I always wanted to be on television, but this isn't exactly what I had in mind."

"Always with the jokes. Even in the hospital," Jesus said.

"Just trying to lighten the mood. Everyone's so glum."

Mary took a wet rag from a bowl on the table and wiped Joseph's brow. "We're just worried about you, that's all."

Joseph closed his eyes as the rag brushed across his forehead. "Would you mind if I had a few minutes alone with Jesus? I'd like to catch up before the nurse comes back."

"Of course. Kids, let's go down to the cafeteria and see what we can find," Mary said.

Mary ushered everyone into the hall and closed the door behind her. The blood pressure machine hummed as the band on Joseph's arm inflated.

"Sit down, son. Let's chat."

Jesus dragged a chair over to the bed and took a closer look at his dad. The dark circles under his eyes were the only color in his face. His cheeks and forehead glistened with sweat.

"I'm going to be honest with you, if that's okay. Man-to-man," Joseph said.

"Sure, Dad. What's up?"

"I don't know what's wrong with me, but it's bad. I can feel it."

There was an uneasy feeling in the pit of Jesus's stomach. "Don't say that. You're going to be fine. The doctors will run some tests and figure this out."

Joseph gave a half shrug. "We'll see. I'm not trying to scare you, but I don't want to sugarcoat it either."

"Does Mom know?"

"You know how your mother is. She's a worrier, and she's stressed enough as it is."

"Then why are you telling me?"

"Because there are some things I need to tell you. Things you need to hear in case something happens to me."

Joseph took Jesus's hand. The strong, calloused hands of his father were now weak and clammy.

"If something happens to me, I want you and James to run the family business. Both of you know your way around a work-bench, and you can take the business to the next level. At least until it's time for you to move on to other things."

"What other things?" Tears were running down Jesus's face.

"I'm not sure, but we both know you're meant for more than woodwork, don't we?"

"No, I'll stay with Mom and take care of her as long as she needs me."

"Son, look at me." Jesus met his dad's eyes. "Your mother will need you when I'm gone, but she'll understand when it's time for you to answer your own calling."

"Because I'm special?"

Joseph smiled. "You knew it when you were a little kid just like you know it now. That's right. Because you're special. I love you, son. I've done my best to raise you right, and I pray to God that I have."

"You have, Dad. You've been the best father I could have ever hoped for. I love you so much."

"Then I've done what I was put on this earth to do."

While the rest of the family ate in the cafeteria, Joseph and Jesus prayed together, cried, and even managed a laugh or two. Jesus thought of all the times his dad had been there for him over the years. Now, it was his turn to be there for him.

***

The doctors couldn't solve the mysterious illness that had taken hold of Joseph's body. Two days later, Joseph fell into a coma and passed away shortly after. Jesus dropped out of college and returned home to take care of his family. With the help of his brother, James, their father's business grew beyond anything Joseph could have ever imagined. Life continued this way for Jesus until God told him it was time to move on to something even bigger.

CHAPTER 5

Jesus, now in his thirties, checked his reflection in the front window, straightened his tie, and rang the doorbell. He rehearsed the upcoming conversation in his mind for the hundredth time. Mary opened the door and rolled her eyes.

"Why on earth are you ringing the doorbell? You have a key for goodness' sake."

"It's early, and I didn't want to scare you."

"Nonsense! You're always welcome in this house no matter what time it is." She glanced at the clock on the wall. "But you are early this morning. Temple isn't for another hour. Come inside and have some breakfast while I finish getting ready."

"That's okay. I already ate."

"Are you sure? I picked up some fresh fruit at the market yesterday. Or how about a muffin?"

"Listen, Mom. I have something I need to talk to you about."

Mary stopped halfway across the kitchen and turned to face him. She brushed a strand of hair behind her ear, the once vibrant black now streaked with gray. "Is everything okay?"

Jesus led her into the living room and motioned for her to sit with him on the couch. "I've spent the last few hours wrestling with the perfect way to tell you this, but I feel like I should just come right out and say it."

"You're scaring me, Jesus. What is it?"

He took a deep breath. "God spoke to me last night. It's time for me to go."

Mary beamed. "Oh, that's wonderful news!"

"You're not upset?" This was not the reaction he'd been expecting.

"Heavens no! Your father and I knew when you were a baby that you were meant for big things. We didn't know exactly what or when, but we knew it probably meant you would have to leave home someday."

"Did God speak to you and Dad too?"

Mary paused. "In a way, yes."

Her revelation floored Jesus. "Why didn't you ever say anything?"

"We almost did, but your father thought it was best to let you work through it on your own. He thought God would reveal everything to you when the time was right, and it looks like he has."

"God told me I'm not fully human. Did you know that too?" Mary nodded. "I don't understand everything he's trying to tell me, but it's slowly coming together."

"Where are you going? When?"

"I'll pack tonight and leave in the morning. God showed me I should visit John, but so far that's all I know."

"Elizabeth said your cousin has quite the following these days."

Jesus hadn't seen his cousin in years, but he'd kept track of him through social media. He was a radical preacher doing things differently, and he was getting a lot of attention, both good and bad.

Mary placed a hand on his shoulder. "Your father would be so proud."

Jesus thought back to the conversation he'd had with his dad at the hospital all those years ago. Now he understood the cryptic message behind those final words. His dad didn't think Jesus was meant for greatness because he was his son. He knew he was meant for greatness because God had told him.

***

The entire family had lunch at Mary's house after temple. It was a weekly tradition that was about to come to an end. Over dessert, Jesus shared the news with the rest of his family, leaving out the part about him being more than human.

Trey showed little emotion. Angela cried. James exploded.

"What about Mom? Are you really that selfish? You can't abandon her," James said.

"He's not abandoning anyone. God has blessed him with a calling, and I want him to follow it," Mary said. "We should all be supporting him."

"It's not a calling. He doesn't even know what he's going to be doing," James said.

"I'll give you my half of the business. You'll have more than enough money to take care of Mom and whatever else the family needs while I'm gone. Trey could be your partner now that he's done with college."

"I don't want to be in the family business," Trey muttered.

"Dad left you in charge to look after Mom," James said. "You're not just failing us. You're failing him."

Mary slammed her hands on the table. "Enough!"

"No offense, Mom, but you're delusional if you think this is a good idea. Leaving because God told him to? Do you hear how stupid that sounds? This is a midlife crisis on steroids. Looks like your perfect son isn't so perfect after all, huh?"

"Don't talk to Mom like that," Jesus said. He had expected James to be a little upset, he had always been a bit of a hothead, but it broke Jesus's heart to see him blow up like this.

"Just get out of here, and go on your fantasy adventure. I'll stay behind and take care of the family."

Jesus looked around the room. "I'm sorry this is so sudden, but I didn't know about it myself until last night." James barked a bitter laugh. "I need to go home and pack, but I hope all of you will come say goodbye before I leave in the morning."

He walked around the table and hugged everyone. James became rigid as Jesus wrapped his arms around him. James slipped out of the embrace and disappeared into the next room.

The car ride home was a solemn one. Jesus prayed that his family would understand why he had to leave, especially James. He also prayed for more clarification regarding his future. Where would he go after visiting John? How was he going to spread God's word? He listened with a still heart but heard nothing.

Jesus pulled into his driveway, shut off the engine, and closed his eyes. God had shown him the first step. He would visit John as instructed, and once he found him, he had faith that God would show him what to do next.

CHAPTER 6

John stood along the bank of the river, preaching to the large crowd standing in front of him. Many were there to be baptized, some had come out of curiosity, and a few had shown up to mock him.

"Many of you are looking to be baptized today for the wrong reasons. You're seeking an insurance policy against God's wrath, but your heart remains hardened against him. You act out of fear rather than a desire to become closer to God. You are nothing more than a brood of vipers! I pray you will truly repent and seek his grace instead of just a get-out-of-Hell-free card."

John was a preacher who was doing things his own way, ignoring the traditional norms of the world. He'd left home after high school and built a log cabin for himself in the wilderness. It wasn't like the majestic log cabins they showed on television or advertised in travel magazines. John's cabin was a single room with only a bed, a stove, a fireplace, and a small wooden table with chairs. A crude outhouse sat several yards behind it.

John made his clothes from the animals he hunted, and he preferred to only eat what he could scavenge. It wasn't unusual for him to dine on locusts and wild honey when his fishing and hunting expeditions came up short.

His appearance matched his rugged lifestyle. His hair, which hung past his shoulders, was unkempt, and his beard was thick and disheveled.

John's decision to live the minimalist lifestyle had not been a popular one. Friends and relatives thought he had lost his mind, and they questioned how his parents could allow him to live such a life.

Zach and Elizabeth understood everyone's criticism. They would have thought the same thing if it weren't for Gabriel's visit to Zach over thirty years ago. He had promised them John was going to bring many people to the Lord. They had always assumed that meant he would become a priest like his father, but they never questioned John's decision to go his own way. Unlike Mary and Joseph, they had been open with John about their encounter with Gabriel. They told him everything they knew and trusted God to take it from there.

John began his ministry by preaching to those who came into the woods. He would visit campsites, greet people on the various hiking trails, and stop to chat with those fishing along the river. Many were apprehensive about being approached by such an unusual man, but John had a calming demeanor that usually put people at ease after a brief introduction.

It wasn't long before John had gained a following. Locals regularly came to see him, and vacationers would often seek him out, word of the woodsman having spread to the surrounding cities. He began holding weekly sermons on the riverbank. The first week he baptized one person. The following week he baptized an entire family. Before long he was baptizing a line of people every week, thus earning him the nickname of John the Baptist.

It thrilled John to see his unique style of preaching resonating with people. He was blunt about their sinful nature, and he also attacked the Pharisees and Sadducees for their rampant hypocrisy. These were two Jewish sects that held religious and political power among the Jews. These men were high-ranking leaders who acted righteous in public but often hid ungodly secrets behind closed doors. They were more concerned about outward appearances than following God with a pure heart.

His preaching was controversial. People began posting videos of his sermons online, and John became an internet sensation.

He gained a group of loyal followers who became his disciples. They were always by his side to help with whatever he needed. They coordinated his sermons, which were now being held three to four times a week, and helped control the crowds.

"Pursue God with all of your heart. Do it sincerely rather than trying to impress others," John continued. "God is love, and by showing love to others, you can know God's heart and draw closer to him." He pointed to a young man on the front row that appeared to be in his early twenties. "What do you do for a living?"

The man was taken aback. "Um, I . . . I work for the IRS."

A wave of boos came from the crowd. John held up his hands.

"Come on, everyone. That's no way to treat a fellow child of God. You shouldn't judge someone based on their profession. In fact, you shouldn't judge people at all. A person's job, their looks, what they wear, what they drive. None of that is your concern. Those of you who judge others so you can feel better about yourselves are no better than the Pharisees."

There was a hush among the crowd. The sting of truth had hit them hard. John turned back to the tax collector.

"Your profession has a bad reputation, and your powerful position intimidates a lot of people. Use that power for good instead of evil. You can show love by only charging what someone legally owes instead of charging extra to line your own pockets. You can show mercy to a struggling single mother by forgiving an innocent tax mistake instead of raking her over the coals with penalties and interest."

John pointed toward the back of the crowd. Everyone craned their necks to see who he was looking at.

"Young lady in the back with the pink hat and black tank top." The woman looked to both sides before pointing to herself. "Yes, you. What do you do?"

She stood up straight and stuck out her chest. "I'm a police officer."

"You can love others by not falsely accusing people and by helping those in need. Don't abuse your power and always treat others with respect. People watch you closely. Make sure they see God through your actions."

John continued preaching with a tireless passion. As the morning transitioned to afternoon, he invited those who wished to be baptized to join him by the water. About twenty people came forward, and John waded into the river while they formed a line in the wet sand. One at a time, he buried their old selves beneath the murky water and brought them out brand new.

Halfway through the baptisms, a lone figure appeared at the tree line in the distance. As the stranger got closer, John noticed him and did a double take. His heart filled with joy when he recognized the man approaching him. Leaving behind those waiting to be baptized, John sprinted along the sand and barreled into Jesus, almost knocking him to the ground. The two men embraced while patting each other on the back.

"It's great to see you, cuz!" John said.

"It's been a while, hasn't it?"

"A while? It's been years since I've seen you."

"Definitely too long, but I've been keeping tabs on you. You're doing some amazing things down here."

John shook his head. "Not me, cuz. It's all God. I mean, look at me. I look like some crazy hippie that's been transported from the past. Not to mention I was terrified of public speaking when I was younger. And now?" John motioned toward the hundreds of people behind them. "Nothing but the hand of God could explain all of this. The same hand that brought you here to see me, am I right?"

Jesus looked like someone had thrown cold water in his face. "What do you know about that?"

"Only as much as the Holy Spirit showed me, which I'm sure is a lot less than what it's showed you."

"What did you see?"

John waived away the question like a man swatting at gnats. "Follow me."

The people watched Jesus with a curious intensity. John chuckled to himself when he thought of how his cousin was about to change their world. With one arm slung over Jesus's shoulders, John addressed the crowd.

"People always ask me if I'm the Messiah, and my answer is always the same. I'm a prophet that preaches God's truth, but I am not the Savior you've been waiting for. There is another who is more powerful than me. Someone whose shoes I am not fit to carry. While I have come to baptize you with water, the one who follows me will baptize you with the Holy Spirt." John pointed at Jesus. "This is your Messiah! This is the one God has sent to save all of mankind, and you are blessed to be the first to hear the wonderful news!"

The crowd became a melting pot of emotions. There were cries of joy, mocking laughter, and looks of disgust. An older woman limped to the front of the crowd with a gnarled finger pointed at Jesus.

"This man is no Messiah. That's blasphemy! May God strike you both dead!"

Jesus took a step toward the crowd. "I have come here today for only one thing. Many of you have already been baptized at the hands of John, and today I humbly ask him to do the same to me."

"Are you kidding me? I'm not worthy to baptize the Messiah. You should baptize me," John said. He had no desire to be the center of attention right now. This was Jesus's big moment.

"This is God's will. Who better to baptize me than the man who is bringing so many people to God?"

A few people left, but the majority crowded against the edge of the water for a closer look. Even those who thought he was crazy couldn't resist an opportunity to watch the event unfold.

Hundreds of phones were held in outstretched hands, everyone eager to post their video online and reap the likes from their virtual friends. People jostled for position. A phone plunged to its watery grave among the chaos.

John and Jesus waded into the river until the water rose above their waists. Facing the crowd, John offered the most heartfelt prayer he had ever given and lowered Jesus into the water. When Jesus resurfaced, a low rumble tore through the sky.

"This is my son whom I love; with him I am well pleased," a disembodied voice said.

The powerful voice seemed to come from everywhere. It sounded like a man, but not quite human. Everyone looked around, confused and frightened. John felt weak in the knees and gripped Jesus's shoulders for balance.

"It's not on my video!" a young man shouted, staring at his phone. "There's no voice!"

One by one, others looked at their phones. Each one revealed the same result: neither the voice nor the rumbling in the sky had been recorded. Some shook their heads in disbelief. Others cried.

A married couple broke to the front of the crowd, hands locked together and tears running down their faces. They dropped to their knees and bowed at Jesus's feet.

Wet sand clung to the woman's hair as she pulled her face from the ground. "It was the voice of God, wasn't it? You're the Messiah!"

"Lord, forgive us for doubting," the husband said. "How could we be so foolish?"

Others joined the couple at Jesus's feet. The doubters hung back, some choosing to mock the believers.

"It was mass hypnosis."

"You all look ridiculous."

Jesus walked among the people kneeling before him. He grabbed outreached hands and touched the shoulders of those he passed. John was in awe as he watched the scene unfold in front of him.

People shouted questions at Jesus, and some tried to follow him. The disciples held them back as John took Jesus deep into the woods toward his cabin.

That night Jesus and John sat around the rickety table eating dinner. John used the last of his cornbread to sop up the remaining broth in the corner of his bowl.

"How long do you plan on sticking around?" John asked.

"I'm not really sure. I just plan on going where God leads me and staying there until he shows me something else."

"How'd your mom take it when you told her you were leaving?"

"Surprisingly well. She said she already knew this day was coming and had prepared for it. Kind of like how you already knew God would lead me here."

John collected the dishes and took them over to the sink. "Mom and Dad always told me I was destined for great things, but about the time I started my ministry, they told me you were going to come along and do something even greater. They were positive our paths would cross in a big way.

"Then I had a vision several months ago. The Holy Spirit showed me you were the Messiah, and that you'd be coming to see me. That's how I knew you were coming. I just didn't know exactly when." John wiped his hands on a dishtowel and threw it across his shoulder. "Now that you're here, you're welcome to stay as long as you want. We'll be a bit cramped, but this place is downright cozy once you get used to it."

A knock at the door interrupted their conversation. John opened it to see two of his disciples standing in the shadows.

"Sorry to bother you so late," one of them said.

"No bother at all. What can I do for you?" John asked.

The other disciple nodded toward Jesus. "We came to see him."

John smiled. "Well, come say hello." The two men hesitated in the doorway. "Come on now. Don't be shy." John ushered them inside the tiny cabin. "Jesus, this is Andrew and John. They're two of my finest disciples, and I'm not just saying that because they happen to be the two standing here."

Andrew's curly blonde hair seemed to glow in the light coming from the lantern on the table. "What we saw today was incredible."

John, the shorter and leaner of the two, stepped around Andrew. "It was God, wasn't it? The voice that called you his son."

"Is that really what brought you all the way out here tonight?" Jesus asked.

The disciples glanced at each other. Andrew nudged John.

"Well, um . . . not really. Andrew and I talked it over, and we were hoping we could be your disciples. We'd like to help spread your message."

Andrew looked at John the Baptist. "If it's okay with you."

John laughed and slapped his two disciples on the back. "Are you kidding me? Of course I'm okay with it. We've been bringing people to God in these woods for a long time to prepare for this very moment. What do you say, Jesus? You won't find anyone more passionate about doing God's work than these two."

"I'd be honored to have them join me," Jesus said. "I'm not sure what I'll be doing yet, but I have a feeling I'm about to find out."

Ready or not, world, here he comes, John thought to himself with a smile.

CHAPTER 7

John and Andrew returned to the cabin the following morning with another visitor. His eyes and hair were different, but there was no mistaking his resemblance to Andrew.

Jesus sat in a patch of wildflowers near the cabin, enjoying the coolness of the morning and preparing his mind for the day ahead. Last night God had placed a very simple message on his heart. He was to preach to the people at the river.

"John's already left," Jesus said.

"We actually came to see you," Andrew said, turning to the newcomer "This is my brother, Simon. We told him about you last night, and he wanted to meet you."

Simon shook hands with Jesus. Simon's calloused hands reminded Jesus of his father's, and he felt a pang of loss at the memory.

"My brother tells me you're the Messiah. Is it true?" Simon said.

Jesus shrugged. "Some people think so. Do you?"

"My brother has spent his whole life waiting for the Messiah, and if anybody would recognize him, it'd be Andrew," Simon said.

"Why don't you join us at the river today and decide for yourself?" Jesus offered.

Simon considered the invitation. "Okay. One day away from the boat won't be the end of the world."

"A sailor?" Jesus asked.

"Fisherman."

"Of course. I should have guessed from your hands."

Simon looked at his palms and laughed. "Yeah, nobody's ever accused me of having a woman's touch."

The four men left for the river. As they crested the hill, they saw hundreds of people swarming the area. A television crew was there with a direct line of site to where John was standing, and several police officers stood along the outskirts of the crowd.

"Is this normal?" Simon asked, sounding hesitant.

Andrew shook his head. "John's popular, but he's not *this* popular."

The four of them squeezed through the crowd and joined John at the edge of the river. He noticed them and held up a megaphone.

"Looks like we're going to need this today, cuz. You've become quite the overnight celebrity." John put the megaphone to his lips. "Can everyone hear me?"

The crowd noise died down, starting at the front and working its way to the back like an invisible wave. Everyone watched as John held out his free hand toward Jesus.

"Look, the Lamb of God!" John said.

Jesus took a deep breath as all eyes turned to him. There were so many people in the audience that needed to hear about God, and he wished there was a more personal way to do it than through a megaphone.

People fell to their knees, lifting their hands and crying out to God. There were also cheers and scattered boos throughout the crowd.

"Some of you have been so desperate for a Savior that you thought I was the Messiah," John continued. "I'm definitely not the one you're looking for, but the one you seek is with me here today. Let me introduce you to Jesus, the Messiah!"

"Liar!" a man from the crowd said.

He lunged at Jesus. Three disciples intercepted him and wrestled him to the ground. A police officer rushed over and slapped a pair of handcuffs on the man.

"Let me at him!" the man said as the officer yanked him to his feet.

"Let him go," Jesus said. "I don't want him arrested."

The officer shook his head while keeping a tight grip on the attacker's arms. "No can do, buddy. This guy's itching to rip your face off, and frankly, I don't want to deal with all the paperwork that would come with letting him do it. You don't have to press charges if you don't want to, but I have to take him down to the station."

"I won't press charges. I'll show him mercy just like God shows mercy to us every day," Jesus said.

The man glared at Jesus with hatred pouring from his eyes. "Screw you and your mercy. You're just a charlatan taking advantage of these gullible people."

He spat at Jesus, missing his face by inches. The officer jerked the man backwards and dragged him to the police cruiser. Jesus felt compassion for the man and prayed that God would show him the truth.

"Stay away from this fraud! You've been warned!" The man continued shouting until the officer threw him in the back of the cruiser and slammed the door in his face.

The name, Terry, exploded in Jesus's mind like a flashbang, and he suddenly knew that a man claiming to be the Messiah had once scammed Terry's mother out of her life savings. It had financially ruined her and left Terry picking up the pieces. It was no wonder his heart was hardened and unreceptive to Jesus being the Messiah.

Jesus was shaken by the vision God had shown him about Terry's life. Was this ability a one-time thing, or was it a gift God would continue to grow inside of him? One thing was certain: the connection between Jesus and God was strengthening by the day.

He looked at the crowd and realized many of them were frightened. "Don't let what you've heard from this man trouble you and don't hold it against him. Instead of judging him, let's pray for him. While God hears a man who prays alone, the prayers of a hundred thunder through the heavens like a herd of buffalo."

Jesus led the group in prayer before preaching a message of love that he hoped would pierce their hearts like an arrow. His words flowed like a casual conversation among friends. Despite not using the megaphone, his voice seemed to reach every ear with ease.

Jesus could hear weeping throughout the crowd. People raised their hands in submission, and hearts were transformed. Jesus asked those who wished to be baptized to come forward. Almost two-thirds of the crowd made their way to the river.

One disciple turned to John. "Everyone's lining up in front of Jesus instead of you. Should we split them up?"

Jesus glanced at them, but John shook his head. "No, let's just thank God we get to witness this. These people are like a bride belonging to the groom, and we are just guests at the wedding. It's now complete."

"What is?"

"My mission in life. Jesus must now become greater; I must become less."

As the brilliant blue sky became dark pink, the disciples arranged for cars to be lined up along the river so their headlights could illuminate the area. One by one, Jesus baptized the hundreds of people ready to give their lives to God. Songs of worship floated through the night, but there was more than just music in the air. The Holy Spirit was alive and well along the river.

Jesus brought the last person out of the water during the early hours of the morning. The long day had exhausted John and his disciples, but Jesus was still going strong. He was filled with an urgency to help all of God's children, no matter how long it took.

After saying goodbye to the last of the crowd, Jesus approached Simon. "Well, what do you think?" Jesus asked.

Simon looked bewildered. "This is the most amazing thing I've ever seen. My brother was right. You're the Messiah."

"You're a good man, Simon, and you have the potential to become even greater. How would you like to be one of my disciples?"

"I'd be honored, but I have my wife and daughter back home that need me. Plus there's the fishing business."

"Don't worry about any of that. You can still tend to those things. Just join us when you can, and we'll go from there. How does that sound?"

"That sounds perfect. Thank you."

"Your name is Simon, but you will be called Peter from now on." Jesus looked at the rest of the group. "Everyone go home, and get some rest. We'll come back later this afternoon and do it all over again."

Jesus left with John the Baptist and disappeared into the woods.

***

After Jesus had left, Simon looked at his brother, Andrew. "Did Jesus just change my name to Peter? Why would he do that?"

Andrew shrugged. "Beats me, but if the Messiah says your name is Peter, then I think you should change your name to Peter, right?"

"I guess so, but how am I going to explain this to my wife?"

Andrew laughed. "Just slip it in between the stuff about meeting the Messiah and him asking you to become one of his disciples. I bet she'll hardly notice."

The disciples shuffled toward the parking lot like zombies, their bodies aching with exhaustion. John collapsed into the backseat of a white Honda Accord. Peter climbed into the passenger seat while Andrew got behind the wheel.

"You guys don't see anything wrong with the name Simon, do you?" Peter asked.

"Not now, *Peter*. I'm tired," John said.

Peter rested his head against the window. "Maybe he knew a Simon that was mean to him when he was a kid or something. Do you think the Messiah can have psychological issues like that?"

"I'm seriously going to kick you out of the car if you don't shut up," Andrew said.

"Okay, okay. I'll stop."

"Thank you." Andrew started the car and smirked. "Peter."

CHAPTER 8

Saw you on the news. Are you out of your mind???? Reporters are calling Mom about the Messiah stuff. Stop this nonsense and come home.

Jesus stared at the text through half-lidded eyes that were crusted at the corners. The text alert on his phone had brought him out of a deep sleep.

Jesus crept past John, who was snoring in the corner of the room. He grabbed a loaf of bread from the cabinet and read the text message for the third time. Jesus devoured a peanut butter and banana sandwich while contemplating his response. He knew his younger brother better than anyone, and responding would only make James more upset. Jesus thought he'd give him a day or two to cool off before answering.

His thoughts turned from James to the dream he'd just had. He was standing in the middle of a vast desert, surrounded by nothing but miles of unending sand and colorless vegetation. The hot wind whipped across his face, blowing bits of sand into his eyes and mouth. Jesus cried out into the void, but the screech of a vulture on a nearby rock was his only answer. He sensed someone watching him but saw nothing other than his own shadow.

From the hot wind to the gritty texture of the sand, everything about the dream had felt real. He was certain the dream had a meaning, but for now it escaped him. All he could do was pray to God for the wisdom to understand it. He went for a walk to clear his mind.

When Jesus returned, John was awake and staring at his phone. "Have you seen today's news?"

"No."

"Man, people are talking about you all over the place. I Googled your name and got hundreds of hits."

"That's nice."

"That's nice? Is that all you have to say? This is downright amazing! You've had more press in the last two days than I've gotten in the last two years. You should be celebrating!"

"This is all because of what God is doing *through* me. We should celebrate him, not me."

"Always so humble. I'm still happy for you, cuz."

There was a knock at the door. Andrew, John, and Peter entered the cabin with a group of people Jesus didn't recognize.

Bags hung under Peter's bloodshot eyes. "I couldn't sleep when I got home, so I started calling my friends and telling them about you. A few of them wanted to come hear what you have to say."

Peter waved the newcomers forward. Judas, Thomas, Philip, and Matthew took turns introducing themselves to Jesus.

"It's an honor to have you join us," Jesus said. "I look forward to hearing what you think of today's message." Jesus knew these men would become his disciples. There was no rational explanation for knowing this with such certainty, but God had impressed it on his heart.

When the men arrived at the river, a crowd twice the size of yesterday's awaited them. John had been right. This was downright amazing.

CHAPTER 9

"What do you want?" Jesus called out. He was in the desert again, searching for the presence he could sense but not see.

"Come to me."

The disembodied whisper was full of evil. It made Jesus's skin crawl.

"Where are you?" Jesus said.

"I am waiting," the voice hissed.

Jesus woke with his heart thundering in his chest and his shirt damp with sweat. He didn't recognize the voice from his dream, but he was certain it wasn't human.

Unable to sleep, Jesus grabbed his phone and snuck outside. The moon was full and bright, lighting a path that wandered deeper into the woods. About a mile in, the trees gave way to a small clearing. The absence of light pollution and city noise reminded Jesus of just how magnificent God's creation was. He got on his knees and held up his hands.

"Father, open my eyes so that I may see your purpose for me, and use these hands to do your work. May you always be with me, Lord, as I stand against those who would come against you."

Jesus continued praying, pausing occasionally to listen for God's voice. It was in those moments of silence God often revealed himself.

As the woods came alive with the sounds of waking wildlife, Jesus checked his phone and saw that it was just past five o'clock.

He thought of his mom, always the early riser, who was probably sitting at the kitchen table with a cup of coffee in one hand and her devotional book in the other. He thumbed through his contacts and tapped on her picture. She picked up on the first ring.

"Good morning, son. Were your ears burning? I was just praying for you."

His heart ached for home at the sound of her voice. "I was hoping you were up."

"You know me. I'm always up bright and early. What's going on?"

"Nothing big. I was just missing you." He swallowed against the lump in his throat.

"Oh, sweetheart. I miss you too. I saw you on the news last night, and I'm so proud of you! I would have called, but I didn't want to bother you. I know you must have a million things going on right now. The kids say they've seen videos of you preaching on the YouTube."

"It's YouTube, Mom. Not *the* YouTube."

"Whatever. I'm too old for all this technology. Trey said he'd stop by to show me how to watch the videos. I bet they're wonderful."

"How's James?"

There was a pause on the other end. Jesus could hear her fingernails tapping against her coffee mug.

"I don't hear from him much since you left. He says he's swamped with running the business. He's still pretty upset, but he'll come around."

"What about the others?"

"Oh, they're fine. They think it's cool to have an older brother on the news, but they don't believe it all just yet. I've tried explaining it to them, but they think I'm drinking the Jesus Kool Aid."

"They've said that?" Jesus's heart sank.

"Well, no, but I can tell. A mother knows. She always knows."

"I don't know how long I'll be out here, but I promise to come home as soon as I can."

"You don't need to worry about coming to see me. I'll be just fine. Those people out there need you right now, Jesus. The entire world does."

After they hung up, Jesus thanked God for his mother's re-assurance. Knowing she supported him gave him the strength he needed to continue his work, even in the face of doubters.

CHAPTER 10

Jesus tossed a black duffle bag into the backseat of his car and shut the door.

"When you coming back?" his cousin, John, asked.

"I'm not sure."

"I still don't understand why you're leaving. We've built so much here," Peter said, looking concerned.

Peter was right. The last month had been incredible. Tens of thousands of people had heard Jesus and John preach, and hundreds were being baptized every day.

The number of disbelievers and antagonists had grown as well. Jesus had refused personal security guards, but the city had provided police protection at every event because of safety concerns.

The popularity of Jesus and John had also attracted the attention of local Sadducees and Pharisees. Because of the mounting inquiries they received about the supposed Messiah, they released a joint statement condemning Jesus and labeling his teachings as heresy. The Pharisees and Sadducees didn't see eye to eye on a lot of things, but on this they were in complete agreement: Jesus was not the Messiah, and anyone who thought he was would face the eternal fires of Hell.

"I'm being called away, and I have to go by myself," Jesus said. "I'm afraid I can't say more than that, but I promise I'll come back as soon as I'm finished."

"What should we do while you're gone?" Philip asked.

"Stay with John. He'll need your help while I'm away."

"I'll do my best, but I'm no Messiah," John said.

Jesus clapped him on the shoulder. "You'll do great. Just like before."

Jesus got in the car and headed north toward a desert he'd never heard of until last night. In his most recent dream, the name and location of the desert had been revealed to him. During his morning prayer, God had instructed him to leave at once and travel alone. He would wander the desert without food or water until God instructed him to return home.

The voice in his dreams still troubled him, along with the fact that God was never in them. Although God had told him to go to the desert, Jesus was certain the dreams weren't from him.

Jesus reached the outskirts of the desert around noon. He noticed a rundown gas station sitting along the highway like a mirage. He stopped for a tank of gas before starting the final leg of his journey.

A few miles later, Jesus turned off the main road and followed a narrow path that was more of a trail than an actual road. His car bounced along the rutted dirt for miles before he felt the presence of God and knew he'd reached his destination.

Jesus killed the engine and surveyed his surroundings. They matched his dream down to the most minute detail. He got out of the car and hollered into the emptiness. A vulture screeched from a nearby rock outcrop. His dreams were morphing into reality.

Jesus could no longer feel God's presence, and it unnerved him. He dug through his duffel bag and pulled out a broad-brimmed hat, a pair of sunglasses, and a light jacket, which he tied around his waist. He left everything else in the car, including a gallon of water and some food. After locking the car, a habit that seemed ridiculous out in the middle of nowhere, Jesus trekked into the belly of the desert.

CHAPTER 11

"And don't think the hypocrisy ends with the Sadducees and Pharisees. There's another hypocrite who deserves to be called out as well. President Herod marries his brother's wife, and the people turn a blind eye to it because they hold him in such high regard. He flaunts his sin in your face and expects you to accept him as a saint worthy of being worshipped. However, there is only one man on Earth we should worship, and it sure isn't President Herod. It's our Savior, Jesus!"

Cameron Herod sat in bed with his iPad resting against his legs, watching the video for the third time. The man known as John the Baptist was on another one of his rants, but this time he'd directed his rant at Cameron. John the Baptist's popularity had skyrocketed with the arrival of Jesus, and his controversial comments were making national headlines. A famous preacher taking aim at the most popular president in American history was a story too juicy to ignore.

Cameron's father, the former president known for the Bloodbath in Bethlehem, had died of a brain aneurysm when Cameron was only thirteen. While possessing all of his father's charisma, he had also learned from his father's mistakes. From a very young age, Cameron had separated himself from his father's views on immigrants and violence. He had adopted the Jewish faith and lived a life based on morality and love. In college, he had fought for immigrant rights, putting himself at the forefront of many famous protests. It was a cause that gained him notoriety among people from all walks of life, and his efforts eventually led to a bill that granted immigrants the same rights as citizens. His popularity grabbed the attention of many politicians who saw a future presidential candidate in the making.

With the help of his new friends, Cameron had worked his way up the political ladder. By the time he became Speaker of the House, his father was a distant memory in the minds of the voters. Thirty years after his father had left office, Cameron was poised to put the Herods back in the White House.

His approval ratings had been strong from the moment he became president, and two years later they remained at unprecedented levels. Cameron's religious beliefs made him very favorable among Jews, which made John the Baptist's latest rant against him even more salacious.

"Are you watching that stupid thing again?" Herodias turned off the bathroom light and slid into bed next to Cameron. She took the iPad from his lap and turned it off.

"Hey!" Cameron said.

"Watching that won't do you any good, especially right before bed."

"Reporters are going to hound me for a response to this. What's his deal?"

"He's just jealous." Herodias kissed his neck and ran her fingers through his hair.

Cameron shrugged away her advances and went to the window overlooking the South Lawn of the White House. "What am I going to do?"

"Just ignore him, and he'll go away."

"And if he doesn't?" Cameron understood the potential PR nightmare this could create if he wasn't careful.

Herodias sighed and rolled out of bed. She stood next to Cameron and slid an arm around his waist.

"Then we worry about that when it happens. Come on, you knew something like this would happen when you married me.

Not everyone is going to approve of the president marrying his brother's ex-wife, but so what? The people still love you."

Cameron and Herodias had been married during a private ceremony inside the White House two months ago. They had made a public announcement the following day, and Cameron hoped his historic popularity would trump any criticism he'd receive as a result of the marriage.

The official story released by the White House was that Herodias had run into President Herod several months ago at a fundraising event. It was the first time they'd seen each other since she divorced his brother, Barrett, years ago, and they had caught up over a cup of coffee. Coffee led to dinner the following week, and over time they had formed a spiritual bond they could no longer deny.

The true story, and the one Cameron was desperate to keep hidden, was a much darker version. Cameron had always lusted after Herodias and dreamed of taking her for himself. Their first adulterous encounter had occurred while Barrett was away on business. The possibility of Cameron becoming the most powerful man in America had been too much for Herodias to resist. The affair lasted for more than a year before Barrett discovered a racy text message on Herodias's phone.

Barrett had driven straight to Cameron's house for a confrontation that had ended in a bloody fist fight. Barrett had threatened to expose his brother and ruin his political career. Cameron did what his father had always done best. He had turned on the charm and convinced his brother to stay quiet. A large sum of money helped sweeten the pot, and Barrett had agreed to fade into the shadows. A quiet divorce had been finalized, and Cameron continued to see Herodias behind closed doors.

Everyone believed the story released by the White House. While they acknowledged the marriage wasn't within religious guidelines, many chalked it up to a mistake worthy of forgiveness. As understanding as the people had been, Cameron knew they would turn on him in an instant if they ever found out the truth.

Now, John the Baptist was threatening to destroy the delicate story he'd worked so hard to create. If he continued calling out the president and drawing attention to his relationship with Herodias, it was possible someone might expose the relationship for what it really was.

"I think I'll call him and see if I can convince him to stop talking about me. Maybe set up a meeting between the two of us and turn on that Herod charm. I'll throw some money at him if I have to," Cameron said.

"Does he look like someone who cares about money? Homeless people have better clothes than that lunatic. Just let it go. If you poke the hornets' nest, you're going to get stung."

"Well, I have to shut him up somehow."

"Then have him arrested if it bothers you that much."

"That's how my father handled things, and look where it got him." Cameron wasn't about to turn into the man he despised.

Herodias pressed her body against his. "You're the most powerful man in the world. You can do whatever you want."

She wrapped her arms around his neck and pulled him into a sensual kiss. The taste of strawberry lip balm, mixed with the intoxicating aroma of her perfume, sent a rush of heat through his body. John the Baptist could wait, at least until morning.

CHAPTER 12

Jesus squinted against the morning sun while arching his back. The nights spent on the unforgiving desert floor were piling up, and the muscles in his back were barking in protest. He'd lost track of how many days he'd spent wandering the desert, but the number didn't matter. He would stay until God told him to go home, whether that be weeks or even months.

Jesus yawned, and blood oozed from his cracked lips as they tore open. His blistered face was peeling, and his ribs looked like miniature speed bumps along his torso, concealed by a shirt too big for his skeletal frame.

Jesus had found just enough food and water to keep him alive. One day he'd found a dry riverbed with a trickle of water flowing underneath the surface. Another time he had come across a pool of water sitting at the bottom of a canyon, shaded by large overhanging boulders. The biggest blessing had come in the form of a freak thunderstorm that provided all the fresh water he could drink.

Food was harder to come by. One day he'd stumbled across a dead snake near some brush, and he'd also managed to kill a sun-bathing lizard. Neither were appetizing when eaten raw, but it was hard to be picky in the scarce delicatessen that was the open desert.

Now, Jesus surveyed a mesa a few miles to his north. The sloped sides looked climbable, and the top would provide a good vantage point to find his next source of water. He hadn't had a drink in over twenty-four hours. His body screamed for hydration.

He stumbled toward the mesa, each step becoming more difficult than the last. The painstaking journey took most of the day, and by the time he reached the base, he was fighting to stay conscious. Realizing he'd never make it to the top without water, Jesus formed his hands into a bowl and drank from the only liquid available. He gagged against the retched taste of his own urine as he forced it down. With the bitter aftertaste still in his mouth, he started the long, excruciating climb.

Jesus crested the mesa at dusk. The view from the top revealed miles of unending desert in every direction. His vision became blurry, and the ground spun beneath him. Staggering to his left, Jesus tripped over his own feet and lost consciousness right before his face slammed into the dirt.

CHAPTER 13

Herodias was nibbling a piece of toast at the kitchen table when Cameron came into the room. She gave him a playful smile and nodded at the plate across from her.

"I had the staff bring up a hearty breakfast for you this morning. I thought you might have worked up quite an appetite." She threw him a seductive wink.

Cameron kissed her and snagged a biscuit off his plate. "It's all set. I have a call with John the Baptist this afternoon."

Herodias frowned. "I thought we agreed you'd leave that alone?"

"That was your idea, not mine."

She banged her fork against the table. "It's not just your future you're messing with, Cameron. I didn't come this far to have some forest hippie destroy everything we've worked for."

Cameron seethed inside. Herodias acted like they were equal partners in his rise to power, but how quickly she forgot that he was already well on his way before they had gotten together. She was riding his coattails, which was fine, but she needed to remember her place. He would remind her if necessary.

Herodias's daughter, Salome, came into the kitchen, sweating and out of breath. "Morning, Mom. Hey, Cameron." She took a bottle of water from the refrigerator and pressed it against her neck.

"You're up early." Herodias's voice was pleasant, but she was shooting daggers at Cameron.

"I've got a big Legal Studies test today, and I couldn't sleep. Thought I'd go for a run to calm my nerves." Salome stood in front of the open refrigerator, fanning her tank top against the cold air. Sweat ran down her neck and disappeared beneath the shirt clinging to her body like a wet rag.

"I'm sure you'll do great. You always do," Herodias said.

Salome had been a straight-A student throughout high school. That, along with her extracurricular activities and outstanding test scores, had attracted full-ride scholarships from all over the country.

Hoping to one day marry the eventual President of the United States, Herodias urged her daughter to consider universities in the Washington, D.C. area, claiming it would be the perfect place for Salome to develop her future legal career. Three years later, Salome was now one of the top pre-law students at Georgetown University.

She had her father's brains, but there was no denying where she got her looks. Salome was a younger version of her mother. She was stunning in every way, and she knew it. Just like her mother, Salome wasn't afraid to use her looks to get what she wanted.

"I guess I better hit the shower before class. I'll see you guys tonight."

Salome tossed the now empty water bottle at the trash can. It bounced off the side and rolled across the floor. While bending over to pick it up, Cameron's eyes worked their way up her legs and lingered. Herodias threw him a glance, and his eyes darted back to his plate. Busted.

CHAPTER 14

"Get up, sleepyhead. It's time for a new day."

Jesus stirred. The voice seemed distant and dreamlike. He tried to focus on it, but his mind slipped back into the comfortable darkness waiting to enfold him like a familiar blanket. For the past twelve hours, he had lingered in a state of unconsciousness closer to death than sleep.

A cold, thin hand gripped his cheeks, and sharp fingernails dug into the soft flesh. Jesus's eyes flew open to see a man staring back at him. Jesus couldn't stop looking into his eyes. They were black and seemed to float in a face so pale it was almost translucent. His gray lips peeled back into a hideous grin, exposing uneven and rotting teeth.

"So we finally meet. I was starting to think you'd never show up," the man said.

"Who are you?" Jesus's throat burned, and his tongue felt like sandpaper against the roof of his mouth.

The man cackled, his gaping mouth exposing a tongue the color of blood. He stood up and sat on a nearby rock. "Oh, I think you know the answer to that. Maybe not when I first called you here, but surely you do now."

Now that his head was clearing, Jesus did know. It was Satan. He could feel the evil radiating from the man like a demonic heat. Fear crept into his mind, and he pushed it away with all his mental might, praying for God to protect him and give him strength.

"Why did you call me here?" Jesus asked, easing himself into a sitting position.

Satan clapped his hands together, rubbing them back and forth. "A man who gets right to the point. I love it!"

Jesus slumped to one side. Satan jumped from his rock and caught him before he collapsed.

"Easy there. Forty days in the desert takes a lot out of you," Satan said.

Jesus straightened himself and shrugged off Satan's grip. Even his touch felt vile. "I'm fine. Just tell me what you want."

Satan paced back and forth. "It's not so much what *I* want as it is what *you* want. Or rather, what you *need*. Look at yourself. I'd say your days are numbered unless you get some food and water soon."

"God will always provide me with what I need."

Satan scoffed. "You call this provision? How great is a God that lets his own son waste away in the dessert? Think about it. Does that make any sense? Maybe he's not the man you think he is."

"I know exactly who he is." Hearing Satan question God's power gave Jesus a renewed sense of courage. He wasn't afraid of this monster.

Satan picked up a handful of rocks and tossed them at Jesus. "Come on, show me how powerful God is. Tell those rocks to become bread. You should be out here feasting like a king, not starving like a peasant."

Jesus picked up a stone, glanced at it, and tossed it over his shoulder, as if bored with the conversation. "The Torah says, 'Man does not live on bread alone, but on every word that comes from the mouth of God.'"

"You want to quote Torah verses? I can do that too." Satan hauled Jesus to his feet and dragged him to the edge of the mesa. "If you're the Son of God, then throw yourself off the edge. It won't hurt you, right? The Torah says, 'He will command his angels concerning you, and they will lift you up in their hands, so that you will not strike your foot against a stone.'"

Jesus looked at him. "It is also written, 'Do not put the Lord your God to the test.'" He saw the frustration burn in Satan's eyes, and it gave him immense pleasure.

Satan shoved Jesus to the ground. "You're insufferable, you know that? I'm here to offer you more than God ever could. I can make you the greatest man on Earth. The world could be yours. All you have to do is bow down and worship me."

Jesus could feel the anger rising within him. Satan could bribe or threaten him with whatever he wanted, but Jesus would *never* bow at his feet. He pulled himself up and pointed a shaking finger in Satan's face.

"Away from me, Satan! For it is written, 'Worship the Lord your God, and serve him only.'"

Satan threw back his head and emitted a demonic screech that filled the desert air. His face pulsed a fiery red. His black eyes burned like embers. The mesa vibrated, and Satan's body shimmered like heat waves coming off asphalt. His shriek turned into a chilling growl, and then he evaporated like a mist.

Jesus fell to his hands and knees, gasping for air. He'd used the last of his strength to stand up to Satan, and now he was beyond the point of exhaustion.

Two pairs of feet appeared beneath him. He looked up, squinting against a brilliant light that was not coming from the sun. The two men standing in front of him looked human except for the white aura surrounding them. One of them smiled and held up a canteen and a lunchbox. The other was holding a first aid kit.

"It's all over, Jesus," the first angel said. "God sent us to tell you it's time to go home."

Jesus closed his eyes and lowered his head. "Thank you, Father."

CHAPTER 15

Herodias stormed through the front doors of the White House, the fake smile she'd worn all night vanishing in an instant. She marched up the stairs, leaving Cameron standing in the doorway holding her purse. She tripped and fell against the handrail. Yanking off her high heels, Herodias screamed a barrage of profanity and flung them down the stairs.

Cameron picked them up off the floor and followed his wife, too embarrassed to make eye contact with the secret service agent standing in the hallway. He was grateful no one else had witnessed her tirade. Given everything that had happened over the last forty-eight hours, neither of them needed a story like this hitting the tabloids.

Herodias slammed the bedroom door in his face. Jumping into a rattlesnake pit was safer than approaching her when she was like this, but leaving her alone would only make her anger grow like a malignant tumor. Cameron took a deep breath and entered the room.

She was standing in front of the television, holding the remote out in front of her like a magic wand. "Channel 4, channel 12, channel 25!"

"Herodias."

"Oh look, Cameron! We even made that trashy gossip talk show on channel 34."

"I know you're upset—"

"Upset? *Upset* was when I told you not to talk to John the Baptist, but you did it anyway. Tonight goes way past upset. I had to listen to everyone ask me about the rumors all evening, and I had to sit there with a stupid grin on my face like it was no big deal!"

Cameron watched the headline scrolling across the bottom of the television. *Sources say President Herod had an affair with first lady while she was married to his brother. Hush money and threats kept it quiet. Story developing.*

The host of the show was hamming it up for her audience. "It looks like the first lady is really just a first hussy!" Cameron winced as the studio audience exploded with laughter. "And don't get me started on President Herod. He walks around with such a righteous attitude when he's been giving the Ten Commandments the middle finger the whole time!"

Herodias screamed at the top of her lungs and heaved the remote at the television. The screen shattered and went dark.

"Look what that backwards hillbilly has done to our lives! He's behind these leaks. I just know it!" Herodias said.

Someone knocked lightly on the door. "Mr. President, is everything okay?"

Cameron locked it. "We're fine. The TV just fell off the mount."

"Would you like for me to send someone up to fix it?"

"No, it can wait until morning. It's been a long day."

There was a pause. "Understood, Mr. President. I'll be down the hall if you need me."

Cameron turned back to his wife as the footsteps faded away. "What do you want me to say? You want me to say you were right? Fine, you were right. I shouldn't have called him. I screwed up."

The phone call had been a disaster. John the Baptist had refused all of Cameron's proposals, even the hush money. Cameron had become so frustrated that he'd even threatened him. The next day John the Baptist had preached about the details of their phone conversation to the crowd at the river.

"Why would the President of the United States waste his valuable time trying to keep me quiet unless there was more to the story than just the inappropriate marriage?" he had asked.

Several days later, an anonymous report claimed Cameron and Herodias had been together while Herodias had still been married to Barrett. The floodgates opened, and within twenty-four hours it became a full-blown scandal, with multiple anonymous sources coming forward.

"You more than screwed up, Cameron. Do you realize what will happen if one of those sources goes on the record?" Herodias screamed.

"Why do you think I was trying to shut him up?"

"And how'd that work out for you?"

"We'll find a way to spin the story. It's not like I'll get impeached over it."

"Impeached? No. Voted out after one term? Definitely. And don't act like that doesn't bother you."

Cameron threw up his hands. "Of course it bothers me! You think I want to go down as a one-term president who spent half his time in office fighting a sex scandal? But what else can I do?"

"Kill him."

"What? You're out of your mind." His wife could be crazy, but this was insane, even for her.

"Am I? Whoever's got the dirt on us is working with him. Kill him, and everyone else gets the message and stays quiet."

"I can't do a complete 180 and become a tyrannical dictator overnight. My father tried that, remember? America won't let it happen again. I won the election despite who my father was, not because of him."

Herodias's face softened. "I know. I just hate what he's done to us, and he won't stop until we're ruined. I want it to go away. I want *him* to go away."

Cameron snapped his fingers, coming up with a plan. "I think you were onto something the other night."

"What's that?"

"I could arrest him and throw him in jail for something. It'd be easy to frame him."

"I thought you didn't like that idea."

"That was before everything blew up. Think about it. We could put him in isolation and interrogate him until we find out who his sources are."

Herodias flashed a genuine smile for the first time all day. "No more of this diplomatic nonsense. Let's shut him up once and for all."

Cameron opened the door. "I better move on this tonight before things get worse."

"Cameron?"

He saw the anger in her eyes was gone; now they were playful. Cameron recognized the look and what it meant. She craved power like a drug, and he had just given her the fix she needed.

"I'll wait up," she purred.

CHAPTER 16

Six masked men, armed and wearing night vision goggles, emerged from the shadows of the forest. They approached the cabin from all sides, three covering the door and one securing each of the windows.

One soldier kicked open the front door while another tossed in a stun grenade. They turned their heads as a loud bang and bright light filled the tiny cabin. The soldiers rushed the room to find John the Baptist stumbling out of bed. They threw a black hood over his head, zip tied his hands behind his back, and dragged him into the depths of the forest, kicking and screaming.

The entire event was over in a matter of seconds, and soon the sounds of the forest returned to normal. The front door swinging open in the breeze was the only sign anything unusual had taken place.

John the Baptist's days of preaching had come to an abrupt end.

CHAPTER 17

God revealed Jesus's full purpose to him as he hiked out of the desert. The bond between the two was stronger than ever, and Jesus felt like they had almost become one.

He now understood that the power of God lived within him, and he was to use that power to display God's truth to everyone. God also showed him his future. It was both awe-inspiring and terrifying, but more than anything he felt humbled to be a part of something so significant. By the time his car came into view, Jesus was ready to begin the next phase of his life.

A rejuvenated Jesus started the car and followed the road out of the desert. While filling his tank at the gas station, he took his cell phone from the glove compartment and scrolled through the numerous texts and voicemails he'd missed over the last six weeks. He saw Andrew had called several times and clicked on his most recent voicemail.

"Jesus, please call me right away. I know we're not supposed to bother you, but I'm sure you've heard by now. We don't know what to do."

Jesus frowned and clicked on the next message.

"Jesus, this is Andrew. John's missing. He wasn't at the cabin this morning, and it looks like someone broke in. We've called the police and wanted to see if maybe he'd reached out to you. Can you—."

Jesus didn't bother listening to the rest. He jumped into his car and sped out of the parking lot.

***

The disciples were waiting for him when he arrived at the cabin later that night. Jesus could see the despair on their faces.

"Where's Peter?" Jesus said, scanning the room.

"He took off when John got arrested," Andrew said.

"Any idea where he's at?"

Andrew poured him a cup of coffee. "Back with his family and the fishing business. He said he was tired of neglecting his wife and kids."

"You want us to tell him you're back?" Thomas asked.

"No, I'll pay him a visit when the time's right." The news troubled Jesus. Peter had become somewhat of an unspoken leader among the disciples, and Jesus would need him for what was coming next.

"Now that you're back, can you finally tell us where you went? You look like you were stranded on a desert island." Andrew wrinkled his nose. "And you smell pretty ripe."

Jesus managed a weak smile. "There wasn't a lot of food or water where I've been."

Matthew brought him a plate of biscuits. "And where was that?"

The smell of freshly baked bread made Jesus's stomach rumble. "I was in the desert facing my demons."

"Are you crazy? It's dangerous to travel alone in the desert. People die out there all the time," Philip said.

"Couldn't you have gone to a Holiday Inn or something?" James asked.

"Do you have any idea how much forty days in a hotel would cost?" Judas pulled up the calculator app on his phone and began plugging in numbers.

"There will be plenty of time to talk about this later, but right now I want to talk about what's next," Jesus said. "It's time for us to leave the river. The work we've done here is good, but there are millions of people hungry for God's word, and we're going to take it to them. I need each of you by my side. I can't do it alone."

"You want us to leave our home? For how long? When?" Thomas said.

"We'll leave in a few days. We'll come back to visit when we can, but I can't promise that it will be often." Even though this would be hard for the disciples to accept, they deserved to know the true cost of following him.

"So are we talking years?" Thomas said with apprehension.

Jesus nodded while he swallowed the last of his biscuit. "Most likely."

The room was silent. Matthew picked at his fingernails. Thomas stared at the floor. Andrew gazed out the window.

"I know most of you have families and jobs to consider. It's a huge sacrifice, but it's a chance to serve God in a way that no one else can. The difficulties you'll face will be nothing compared to the rewards awaiting you in Heaven. I don't expect an answer tonight, so think it over and come back to me with your decision."

After the disciples left, Jesus collapsed into bed and thought about John. His cousin's face was plastered all over the television and newspapers. The FBI had arrested him on charges of planning to assassinate President Herod, but officials weren't releasing any details.

Visiting John was out of the question. The government wouldn't risk letting him speak to anyone right now. The only thing Jesus could do was take his disciples and spread God's word across the country. It's what John would want, and it's what God had called him to do.

CHAPTER 18

Mary walked across the front lawn to greet the two vans pulling into the driveway. Jesus's siblings were standing behind her, except for James. He had refused to be there when Jesus arrived. Mary threw her arms around Jesus as soon as his feet hit the pavement. It felt wonderful to have her son back in her arms again. She had missed him terribly.

Eleven disciples got out of the vans. Everyone but Peter had decided to follow Jesus.

Mary ushered them inside the house, where she had warm food and cold drinks waiting for them. Jesus introduced each of the disciples to his family: Andrew, John, James, Philip, Thaddeus, Bartholomew, Thomas, James, Matthew, Simon, and Judas.

Mary couldn't stop smiling as she listened to her son talk about his adventures over the last couple of months. She imagined how proud Joseph would be if he could see what his son had become, and it brought tears to her eyes.

The conversation took a somber turn when Jesus brought up John. He explained their cousin was innocent, and none of what they'd heard on the news was true. Although Mary believed him, his siblings had their doubts. Every news station in America had dragged John's name through the mud. Believing Jesus's version of the events was a hard pill to swallow.

"Will you boys be joining us at the wedding this evening?" Mary said once the conversation turned to small talk. The son of

Mary's closest friend was getting married, and they had all been invited to the wedding.

"Wouldn't miss it," Jesus said.

"Wonderful! Everyone will be so excited to see you." Mary glanced at the clock. "I better get ready. It's going to be quite the event, and we don't want to be late."

***

The wedding was elaborate, with hundreds of guests filling the room. The father of the bride was a wealthy business tycoon, and he had spared no expense. Held inside a massive ballroom, the celebration included a string quartet, ice sculptures, food that was hard to pronounce, and bottles of wine that cost more than some people made in a month. It was like a scene straight out of a fairytale.

Aside from the bride and groom, Jesus was the most popular person in the room. Everyone wanted to speak with the man who had become a national sensation. As the wine flowed, people lost their inhibitions. Courteous inquiries became questions dripping with sarcasm, and they mocked the claims of Jesus being the Messiah. The biting words of his friends and neighbors stung like a thousand hornets.

At one point he excused himself from the table and went to the restroom to compose himself. As he was washing his hands, James exited the nearest stall and locked eyes with Jesus through the mirror.

"Well, if it isn't my big brother, Jesus! Oh, excuse me. Can I still call you that, or do I have to call you Messiah now?"

Jesus dried his hands and extended one to his brother. "It's good to see you, James."

James gripped his hand and pulled him into a hug. "I'm so glad you could find time in your busy schedule to come see us. It's an honor to be in your presence." His breath was heavy with alcohol.

"You're drunk."

James gasped. "How'd you know?" He looked around the room and whispered, "Did God tell you that?"

"Very funny. Look, I miss talking to you. I was hoping we could catch up while I'm home."

"Hey, I'm not the one ignoring texts and phone calls. You're the one that's gone off the grid, buddy." James staggered to one side and bumped into the urinal.

"I'm sorry about that. I didn't have my phone with me," Jesus said.

"For a month? Yeah right. Why'd you really ignore us?"

"I was in the desert on a spiritual journey. God showed me my life's purpose."

James cackled, leaning against the wall for support. "And you think *I'm* the one who's drunk?" He let out a hiccup that turned into a belch. "I hope you haven't been telling other people that story. They'll think John the Assassin is the normal one in our family."

The barrage of hurtful words coming out of James's mouth were painful to hear, but rather than getting angry, Jesus was only worried about his younger brother. It was obvious he was going through a difficult time.

James stumbled over to the sink. He splashed water on his face, dried it with a wad of paper towels, and walked to the door.

"James, wait. Let me drive you home so we can talk."

"We can talk tomorrow. I'm going back to the party."

"I'm leaving tomorrow."

James let go of the door. "Of course you are. Did God say anything about abandoning your family? Is he cool with that?"

There wasn't an answer that would satisfy him, so Jesus stayed silent. James shook his head.

"What's your end game? What are you after that's worth all the pain you're causing? I'm the only one who will say it to your face, but we all think you're crazy."

"My end game is to save as many people as I can while I'm here. I want the world to know God and to accept him as their Savior."

James snorted in disgust. "Whatever you say, big brother. Just do me a favor. Next time you're in town, don't bother looking me up. We're through."

James stormed out of the bathroom. Jesus locked himself in a stall and cried. He had prepared himself for the hardships that would come with following God's plan for his life, but no amount of preparation could protect his heart from the pain of being rejected by his family.

When he returned to the table, only his disciples remained. The rest of the crowd had drifted away in search of other entertainment.

Mary hurried over to the table and sat down next to Jesus. "They've run out of wine. Can you believe it?" Mary looked over her shoulder. "The bride looks like she's about to cry, and her father is so embarrassed."

Andrew stood up. "I'll go get some more. How much do they need?"

"That's very sweet of you, dear, but the wine isn't exactly the kind you can buy at the liquor store," Mary said.

"Millionaire problems," Judas said.

Mary smiled. "I know it sounds petty, but can you imagine if that were your little girl? You'd want everything to be perfect for her big day."

Jesus leaned over and kissed her cheek. "I'll take care of it, Mom." What better place to display God's power than in the presence of his mom? He turned to his disciples. "Take all the empty wine bottles you can find and fill them with water. Then take them over to the bride's father."

"I don't think anyone's drunk enough to be fooled by water in wine bottles. We're better off going to the liquor store and buying some of the boxed stuff," Thomas said.

"Trust me. Fill them up," Jesus said.

The disciples collected the empty bottles from the bar and carried them over to the back table, where they filled them with water from the dispensers. With a full bottle in each hand, the disciples walked to the head table and placed them in front of the bride's father.

"What's this?" The bride's father picked up a bottle and frowned.

Thomas faded to the back of the group, muttering something about boxed wine. Andrew cleared his throat and stepped forward.

"Sir, we heard you were out of wine and thought you could use this."

The man poured the liquid into a glass. The disciples watched as red wine flowed from the mouth of the bottle. He took a sip and smacked his lips.

"This is even better than the other stuff." He examined the label. "It says it's the same thing, but there's no way. Where'd you get this?"

"I saw them filling those with water," a woman said.

"I see someone's had enough to drink," the bride's father said. "Does this look like water to you?"

Everyone at the table laughed. The groom and his friends gathered up the bottles and took them to the bar. A few of the guests snagged a bottle for themselves and hurried off to their tables.

"I don't know where you got this, and I guess I don't really care. The important thing is you boys saved my daughter's wedding. I owe you big time."

He came around the table to thank each of the disciples. Thomas pushed his way to the front, eager to accept the gratitude. Jesus couldn't help but smile.

When the disciples returned to their table, Mary was holding Jesus's hand between both of hers. Her smile was radiant.

"What just happened? Did you do that?" Bartholomew asked Jesus.

Thaddeus, who had been standing in a dazed silence, shook his head and ran his fingers through his hair. "That was unbelievable. I mean, you literally turned water into wine, didn't you? That was a miracle!"

"He's the Messiah. Are you really surprised?" Andrew said.

Mary squeezed Jesus's hand. "He's also my son."

Jesus felt a wave of love wash over him. Regardless of what happened with James, or anyone else for that matter, at least his mother would always be there for him.

CHAPTER 19

Peter came up from below deck with his hands full of cleaning equipment. He dropped it on the deck and arched his back with a grimace. Kneading his knuckles into the small of his back, he lifted his face toward the cool breeze.

"Long day?"

Peter jumped. He looked down at the dock and saw Jesus staring up at him.

"Jesus?" Peter hopped over the side of the boat, landing on the wooden dock with the grace of a seasoned acrobat. "What are you doing here?"

Jesus surveyed the boat. "I was hoping you'd take me for a ride. I've never been on a fishing boat before."

Peter eyed him suspiciously. "You came all the way out here for a boat ride?"

"It's not the only reason, but what do you say? Do you have time to take me on a little expedition?"

Peter chuckled. He'd play along with Jesus for now. He lifted his ball cap and wiped the sweat from his forehead with a stained rag. "Sure, why not? But the rest of the crew's already gone home. We won't be able to do much."

"Never underestimate the power of two men, Peter."

Peter untied the ropes from the dock cleats and helped Jesus board the 50-foot vessel. The white paint was chipped and fading in most places. The seats were worn, and the equipment was years past its prime.

"She's not much to look at, but she gets the job done," Peter said as he made his way to the bridge.

"Does she have a name?"

"The Annabelle. Named it after my wife. I had a second one named after my daughter, but I had to sell it a couple of years ago to make ends meet."

"I'm sorry to hear that."

Peter brought the engine to life and shrugged. "It is what it is. There aren't any guarantees in the fishing business. The rewards are great, but so is the risk."

The boat puttered its way out of the harbor. Once it cleared the final dock, Peter increased the throttle.

"How's business these days?" Jesus called over the roar of the engine.

"Pretty good, but this week has been brutal. My traps keep coming up empty, and my nets aren't catching anything but sneakers and old tires."

They sat in silence, content to let the motor do all the talking. With the shoreline now far in the distance, Peter brought the engine to a slow idle. He was tired of dancing around the unspoken elephant in the room. He wanted to get it all out in the open.

"You're wasting your time if you came all this way to convince me to come back."

"We need you, Peter. *I* need you."

"Andrew told me about your plans. I think it's great. I really do. But I've got a family to worry about. I can't just abandon them to travel around the country."

"I know it's a huge sacrifice."

"It's not just that. I mean, look what happened to John. You think that won't happen to you and the disciples too? If they were annoyed with John, then they're going to hate you."

Jesus pointed to a pile of green netting at the back of the boat. "Is that what you use to catch the fish?"

Peter frowned. "Huh? Yeah, one way, but if you think—."

"What are the other ways?"

Peter sighed. Why was Jesus changing the subject? Nothing was going to make him change his mind, certainly not a Q&A on fishing techniques. But Jesus was the Messiah, and the least Peter could do was humor him.

"If we have a small crew, then we toss out those nets by hand. If we have a full crew, then we use the bigger ones over there on the reel. Then there's the traps I was talking about that we leave out overnight."

"Let's lower the smaller nets for a catch."

"I wish it were that easy, but that's not how it works. This isn't a good spot for trawling, and even if it was, it wouldn't matter. Like I said, I've been out here with a full crew for over a week and haven't caught a thing."

Jesus's eyes drifted toward the nets and then worked their way back to Peter's face. Jesus raised his eyebrows.

Peter sighed again. "Alright, but it won't do any good."

With Jesus's help, Peter cast the net into the water. He went to the wheel and pushed on the throttle. The lines tightened, and the net ballooned out against the current.

"Okay, that's good. Shut it down," Jesus said once they'd gone a few hundred yards.

Peter idled the engine and returned to the back of the boat. "That's really all there is to it," he said as he hauled in the net.

"Well, there's a little more to it than that. There's a science to finding the right spots, and you have to leave the nets out longer than—" The net stopped moving. Peter pulled harder, but it wouldn't budge. "It must be caught on something. Can you give me a hand with this, Jesus?"

Jesus took the other end of the net, braced his foot against the side of the boat, and pulled. The net made its way back into the boat one grueling inch at a time. Veins bulged from Peter's forearms, and sweat poured down his face. As the bulk of the net rose out of the water, Peter saw hundreds of fish sparkling in the evening sunlight.

"What in the world?" Peter said.

The two men wrangled the overflowing net into the boat. The fish poured onto the deck like cement from a mixer. Peter collapsed onto a bench, panting as the fish stacked up around his ankles.

"How'd you do that? There's no way this many fish were underneath us. No way." Peter's voice was shaky. "Andrew told me about the water into wine thing, but I thought he was making it up so I'd come back. But it was true, wasn't it? You can do miracles."

"Come back with me, Peter."

Peter fell to his knees, paying no attention to the fish floundering around him. He didn't know how he could leave his wife and daughter behind, but he had to do it. After what he'd just seen, it wasn't even a choice.

"I'll do whatever you want, Lord. Anything!" Peter said.

Jesus helped him to his feet. "You're a great fisherman, Peter, but with me you will become a fisher of men." He put his arm around Peter and smiled. "Now, show me what to do with these fish."

CHAPTER 20

"Daddy!"

A young girl sprinted to the front door, blonde curls bouncing against her shoulders. She squealed as Peter lifted her into the air and covered her freckled cheeks with kisses.

"Shoo wee, Daddy! You stink."

Peter laughed and lowered her to the ground. "But it's a good stink, Olivia. It's the smell of fish, which in this house is the smell of money."

"Don't you stink up my house, mister. I spent all day cleaning this place."

Peter looked up to see his wife, Annabelle, leaning against the archway. Her hair was pulled back in a ponytail, her tank top spotted with dust. Peter thought she looked beautiful, and his heart ached at the thought of what he was about to tell her.

"I helped too!" Olivia said.

Annabelle smirked and mouthed the word *helped* while adding air quotes with her fingers.

"And you did a fantastic job," Peter said.

"Who's that?" Olivia asked, pointing outside.

Annabelle looked horrified. "You brought a guest? Simon, why didn't you tell me? I'm a mess!" She swatted his arm with her dust rag.

"Sorry. It was kind of last minute," Peter said.

She preened her hair and smoothed the wrinkles from her tank top. "Well, aren't you at least going to introduce us?"

"Oh, right. Jesus, I'd like you to meet my wife, Annabelle, and my daughter, Olivia."

Jesus stepped from the shadows and into the entryway.

Annabelle's eyes widened. "*The* Jesus? In my house?"

Jesus shook her hand. "It's nice to meet you, Annabelle. I apologize for showing up unannounced. I hope you don't mind."

"Don't be silly. Come on in."

Jesus got down on one knee and held out his hand. "It's nice to meet you too, Olivia."

She giggled while shaking his hand. "You want to see my room? I have a princess castle and lots of Barbies and a Wonder Woman doll."

"Olivia, honey. Leave Jesus alone," Annabelle said.

Jesus laughed. "It's alright. I'd love to see her room. She can show it to me while the two of you talk."

"Come on!" Olivia grabbed Jesus's hand and pulled him toward the hall. "I have a dog in my room too, but he's not real. Daddy says we can't have a real dog, but Mommy says he might change his mind someday."

Annabelle looked at Peter. "Talk about what?"

Peter's heart sank.

***

Olivia held out a pink teapot. "Would you like some more tea?"

"Why, that would be lovely, princess Olivia. Thank you very much," Jesus said.

He pushed his teacup across the table so Olivia could pour him some more invisible tea. Jesus remembered having similar tea parties with his sister, Angela, when she was younger, and he smiled at the memory. He brought the cup to his lips and blew across the top.

"Very hot," Jesus said.

Olivia giggled and blew into her own cup as well.

They could hear Peter and Annabelle through the adjoining bedroom wall. Their voices grew louder as the conversation progressed. Olivia's face clouded.

"They better be quiet, or they'll wake Grandma. Mommy said Grandma needs lots of rest."

"Your Grandma is here? Is she sick?"

Olivia nodded. "She has a fever. Mommy said I can't see her cuz she's cages."

"Contagious?"

"Yeah."

A thought that was not his own entered Jesus's mind. "Don't worry. I bet she'll get better real soon."

Annabelle stormed into the room, mascara running down her face like war paint. "He can't go with you. I'm sorry, but he can't leave us." Peter put his arm around her, but she pulled away. "I mean it, Simon. You can't leave. This is the stupidest idea you've ever had."

"Mommy, you're not supposed to say stupid."

Annabelle glared at her daughter. "Not now, Olivia."

"I told you it's just for a little while. The money from today's catch will hold you over until you can sell the boat," Peter said.

"Sell the boat? You really have lost your mind," Annabelle said, looking horrified.

Peter gave Jesus a pleading look. "Tell her what you did with the fish. She doesn't believe me."

Annabelle frowned. "Forgive me if I don't believe you made magic fish jump into my husband's boat."

"I didn't say they were magic fish." Peter looked at Jesus. "I didn't tell her they were magic fish."

Jesus got up from the table. He could feel the Lord guiding him. "Annabelle, where's your mother?"

"My mother?"

"Olivia told me she's sick. I'd like to see her."

"I'll show you where she is!" Olivia ran out the bedroom door.

"Olivia, no!" Annabelle cried.

"Shhh. Let him see her. It's okay," Peter said.

Jesus followed Olivia to the other side of the house, with Peter and Annabelle trailing behind them. Olivia stopped at the edge of the living room and pointed at the closed door facing them.

"She's in there."

"Olivia, why don't you wait in the living room?" Annabelle said.

"But Mooommmy!"

"Listen to your mother," Peter said.

Olivia stuck out her bottom lip and threw herself on the couch. "Fine."

Annabelle looked skeptical as she lightly knocked on the door and pushed it open. "Mom, there's someone here to see you."

An older woman with sunken features was lying in bed under several blankets. Her white, thinning hair was spread across the pillowcase like a delicate spider web.

"How are you feeling?" Anabelle said.

"Achy." Her voice sounded like she'd swallowed a handful of gravel.

Annabelle looked at the clock. "It's almost time for some more medicine, and then maybe you can eat some soup."

The woman's eyes fell on the stranger behind Annabelle. "Jesus."

"You recognize him?" Peter asked.

She pointed to the corner of the room. "From the TV."

Jesus sat on the edge of the bed. "It's nice to meet you, Elaine."

Annabelle looked at Peter. "How does he know her name?" Peter shrugged and shook his head.

"I hear you're not feeling well," Jesus said.

"Darn medicine doesn't even help," Elaine said.

Jesus smiled and took her hand. "You won't be needing any more medicine. You're all better now." He could feel the power of the Holy Spirit working through his body and into Elaine's.

Elaine's eyes grew wide. "I don't believe it. I feel completely normal." She swung her legs over the side of the bed and hopped to the floor.

"Mom, get back in bed," Annabelle said, looking frantic.

Elaine examined her face in the mirror above the dresser. "I look like my normal self again."

Annabelle felt her mother's forehead. She looked at Jesus with uncomprehending eyes. "Her fever's really gone. How is that possible?"

"See? It's like the thing with the fish. Do you believe me now?" Peter asked.

Elaine gripped the side of the dresser and eased herself to the floor.

"Mom, what are you doing?" Annabelle said.

"A man sent from God just healed me. What do you think I'm doing? I'm getting on my knees to worship him."

"Get up, Elaine. You don't have to kneel." Jesus helped her to her feet, touched by her display of reverence.

Elaine smiled and kissed his cheek. "God sent you to save the world, and here you are healing an old woman past her prime. Why?"

"Your problems are just as important to God as everyone else's," Jesus said. He could feel how much the Lord loved this woman.

She patted his hand. "Well, I'm mighty thankful for what you just did. Why don't you stay for dinner as my way of saying thanks? I make a mean chicken fried steak."

"I'd love to," Jesus said.

"Wonderful!" Elaine grabbed a tattered robe from the back of the closet door and excused herself to the kitchen.

Peter cleared his throat. "Annabelle, I have to—"

"I know," she interrupted, her body trembling. "You have to go." She glanced at the bed where her mother had just been.

Olivia burst into the room. "Grandma says you're staying for dinner. I told her you have to sit by me!" She wrapped her arms around Jesus's leg. "Will you play in my room until it's ready?"

The heaviness of the moment lifted, if only temporarily. Jesus understood how difficult this was for Peter, but he was certain it was all part of God's plan. Jesus smiled and took Olivia's tiny hand in his.

"I'd be delighted."

CHAPTER 21

There was a loud knock on the iron door, and John lifted his head from the table. The chains around his arms scraped against the metal chair. President Herod entered the room, flanked by a pair of prison guards.

"How are you doing, John?" he said.

"Like you care."

John had been in solitary confinement for over two weeks without a lawyer or even a phone call. What they were doing was illegal, but he was powerless to do anything about it.

Herod grabbed a chair and sat across from him. "Oh, I care very much, John. I don't want you wasting away in here. In fact, I don't want you in here at all. Just cooperate, and you'll be back in your cabin by tomorrow morning."

"I'll tell you the same thing I've told everyone else. I have nothing to do with the leaks. I don't know where they're coming from, but they're not from me." He was telling the truth about the leaks, but he'd be lying if he said he wasn't glad someone had done it.

"So it's just a coincidence that everything came out right after we had our little talk about you slandering me?"

John shrugged. "Like I said, it wasn't me. And for the record, it's not slander if it's true."

He watched as Herod tried to compose himself. Knowing that he was pushing the president's buttons gave him immense pleasure.

Herod leaned across the table. "Come on, John. Help me help you."

John held up his chained wrists. "I think I've had all the help I want from you."

Herod pounded his fists on the table. "Lock him back up! We're through here!"

He stormed out the door and slammed it shut behind him. The hissy fit gave John a strong sense of satisfaction. As the guards prepared to take him back to his cell, John did the one thing that came natural to him: he preached the word of God.

CHAPTER 22

Matthew hopped into the van with a plastic bag clenched between his teeth and his arms full of bottled waters. He let the bag fall to the floor and tossed a bottle to each of the disciples.

Judas dug through the bag, his eyes widening. "Beef jerky, chips, candy bars. For crying out loud! How much did you spend?"

"I don't know. The receipt should be in there somewhere."

"What do you mean you don't know? What part of a budget do you not understand?"

Matthew wasn't in the mood for one of Judas's finance lessons. "Most of it. That's why I'm a painter and not an accountant."

"Hardy har har. Very funny." Judas said.

Thomas appeared in the doorway with a bag of chips. "Thaddeus said the Snickers are in your van. Anyone want to trade for some Funyuns?"

"There's more in the other van?" Judas looked through the back window and saw Peter downing a bag of M&M's.

Matthew shrugged. "They've got to eat too."

Judas grabbed the bag of snacks and hopped out of the van.

"Hey, where are you going?" Matthew said.

"I'm getting our money back." Judas snatched the bag of Funyuns out of Thomas's hands.

Matthew watched him confiscate the uneaten items from the other van and march toward the gas station. He thought

Judas would make a great captain of the fun police. The guy was a real buzzkill.

The group of thirteen had been traveling together for a few months, and like any family spending a lot of time together, they sometimes wore on each other's nerves. Traveling thousands of miles in close quarters was difficult under normal circumstances, and these last few months had been anything but normal.

The disciples had left their families and jobs to travel the country with nothing more than a bag of personal belongings, a small amount of money, and two vans older than the men riding in them. They'd hitched a rickety trailer behind one van to hold their meager supplies.

With no definitive plan in place, the disciples relied on Jesus's guidance as they traveled across the country. One day Jesus would preach in front of hundreds of people at a large temple, and the next he would minister to a small group at a local homeless shelter. No venue was too great or too small when it came to Jesus preaching the word of God.

Matthew watched Jesus's popularity skyrocket as people heard about his supposed miracles. There were rumors of him healing the sick, but those were vague and lacked evidence. The story of Jesus turning water into wine had also become popular, but most people dismissed it as an urban legend.

There were three incidents, however, that even the greatest skeptics had trouble dismissing. The first had occurred two weeks into Jesus's travels. He was in the middle of a city park, preaching on a wooden stage normally reserved for theatrical performances, when two blind men approached the front of the stage with the help of a friend. They began yelling for Jesus to heal them. As the disciples were about to escort the men away, Jesus stopped preaching and left the stage to stand face to face with the strangers.

"Do you believe I can heal you?" Jesus asked.

"Yes!" the men cried in unison.

Jesus placed the tips of his fingers on the eyes of the first man. When he pulled them away, the man opened his eyes and immediately closed them again.

"It's so bright!" the man said.

Jesus then touched the eyes of the second man as well. Little by little, both men opened their eyes. As the world revealed itself to them for the first time, they cried while lifting their hands to the heavens. An excited murmur worked its way through the crowd. Many were convinced they had seen a miracle. Others claimed the men were actors planted there by Jesus.

Several people recorded the event on their phones, and the story went viral. Friends and family of the two men came forward to confirm that both had been blind since birth. Medical reports also verified the claims. Despite all the evidence and multiple eyewitnesses, most people wrote it off as a hoax.

The second documented miracle had occurred a couple of months later while Jesus was preaching in a temple. A man had approached Jesus and handed him a note stating he was mute and possessed by demons. Jesus studied the man for a moment and then laid his hands on him. The man collapsed to the ground and began rolling around on the floor. He emitted a growl that seemed to come from the fiery pits of Hell rather than his own throat. In a voice that was not his own, the man uttered words so vile that several people left. A shiver ran up Matthew's spine, and he felt a dark and foreboding presence inside the temple.

Jesus ordered the man to be quiet and get up. The man's vulgarity stopped at once, and the presence Matthew had felt vanished in an instant. The man got to his feet and thanked Jesus with a voice he had not used in years.

While most of the audience applauded the healing, not everyone in the crowd was pleased. Like John the Baptist, Jesus was often critical of the Pharisees and Sadducees. Several of them were in attendance that evening, and they rushed to the front of the temple, criticizing everyone for celebrating what Jesus had done. They said the act was satanic, calling it the work of the devil instead of God.

The last miracle had occurred a week ago in a small town with a single traffic light. A man approached Jesus at the town's post office and begged him to heal his deaf and mute son, who suffered from frequent seizures.

"How long has he been like this?" Jesus asked.

"Since he was a baby. Please heal him if you can."

"If I can? Everything is possible for those who believe."

"Oh, Lord! Help me overcome my unbelief!" the man cried.

Jesus placed his hand on top of the boy's head. "Evil spirit, I command you to come out of this child and never return!" His voice boomed up and down Main Street.

The boy collapsed and began to shriek and convulse, just like the man in the temple. After several terrifying minutes, the boy grew still. He looked like a corpse, and for a moment Matthew thought he was dead.

Jesus bent down and took the boy's hand. Matthew watched in awe as the boy opened his eyes and spoke. The crowd went crazy. People cried out to Jesus, begging him for their own personal miracles.

All of these miraculous events led Jesus and his disciples to where they were today. Temples and parks were no longer big enough to hold the crowds. He was now speaking in concert halls and gymnasiums, the latter being their current destination now that Judas had returned the snacks.

Andrew pulled up Google Maps on his phone as they left the gas station. "The school is less than ten minutes from here."

Jesus nodded and followed the automated voice's instructions. Although they couldn't afford to rent the larger facilities, many people offered their venue for free in exchange for the opportunity to host the man who had become one of the most popular people in the world. It was free advertising at its finest.

The school's parking lot was already overflowing when Jesus and his disciples arrived. There were several police cars and fire-trucks parked out front, and people were crammed around the entrance. *Just another day at the office*, Matthew thought to himself.

The vans pulled around back, where a short, plump man was waiting for them outside the fire exit. He waved them over with a meaty hand.

"You must be Stanley," Jesus said.

Stanley nodded. "Please, hurry inside." Once through the doors, Stanley wiped his brow with a handkerchief. "What a day. I've been praying for a large turnout ever since you agreed to come to our city, and God has certainly provided. There's got to be at least two thousand people here!"

Stanley led them down a hall and into the school's entryway. They could see hundreds of people standing outside the glass doors. Matthew felt like a rockstar, and in a way he thought they were. Religious rock stars.

"Man, look at all those people waiting to get in," Philip said.

"Those are just the ones we turned away. Everyone else is already inside," Stanley said.

The disciples watched four teenage boys arguing with one of the security guards outside. Another boy sat quietly in a wheel-chair next to them. The security guard shook his head while crossing his arms across his barrel chest. One boy lowered his head, grabbed the wheelchair, and worked his way back through the crowd. The other boys fell in line behind him.

"Can't we let those kids in?" Peter asked.

"I'm afraid not. We're already at capacity, and the fire mar-shal would love a reason to shut this place down." Stanley turned to Jesus. "He's not a fan of yours."

They continued toward the gymnasium, a crescendo of noise reaching out to them as they got closer. Stanley stopped outside a set of closed double doors.

"There's a microphone at center court and a row of chairs on the sideline for the disciples. Are you guys ready?"

Stanley pulled open the door in front of him. The place erupted into a deafening cheer as Jesus stepped onto the court. He walked around shaking hands with those in the front row, much to the dismay of security.

Jesus took his place at center court and began preaching. The crowd was mesmerized from the beginning, hanging on his every word. Matthew took a moment to appreciate how far they'd come. The crowds continued to grow with each passing day, and their passion for God's word was growing along with it. God was doing something amazing through Jesus and the disciples. He felt blessed to be a part of it.

About an hour into the message, a loud noise from above interrupted Jesus. Everyone looked up to see a group of boys yanking one of the skylight windows off the ceiling.

"It's those kids from earlier!" Thaddeus said.

One boy peeked through the opening and waved to the on-lookers, a mischievous grin plastered across his face. The laughter and cheers from the audience drowned out the shouts coming from the police. The boys carried their friend from the wheel-chair over to the skylight and sat him on the edge. They grabbed a set of ropes and tied them around him.

"Hold it right there!" shouted one of the police officers.

As the officer raced out of the gym, the boys eased their friend over the edge and slowly lowered him to the ground. His weight shifted, causing him to flip upside down like a circus ac-robat. The crowd gasped.

Matthew's heart filled with dread. Only a teenager with a misguided sense of invincibility would try such a reckless stunt. The kid was going to get himself killed.

The police officer appeared on the roof next to the boys. With their crippled friend now at the point of no return, the officer had no choice but to grab a rope and help lower him to safety.

Jesus and his disciples waited underneath the opening along with several police officers. When the boy was within reach, they grabbed his shoulders and eased him to the ground. The crowd burst into applause. The boys on the roof exchanged high-fives and pumped their fists in the air. Even the police officer managed a relieved smile before giving them a stern lecture. Matthew's heart was racing; they had dodged a bullet.

Once they untied the boy, Jesus knelt beside him with a microphone in his hand. "Son, your sins are forgiven."

"No!" came a cry from the bleachers. A priest in colorful garments ran down the steps of the gymnasium, holding his robe above his ankles as he went. "How dare you!" the priest said as he reached the edge of the basketball court.

Police officers moved to block the priest's path, but Jesus insisted they let him through. The priest gave the officers an indignant look as he pushed past them. He marched up to Jesus and snatched the microphone out of his hands. Matthew rolled his eyes. These guys were such a pain.

"This is blasphemy! Nobody but God can forgive sins." The priest turned to the audience. "Don't you see he's nothing more than a wolf in sheep's clothing? If you follow this man, he will lead you straight to Hell!"

A chorus of boos poured from the bleachers. Jesus held out his hand. The priest slapped the microphone into it.

"Why do you say that? Is it easier to tell this paralyzed boy his sins are forgiven, or to tell him to get up and walk?" Jesus said.

"Don't be ridiculous. What does that even mean?" the priest said.

"Which one is easier?" Jesus pressed.

"Of course it's easier to tell him his sins are forgiven, but that doesn't mean you have the authority to do it."

Jesus turned to the boy. "What's your name?"

"Landon."

"And why did you come here today, Landon?"

217

"Well, sir, I got in a wreck a few years ago, and now I'm paralyzed from the neck down. My friends heard about all the miracles you've been doing and thought maybe you could fix me."

"But you couldn't get in?"

"No, sir. The place was already full when we got here, but my friends wouldn't give up. Brad drove home real quick and came back with some ropes from his dad's shed."

"That's me!" came the distant voice of one boy hovering over the skylight. Thunderous applause and whistles worked their way up to Brad.

"I want you to get up," Jesus said.

Landon's eyes grew wide. "Really?"

"Do it!" Brad said.

"Do it, do it, do it!" The crowd's chant picked up momentum and echoed off the walls.

Landon's feet twitched like someone had pricked them with a needle. Then his left leg suddenly jerked to one side. Landon cried as he lifted both legs into the air. He stared at them like he was seeing them for the first time. The excitement in the gym was electric. Landon's friends jumped up and down on the roof while hugging one another.

Matthew watched the boy in stunned silence. He'd seen Jesus do a lot of miracles, but this was taking it to a whole other level. A paralyzed boy was moving his limbs. It was incredible! The childlike faith of these boys was paying off in a big way. Matthew wiped away the tears rolling down his cheeks.

Landon turned over and pushed himself to his feet. He took a few tentative steps and then ran around the perimeter of the court.

Jesus held out the microphone to the priest, his eyebrows raised. The priest shook his head and stormed out of the gym.

Jesus invited anyone who wanted to give their life to God to come down and be baptized in the swimming pool set up in the far corner of the gym. Hundreds of people poured onto the court.

Worship music played over the loudspeakers as Jesus and his disciples baptized thirteen people at a time. Landon's friends joined him at the edge of the pool, where they waited for the last person to be baptized before entering the water themselves.

CHAPTER 23

Cameron sat behind his desk in the Oval Office, listening to a conference call on the latest bill being pushed through Congress. Salome was perched on the edge of his desk, scrolling through her Instagram feed. Her sundress rode high on her thighs, and Cameron leered at her tanned legs with a longing that both shamed and excited him. He could never act on his desire for her because there was no way she would ever go for it. Or would she? Wasn't Salome always flirting with him? And wasn't her dress pulled up a little too high to be unintentional?

"Ahem!"

Cameron looked up to see Herodias standing in the doorway. "Um, I'm going to have to call you back." He hung up the phone and hurried over to her. "Hey, good looking! What are you doing here?"

"Gross," Salome said.

Herodias held up a stack of papers. "I thought I'd swing by so we could discuss this. What are you doing?"

"Getting ready to take Salome out to lunch to celebrate the end of her semester."

"How very thoughtful of you." Herodias's voice was flat. "Salome, dear, could you excuse us for a second?"

Salome slid off the desk and left the room without looking up from her phone. When the door clicked shut behind her, Herodias hurled the papers at Cameron. They hit his chest and scattered across the carpet like giant pieces of confetti.

"What's with you?" Cameron said, bending down to collect the papers.

"Poll numbers, Cameron. Hot off the press! Have you seen them?"

"Not yet."

"They stink now that your stupid brother told the press about our affair. I hope you get that hush money back because you're going to need it when you're out of a job."

Cameron winced. Things had continued to unravel since the arrest of John the Baptist. Reporters were relentless in chasing down the rumors, and they pressured Barrett with constant phone calls, emails, and visits to his house. It got so bad that Barrett had gone into hiding to avoid the media circus. Reporters are like hound dogs, however, and it only took a couple of weeks for one of them to track him down. That had been Barrett's breaking point, and he had vomited every little detail about the affair to the reporter: the fist fight with his brother, the attempts to cover up the affair, even the money Cameron had paid him to keep quiet. Everything was now out in the open.

Cameron had avoided the press while the scandal exploded, leaving his press secretary to take the heat on his behalf. Although none of what he did was illegal or grounds for impeachment, it had tainted his image beyond repair. Everything people had assumed about him was a lie. He was an immoral fraud.

The scandal opened doors into other areas of his life as well. People scrutinized the arrest of John the Baptist. The administration had yet to provide any evidence of his assassination plot, and some questioned if they had only arrested him because of his public shaming of Cameron's relationship.

"It's just a poll. They're not always accurate."

"It's not just a poll, Cameron!" She spat his name like it was a mouthful of rotten meat. "It's ten polls, and they all show the same thing. Did you know your opposition wants you in office more than your own party? Why do you think that is?"

"Because I'll be a layup in the next election."

"Ding ding ding! Very good, honey."

"Did you just come here to rub this in my face, or do you want something?"

"I want you to act like a man! You've given up, and it's pathetic."

"You said it yourself. I'm finished. What else can I do?" he said through gritted teeth.

"How about sticking it to the man responsible for this mess?"

"Who, Barrett?"

"No, you moron. John the freaking Baptist."

Cameron tossed the poll numbers onto his desk and sighed. "You're still hung up on that guy? It's over. We've done everything short of waterboarding him, and he hasn't admitted a thing. All we've managed to do is make the public suspicious of why he was arrested, which was *your* brilliant idea, I might add."

Herodias slapped him across the face. Her wedding band left a red welt just below his right eye. Cameron stood in stunned disbelief. Herodias had always been verbally abusive when upset, but physical violence was a line she'd never crossed, until now.

"Don't you *ever* try to pin that on me! I said to kill that psycho. You could have made it look like a random murder, but no! You had to do it your way. Your father would be so proud."

"You know what the best thing about being a one-term president is? I can divorce you four years earlier than I thought." Cameron knew that would sting her cold, black heart, and it made him happy. The horrible she-devil deserved it.

Herodias raised her hand, and Cameron flinched. She gave a maniacal cackle and turned to leave.

"Have fun on your lunch date," Herodias said, slamming the door behind her.

CHAPTER 24

Jordan stood before the Sanhedrin, a council of Jewish leaders whose members were the top Pharisees and Sadducees in the country. Like the rest of the Sanhedrin, Jordan lived a lavish lifestyle of large homes, expensive cars, and the finest clothes. The Sanhedrin were led by their high priest, Caiaphas, who was currently sitting at the head of the table.

Jordan, with remote in hand, played the video on the screen behind him. After seeing the news story last night, he knew he had to get it in front of the rest of the Sanhedrin ASAP.

"Good evening, and thank you for joining us. I'm Allie Lawson."

"And I'm Max Henegan. Tonight we begin the ten o'clock news hour with a story that continues to captivate the country."

"That's right, Max. Jesus has done it again. This time supposedly healing a paralyzed boy, Landon Riggs, who was lowered through the gymnasium roof at Lincoln Memorial High School earlier this afternoon."

The station cut to a video showing Landon suspended above the basketball court. Jordan noticed several of the Sanhedrin raise their eyebrows at the scene playing out before them.

"This video was sent to us by one of our viewers. You can see the boy dangling upside down as he's lowered to the ground."

The video jumped ahead to when Landon was getting to his feet.

"And here he is standing on his feet after claiming to be paralyzed. A remarkable video, to say the least. We now go live to Christine Sanders, who is on the scene with the latest. Christine?"

"Thank you, Allie. I'm standing outside Lincoln Memorial High School, where just hours ago, Landon Riggs was lowered through the roof in a desperate attempt to get him in front of the man many people believe can heal the sick."

The Sanhedrin watched as an earlier interview between Landon and Christine replaced the live feed. Jordan saw Caiaphas leaning forward with intense interest.

"If I'm being honest, I didn't really think he was going to heal me. I believe in God and everything, but no way could Jesus make me walk again. My spinal cord got all messed up in a car accident, and I've been paralyzed ever since," Landon said.

"But he healed you?" Christine asked.

"I'm standing, aren't I?" Landon did a little dance and laughed. "Yeah, he healed me. First, he said my sins were forgiven, and then he told me to get up. I thought he was crazy, but my legs started moving, and the next thing I knew, I was running around the basketball court."

"And what do you say to those who think this is all some sort of trick?"

"With all due respect, they don't know what they're talking about. Ask anyone in this city that knows me. Heck, ask my doctor. They'll tell you. Jesus is the real deal. Glory to God!"

The station returned to a live shot of Christine.

"We spoke with Landon's doctor, who confirmed the paralysis, but the story is far from over. Some scientists claim this is nothing more than the placebo effect, also called the power of suggestion. They say while Landon may have been paralyzed, it's possible it wasn't a permanent condition.

"Religious leaders have thrown their hat into the ring as well, claiming this was the work of the devil. In what might be the unlikeliest of alliances, many satanic groups are also supporting the theory. Despite the conflicting opinions, one thing we can all agree on is this is an incredible story. Max, Allie, back to you."

The station returned to the news desk.

"Thank you, Christine," Allie said. "Jesus is no stranger to controversy. Critics have explained away his other miracles as sleight of hand, mass hallucinations, and even edited videos. Computer experts have successfully recreated some of his recorded miracles, showing just how easy it is to make them look real."

"What's your take on it, Allie?"

Allie laughed. "We're not going there, Max. I get enough hate mail as it is."

Max gave a hearty laugh of his own. "Fair enough. In other news—"

Jordan paused the video and faced the Sanhedrin. "This is just one example of what aired across the country last night. A quick Google search pulls up hundreds of other videos just like it. Jesus has gone from a nuisance to a downright threat. He insults us at every opportunity, and now he's forgiving sins in the name of God while convincing people he can perform miracles. People are questioning our authority. We have to put a stop to this."

The council murmured amongst themselves while Jordan let the severity of the situation sink in.

"Do you have a plan on how we should deal with him?" Caiaphas asked.

"Yes, Your Excellency. I propose we launch a full-scale operation to undermine Jesus at every opportunity. We'll have groups of Pharisees and Sadducees follow him wherever he goes. They'll trap him with tough theological questions and call him out publicly whenever he breaks a Jewish law. Essentially, we'll expose him for the fraud that he is."

Caiaphas leaned forward, resting his elbows on the table. "Your plan has merit, but it requires diligent preparation. Jesus is very popular, and we don't want to appear unfairly hostile toward him. I recommend you come up with a detailed plan to present at next week's meeting for our approval."

This was exactly what Jordan had been hoping for. It was a chance to show Caiaphas what he could do and position himself to become the next high priest. The following week, the Sanhedrin unanimously approved Jordan's plan, and the attempt to discredit Jesus was underway.

CHAPTER 25

John sat in one of the booths lining the wall of the prison's visitation room. Preston, one of John's original disciples, sat across from him, separated by a reinforced plexiglass window. John picked up the phone hanging on the wall next to him and pressed it to his ear.

"It's good to see you, Preston."

"You too, John. We've been worried about you. We didn't even know if you were still alive."

"I guess Herod got worried about people thinking I was dead. That must be why they finally let me talk to someone after all these months. What a bunch of fools."

Preston looked at the two guards standing behind John. "I don't think we should talk about things like that."

John looked over his shoulder. "What, are you worried about these guys? What are they going to do, arrest me?" John couldn't care less what the guards saw or heard. He'd been isolated, sleep deprived, starved, and mentally abused. He stopped caring about what they thought of him a long time ago. "So how are things at the river?"

"We've been doing the best we can, but it's getting bad. Now that you and Jesus are gone . . . well, it's just not the same. The crowds have gotten pretty small."

"How many?"

"Ten, maybe twenty on a good day."

John leaned his forehead against the glass and sighed. "Have you talked to Jesus lately?"

"Not since he left the cabin. He's traveling all over the country with twelve of the disciples. He's healing people, John. It's unbelievable. People are converting by the thousands."

"So I've heard. I keep waiting for him to break me out of here with one of his miracles. I'm supposed to be out there paving the way for the Messiah."

A guard snickered and tried to cover it up with a cough. That would have angered John a few months ago, but now he almost understood the skepticism. There had been plenty of time for Jesus to do something about John's situation, but so far he hadn't so much as lifted a finger.

"I could call him for you. See if he'd come visit you," Preston said.

"They'd never let him anywhere near this place unless it was to throw him in a cell next to mine, but I do want you to call him. Tell him I want to know if he's really the Messiah, or if we should expect someone else."

"John, he's the one. You know that."

"Just ask him, okay? I need to hear it from him." Doubts had infected John's mind like a tumor, and they were growing with each passing day. He needed some reassurance from Jesus.

"Time's up," one guard said.

"Just tell me what he says," John said hurriedly as the guard took the phone from his hands.

***

Jesus listened on his cell phone as Preston relayed John's questions to him from the parking lot of the prison. His heart ached for his cousin. He wished there was more he could do for him, but God had made it clear that he was to focus on his preaching instead of John's situation.

"Tell him everything you've seen and heard," Jesus said. "Tell him the blind receive sight, the paralyzed walk, diseases are cured, the deaf hear, and the good news is proclaimed to the poor."

"I already told him you were doing miracles. I think he's looking for something more specific about his own situation. He's frustrated about being stuck in jail."

"Then tell him not to give up on me just because I'm not meeting his expectations at the moment." Jesus prayed that John would stay strong and continue to have faith that everything would work out for God's glory.

"Anything else? Maybe something about you being the Messiah?"

"No. He already knows the answer to that."

"Okay, I'll tell him."

"And Preston?"

"Yeah?"

"Don't discount what you and the others are doing at the river. Comparison can be an evil thing. God rejoices in saving one soul just as much as he does a hundred. You and the others will be richly rewarded in Heaven for what you're doing."

Jesus ended the call as the vans pulled into the parking lot of a large temple, where a crowd of people waited outside to greet them. It was the Sabbath, and Jesus had agreed to spend the day preaching at multiple services so people would have plenty of opportunities to hear his message.

A man pushed his way through the crowd as Jesus walked toward the temple's large, ornate doors. He thrust out a withered hand with fingers bent into a crude claw. "Take pity on me, Jesus! Heal my hand so I can work and support my family again."

Jesus reached out to the man, but a group of Pharisees inserted themselves between the two.

"Wait!" one of the Pharisees said. "Do you think it's lawful to heal someone on the Sabbath?"

Each of the Pharisees wore a smug look. Jewish law proclaimed the Sabbath to be a day of rest, and any type of work, including healing, was a sin.

The Pharisees and Sadducees scrutinized everything Jesus did in the hopes of making him look like a sacrilegious fraud, but it didn't concern him. Whatever he did came from God, and God wouldn't let the plans of men disrupt his own divine agenda.

"If you saw a puppy fall into a hole on the Sabbath, would you rescue it?" Jesus asked. When none of the Pharisees answered, Jesus addressed the crowd standing around them. "What about all of you? Would you save it?" Everyone nodded their heads. "How much more valuable is this man than a dog? Is it lawful to do good on the Sabbath or to do evil? To save a life or destroy it?" He turned back to the disfigured man. "Come here and stretch out your hand."

The man stepped around the Pharisees and offered his hand to Jesus. Jesus touched it, and the fingers straightened at once. The man stared at his hand in amazement.

"It's healed! It's completely healed! Thank you, Jesus! Thank you!" The man began to weep.

Jesus hugged him and walked with him into the temple, asking him about his work and family. He gave a parting glance to the Pharisees, feeling pity for their hardened hearts. The crowd had already turned on them, criticizing the Pharisees for their lack of compassion. Their plan to discredit Jesus had suffered its first blow.

CHAPTER 26

Herodias stared out the limousine window, watching the street-lights zip by like oversized lightning bugs. Beneath the outer beauty and elegance she worked so hard to maintain, there was an unquenchable rage burning deep inside her. Herodias's hatred for Cameron had grown to where she could no longer stand to be in the same room with him, and would only do so for the occasional public appearance. Even those were becoming less frequent these days. Cameron still had two years left in office, but now that his re-election was out of the question, she didn't see the point in continuing to pretend like they were a perfect, happy couple.

His own party had abandoned him like a sinking ship, and members of Congress were declining his endorsement for the upcoming midterm elections. He'd become a lame duck halfway through his first term.

Herodias's days of making Cameron look good were dwindling. The only reason she was still with him was to preserve what little dignity she had left. To turn tail and run would make her look weak, and she refused to appear weak. A liar? Fine. A home wrecker? Fair enough. A power-hungry leech? Whatever. But weak? Never. She'd see this thing through to the end, and if she played her cards right, there'd be a multimillion-dollar book deal waiting for her at the finish line. Until then, she would spend her remaining days in the White House seeking revenge on those who had caused her downfall, and there was one primary target in her crosshairs.

She turned from the window and looked at her daughter. "Salome, honey, can we talk?"

Salome was adjusting the filter on the selfie she'd taken a few minutes earlier. "Sure, Mom. What's up?"

"And can you look at me while we're talking?"

Salome turned off the phone and placed it in the empty seat next to her. "Better?"

Herodias nodded. "I feel like we never talk anymore since you found out about the affair. I know I only have myself to blame for that, but—"

"Mom—"

"I know, I know. You don't want to talk about it, but we're growing apart, and it's killing me. I miss my little girl."

Herodias looked away, forcing a sniffle while dabbing at eyes that were bone-dry.

"Mom, don't cry." Salome scooted closer to Herodias. "I've had a lot of stuff to work through, but I'm not a little kid anymore. I know marriages go bad, and people make mistakes. I hate what you did to Dad, but that doesn't mean I don't love you."

"I hate myself for what I've put you through, and then I've made it even worse by letting Cameron get to me."

"What do you mean?"

Herodias glanced at Salome and looked away. "Nothing. I shouldn't have said anything. I'm just upset."

"No, what did Cameron do?"

Herodias took her daughter's hand. "If I tell you something, do you promise to keep it a secret? You can never tell a soul, especially Cameron. He'd . . . well, I'm not sure what he'd do if he found out I told someone. He's been so angry lately."

Salome's face hardened. The young and carefree look from her Snapchat filters was gone. "I won't say a word. What happened?"

"He's leaving us, Salome. He's going to file for divorce when his term is up. I did everything I could to make him happy, but it wasn't enough. He's the one that leaked everything about the affair. That's how desperate he is to get rid of me. Oh, this is all my fault!" Herodias burst into tears. Her lies were so real that even a small part of her believed them.

Salome pulled her mom into her arms. "Don't cry, Mom. How is this your fault? Did he tell you that?"

"He beats it into my head every chance he gets."

"Tell me about the rest. What about the leaks?"

Herodias sat up and composed herself. "His plan was to leak the affair and spin it so I came out looking like the bad guy. He'd concocted some crazy story about me blackmailing him into the relationship with the help of your father."

"That's crazy! How did he expect anyone to believe that?"

"I'm not sure. I only know that much because one of his staff members got a guilty conscious and warned me." When it came to lying, Herodias knew the fewer details there were, the better.

"Who?"

Herodias shook her head. "I can't tell you that. This person literally put their life on the line for me. I can't risk their name getting out."

"So what happened? It clearly didn't work."

"He had some agreement with John the Baptist where he would leak the affair in exchange for a lot of money. John's arrest was part of their plan, but I don't know what their end game was. All I know is they didn't plan on reporters hounding your father until he broke and gave up the real story. The whole thing blew up in their face, and Cameron's been on the rampage ever since."

"What else?" Salome's voice was shaking.

"Last week . . . oh this is so embarrassing I don't even want to say it."

"Tell me."

"He told me you two were having an affair."

"Mother!"

"I know it's crazy. I tell myself it's all nonsense, but then I see things like you two having lunch together, or the way he stares at you when you're working out."

"That sick pervert! I swear nothing is going on. I'm his niece for crying out loud! His stepdaughter!"

"I'm so sorry. I shouldn't have said anything. He's an evil man, Salome."

"I'll kill him."

"No! You promised you wouldn't say anything."

"What he's doing is unforgivable. We can't let him get away with this."

"We? You mean you'd help me?" Herodias was impressed with her convincing performance. She wondered if maybe she'd missed her calling as an actress.

Salome's hardened face gave way to tears. "Of course, Mom. I've always got your back. If that creep has the nerve to hurt you and spread a bunch of filthy lies about me, then I say let's get him."

Herodias hugged her daughter tight. "I love you so much."

"I love you too, Mom. Now, what can we do to make him pay?"

An evil smile crawled across Herodias's face as it rested on Salome's shoulder. She caught her reflection in the window and relished the look. "We'll think of something, dear."

Mission accomplished.

CHAPTER 27

After a morning of feeding the homeless at the local shelter, Jesus surprised the disciples by suggesting they take the afternoon off to enjoy a movie at the local theater.

"Our work is important but so is rest. Our body is the Lord's temple, and we should treat it that way," Jesus said. He noticed the men were getting a little burned out, and it was important to keep them energized for the work that lay ahead.

None of his disciples argued the point. The past few weeks had been a hectic blur of preaching, baptizing, serving, and traveling. All of them agreed they could use a break.

Following a double feature, Jesus and the disciples walked out of the movie theater and into the blinding afternoon sunlight. They heard a commotion across the street and noticed a crowd of paparazzi yelling questions at an unseen celebrity.

With his curiosity piqued, Jesus led the disciples across the street for a better look. The man in the middle of the chaos was wearing a colorful Hawaiian shirt with the top three buttons undone. His gold chain sparkled through a carpet of thick, black chest hair.

Matthew squinted, his eyes still adjusting to the light. "I think that's Randy Wood."

"Randy Wood?" Jesus said.

"Yeah, he's that famous adult film director who's always doing crazy hijinks for publicity."

Jesus raised his eyebrows. "You know this man?"

"Um, I mean, not really. It's not like I watch his stuff. I've just seen him on TV." He looked at the other disciples. "Come on, guys. You know who he is, right?"

Jesus gave him a playful slap on the back. "I'm just messing with you. I know who he is. What do you say we go say hello?"

"Are you serious?" Peter asked.

"Of course." Jesus started toward the crowd. The disciples looked at one another, shrugged, and followed him.

A young man, wearing an oversized t-shirt and backwards ball cap, shoved his way to the front of the crowd and stuck his cell phone in Randy's face. "Hey, Randy. Any truth to the rumor that you've signed an A-list celebrity to star in your next film?"

Randy shook his head while continuing to sign autographs, his ponytail swinging back and forth like a pendulum. "My lips are sealed until we finalize things."

"So there is something to the rumors then?"

That brought a sly smile to Randy's face. He looked up to respond and became distracted by a group of people lingering at the back of the crowd.

"Well, I'll be. Is that the one and only Jesus and his holy rollers?" Randy said.

There were cries of excitement as people followed Randy's gaze and saw Jesus standing there with his disciples. The crowd parted like the Red Sea to give Jesus a clear path to Randy. A meeting between the alleged Messiah and one of the sleaziest men in America was an event the paparazzi were happy to accommodate. The photographs and videos would sell for record prices on the open market.

"You must be lost. I don't think I'm the kind of guy you want to be seen with," Randy said.

Jesus extended his hand. "On the contrary. It's a pleasure to meet you."

Randy studied it with mock concern. "I won't burst into flames or anything if I touch you, will I?"

The paparazzi laughed as the two men shook hands. Everyone pressed in closer, the cameras flashing like a lightning storm.

"What's your angle, Jesus? Are you here to convert me? I'm afraid my soul's a lost cause."

"No, nothing like that. My friends and I were about to go to dinner, and I was hoping you'd join us. I'd love to hear your story." Jesus saw the uncomfortable looks on his disciples' faces and realized they still had a lot to learn about loving *all* of God's children.

"My story?" Randy looked amused. "What's the catch?"

"No catch. Just dinner. What do you say? You're welcome to bring some friends if you'd like."

Randy laughed. "The press would eat their young to run a story about us hanging out together." He leaned in and whispered into Jesus's ear. "And I'm a sucker for free press."

"Then it's settled. Name the place, and we'll meet you there in half an hour," Jesus said.

Randy shrugged. "Sure. Why the heck not?"

***

La Mesa's was a madhouse. The owners had reserved the back patio for Jesus and Randy, but there were people crammed all along the wrought iron fence surrounding it. Inside the restaurant, customers pressed themselves against the windows, their breath fogging up the glass.

Several tables had been pushed together to accommodate the large group. Jesus noticed the scantily clad women sitting next to the disciples initially unnerved them, but they soon discovered there was more to the women than just their outward appearance. The two groups were quite the juxtaposition, but there was a lot of common ground between them.

A waiter brought out a tray full of chips and salsa. Everyone dug into the baskets without giving it a second thought.

"Hey, Jesus!" cried a voice from the crowd. "Why don't your disciples follow the Jewish law instead of eating their food with unclean hands?"

Jesus scanned the crowd and locked eyes with the Pharisee that had spoken. Jews were not supposed to eat until they had ceremonially washed their hands, a tradition of pouring water onto one's hands followed by a blessing.

Jesus plucked a single chip from the basket and popped it into his mouth. Some onlookers gasped at the blatant disregard for the sacred tradition. The Pharisee's neck turned red, the color working its way up his face like a thermometer.

Jesus took his time chewing, swallowed, and then pointed at the Pharisee. "Isaiah was right when he prophesied about you."

The Pharisee snickered. "The great prophet, Isaiah, prophesied about me? I must have missed that in all my years of study."

"Not you specifically, but hypocrites like you. Remember what Isaiah said? 'These people honor me with their lips, but their hearts are far from me. They worship me in vain. Their teachings are but rules taught by men.' Does that remind you of anyone?"

The Pharisee appealed to those standing around him. "Do you see how he disrespects those of us who serve the Lord? And you call him the Messiah?"

"Listen to me, everyone," Jesus said, ignoring the Pharisee. "Nothing that enters a man from the outside can make him unclean."

"You sound like a fool!" the Pharisee said.

"Do I? It's what comes *out* of a man that makes him unclean. Evil thoughts, sexual immorality, theft, murder, adultery, greed, malice, deceit, lewdness, envy, slander, arrogance, and so on."

The Pharisee gave a bark of laughter. "Are you really going to sit here and lecture me on sexual immorality and lewdness when you're surrounded by these sinners? These hookers?"

Jesus took a deep breath and felt the Holy Spirit guiding him as it always did. "It's not the healthy who need a doctor, but the sick. I have not come for the righteous, but for the sinners. What if you had ten kids and lost one of them? Wouldn't you leave the nine to go looking for the lost one? God is the same way. There will be more rejoicing in Heaven over one sinner who repents than over ninety-nine righteous people who don't need to repent. The Lord loves everyone, including my guests here today. They're not without sin, but show me someone who is." Jesus stood up and faced the Pharisee. "We can start with you if you'd like. Shall I reveal your sins? The ones clean hands cannot hide?"

Randy exploded with laughter, pounding the table hard enough to rattle the nearby silverware. "I say let's hear it, Jesus. What's the man done? Stolen from the temple? Murdered someone? Watched one of my films? Have you been naughty, Mr. Preacher Man?"

Randy's friends laughed along with him. Even some of the disciples snorted.

The Pharisee balled his hands into tight fists. "Your day's coming, Jesus."

Already knowing his ultimate fate, the ominous threat rocked Jesus more than anyone there realized. The Pharisee shoved his way through the crowd, the tail of his colorful robe trailing behind him. Jesus returned to the table and helped himself to a handful of chips. Randy slapped him on the back.

"You're alright, Jesus. I was wrong about you. I mean, I don't buy into that God stuff you're pedaling, but you're not like the rest of the religious people who think they're better than everyone else."

"Not everyone is like that Pharisee," Jesus said. It broke his heart to know how much damage a hypocrite's actions could do to an unbeliever's spiritual fate.

"You might be right, but the loud ones sure are. And those are the only ones I've ever talked to until today. You've earned my respect, Jesus. I tell you what. Since you've been nothing but kind to me and my girls, the least I can do is come to that big revival of yours later this week. I'm a lost cause, but you might rub off on one of these ladies. Plus, more publicity, right?"

"I'd be honored to have you join us," Jesus said, thrilled to have an opportunity to preach God's word to Randy and his friends. "I'll save you some seats right up front."

"Looking forward to it. Now, let's order something. I'm starving!"

CHAPTER 28

Cameron dug into the colorful bag and revealed a blue box with gold lettering across the front. His eyes lit up as he pulled out a glass bottle full of brown liquid.

"A bottle of Macallan? You spoil me, Jackson." Cameron said.

Jackson, a broad-shouldered man in uniform, puffed on a cigar. "Only the best scotch for the birthday boy."

"Well, let's break this bad boy open and have a taste," Cameron said.

The men sitting around the bar cheered. Cameron's most trusted officials and military commanders had come together to celebrate his birthday. After a steak dinner in the White House dining hall, the men had moved into what Cameron liked to call his man cave. A pool table, dart board, and poker table were scattered throughout the room. A giant television hung on one wall, surrounded by some of the most comfortable furniture money could buy.

The men were already several beers into the evening and feeling good. Cameron steadied himself while pouring a splash of scotch into each glass.

They took their drinks over to the couches, where they exchanged exaggerated stories and crude jokes at an ever-increasing volume. The alcohol continued to flow, and by midnight they were all somewhere between buzzed and hammered.

There was a knock at the door. It opened about a quarter of the way, and Salome's head peeked through the opening.

"Mind if I join the party?" She stuck out her lower lip.

Cameron rose from the couch and stumbled over to her. "Come on in! What's wrong?"

Cameron ogled her as she entered the room. She wore a tight black dress that stopped less than halfway down her thighs. A sparkling diamond necklace drew attention to her plunging neckline. He thought she had never looked more beautiful.

"Alan dumped me," she said as she walked over to the bar and poured herself a glass of wine. Every set of eyes in the room followed her.

"Alan? I didn't know you were seeing someone," Cameron said.

Salome shrugged. "We've only been out twice. Hardly worth mentioning. Except tonight he was supposed to take me to that new French restaurant everyone's been raving about. I got all dressed up, and then he calls to tell me we should just be friends."

Cameron took her hand and led her over to the couch. An upset and rejected Salome? Alcohol? He sensed an opportunity.

"Forget about that jerk. You can do better than him," Cameron said.

Salome sank into the couch and drained her glass in a single gulp. "What's wrong with me? Why don't guys like me?" She crossed her legs while Cameron watched with a lustful greed.

"There's nothing wrong with you, Salome," Jackson said. "You're a smart and beautiful woman. That can intimidate a lot of guys."

Salome batted her brilliant, blue eyes at Cameron. "Is he right? Am I beautiful?"

Cameron swallowed hard. "Yes." There were a million salacious thoughts running through his mind, but that was all he could manage to say.

"You're so sweet." She kissed him on the cheek. "Come on, let's do some shots!" She leapt to her feet and grabbed Cameron's hand.

"I don't know. I've already had a lot to drink."

"Don't be silly. I've had a rough night, and I'm not drinking alone." Salome looked over her shoulder. "What do you say, guys? Want to join me?"

Cameron's friends rushed to the bar while Salome dragged Cameron over to the liquor cabinet. One shot turned into several, and before long Cameron was slurring his words and seeing double.

Salome took her cell phone out of her handbag and plugged it into the room's stereo system. A slow and seductive song poured from the speakers. She wrapped her arms around Cameron, her lips inches away from his.

"Dance with me."

Cameron's heart thundered in his chest. He gave her an unsteady nod, and she led him away from the rest of the group.

Salome rested her head against his shoulder. "Thank you for an amazing evening. You've made me feel good about myself again."

Cameron could feel every curve of her body pressed against his. Nothing had ever felt so wrong and so right at the same time. It sent a shiver through his body.

He looked over at his buddies. They were all making various gestures of approval. Salome noticed them and wagged a seductive finger.

"You boys behave yourselves."

Testosterone-fueled laughter exploded from the group, and Salome leaned into Cameron once again. He stumbled backwards and bumped into the arm of the couch, sending both of them tumbling over the side. He landed on his back, pulling Salome down on top of him. She quickly pushed herself into a sitting position, the strap of her dress sliding off her shoulder.

Cameron would never have another opportunity like this. He didn't care if his friends were there or not. It was now or never. "I want you," he panted.

"You do?" she said with a flirtatious smile.

"Please. I'll give you anything you want."

Salome giggled. "Anything I want? I don't think you're *that* powerful."

Cameron stood up, steadied himself, and gestured toward the window. "Everything out there belongs to me. I can make anything happen with a single phone call. So tell me your greatest desire." He gave her what he hoped was an irresistible smile. "Because you already know mine."

Salome adjusted her dress and made her way over to the bar. Her flirtatious smile was replaced with a conniving look Cameron recognized at once; she looked just like her mother.

"I want John the Baptist's head on a silver platter, and I want it brought to me right here." She slapped the top of the bar.

"That's ridiculous," Cameron said.

Salome raised her eyebrows. "Are you saying you can't do it?"

"Of course I can do it, but what a stupid request! Out of everything you could ask for, you pick that?" Her answer had caught him off guard, and now he was floundering.

Salome looked at his friends. "It sounds like he's not as powerful as he thinks."

"Shoot, I'll do it for you if he won't," one of them said.

"Are you going to let her call you out like that?" another one slurred.

Cameron's face was hot, but it wasn't just the alcohol. Anger, embarrassment, and lust swirled through his mind like a category five hurricane, clouding his thoughts. He cursed and pulled his cell phone out of his pocket.

"You don't think I'll do it, but I'll show you. Be careful what you wish for, sweetheart."

***

Several soldiers rushed into John's cell and threw him to the ground. They zip-tied his hands behind his back and carried him to a small, windowless interrogation room similar to the one he'd spent plenty of time in over the last few months. There was only one slight difference most people would have missed, but John did not. The room didn't have any cameras.

A soldier slammed him against the table, shoving his face into the cold, hard steel. John was in trouble, but he wasn't going down without a fight. He kicked his foot out behind him, connecting with the soldier's right knee. The man howled in pain, and a second soldier hammered his fist deep into John's ribs. While gasping for breath, several pairs of hands lifted John onto the table and pinned him on his back. He tried to squirm out of their grip, but it was a fruitless attempt. The wounded soldier limped over to him, his right hand clutching an 18-inch bowie knife.

John's eyes widened. "Wait! You can't do this! It's not my time! Jesus will save me! I'm supposed to—"

The solider plunged the knife into John's throat. There was a sickening gurgle as warm blood spilled onto the table. His mouth opened and closed like a suffocating fish while his feet thumped against the stainless steel beneath them.

John's final thoughts were of Jesus. Why had he never come back for him? Why did he let this happen? What was the point of all of this?

The soldier pulled the knife out of John's neck, shoved it in again, and began to saw.

***

Cameron paced the room like a caged lion. He was certain Herodias was behind all of this. She had become obsessed with murdering John the Baptist, and it explained why Salome would make such a random request.

The one thing still puzzling him was why Salome would agree to it. What did she have to gain from doing this? Cameron saw her sitting at the bar with a glass of wine, one shoe dangling from her foot. She noticed him staring and lifted her glass in a toast.

He'd been tricked, but he'd have the last laugh. He'd get to the bottom of this, and then they would pay. Oh boy, how they'd pay.

A knock at the door interrupted his thoughts. A soldier entered the room holding a dome-covered platter. Cameron took the platter and carried it over to the bar. He savored the horrified looks that greeted him. Even Salome looked like she was having second thoughts about her request.

Cameron banged the platter on the bar. "Bon appétit!"

He yanked off the cover and exposed John the Baptist's head sitting in a pool of congealed blood. Cameron recoiled in disgust. Salome vomited.

***

Over in the White House security room, Herodias had spent the entire evening watching the events unfold from the safety of the security monitors. John the Baptist was finally dead, and Cameron's attempt at infidelity was on tape for the whole world to see. Now, she was moments away from bursting into the room and rubbing Cameron's Salome fantasy right in his face. She was giddy with anticipation.

CHAPTER 29

Jesus closed his eyes in the back of the pontoon boat as it skipped across the lake. Yesterday's news of John's death had hit him hard. God had shown him it was coming, but that didn't make it any easier to digest. The media was reporting John had hung himself in his cell, but Jesus knew the truth.

To make matters even worse, he'd received an email from his brother, James, blaming him for their cousin's death. James also mentioned their mother was worried sick, and it would be Jesus's fault if she ended up having a heart attack or a stroke.

Mary had insisted she was fine. "Keep doing God's work and follow your heart. I'm so proud of everything you're doing," she'd said over the phone later that day.

After he'd spoken to his mom, Jesus had tried to find a quiet place to pray, but his celebrity status made that a difficult task; people recognized him everywhere he went. He ended up retreating to the edge of an enormous lake, where he ran into an older couple walking their dog along the shore. They had recognized him at once and introduced themselves. The woman had sensed he was troubled and asked if everything was okay. Touched by the woman's compassion, Jesus had opened up about his cousin's death and why he was walking the lake alone. The man had told him about a deserted cove on the far side of the lake and insisted Jesus borrow his pontoon boat for the day to get there.

Now, his disciples were escorting him to the cove, where they would drop him off and spend the afternoon anchored on the water, giving Jesus as much alone time as he needed.

"Oh no," Thaddeus said as the cove came into view.

People were packed along the shore, cheering and waving at the approaching boat. Those waiting in their vehicles honked their horns.

"How'd they know we were coming?" Andrew said.

Peter shook his head. "It doesn't matter. Let's get out of here."

"No." Jesus's hand fell on the wheel. "These people are like lost sheep looking for a shepherd. They need us."

"They can wait," Peter insisted.

"I'm the one that can wait. Take me over there."

People swarmed the boat as it pulled up to an aging, wooden dock that creaked under the weight of the crowd. Everyone shuffled toward Jesus like zombies chasing fresh meat. Voices cried out for Jesus to heal them, bless them, or perform a variety of other specific miracles.

Jesus smiled and waved as he exited the boat. Although he appeared fine on the outside, his insides were a battlefield of emotions. His heart was full of love for those that had come all this way to see him, but it also ached for the loss of his beloved cousin.

Jesus walked along the shore until he found a boulder high enough to see the surrounding area. With the help of his disciples, he climbed on top of the rock and surveyed the rapidly growing crowd.

He spent the next two hours preaching a message of love, repentance, and acceptance from atop the boulder. Afterwards, he sat down and asked if anyone had any questions. The impromptu Q&A session was not a normal part of Jesus's sermons, but today he felt called to do things a little differently.

"What's the greatest commandment?" one man asked after raising his hand.

"Love the Lord your God with all your heart and with all your soul and with all your strength and with all your mind," Jesus said.

"What's the second greatest?" a little girl said, giggling.

Jesus smiled down at her. "Love your neighbor as you love yourself."

"So basically love is the most important thing?" the first man said.

"All commandments depend on love. If you follow these two, the others will naturally fall into place," Jesus replied.

An older woman standing near the boulder raised a frail, shaking hand. "How many of us will go to Heaven?"

"The gate to Heaven is narrow. Many will try to get in but won't be able to. They'll beg God for mercy, but he will say, 'I don't even know you.' So be passionate about loving and following God, because the road to Hell is much wider than the road to Heaven."

"What's your opinion on divorce?" another woman asked, twisting her wedding ring while staring at her feet.

"God made man and woman to become one, and you should not separate what God has joined together. Anyone who divorces their spouse and remarries, except for unfaithfulness, is committing adultery."

This brought an uncomfortable silence from the group. People's eyes drifted away from Jesus, married couples held hands, and people kicked at the dirt beneath their feet. This was a hard truth for them to hear. The divorce rate was around fifty percent, and even the half that stayed together weren't always faithful. It was a rampant sin that had become too common, and even accepted, among many of the religious groups. Jesus hated seeing families torn apart because of it, and he refused to ignore it.

A man running through the crowd broke the silence, the coattails of his expensive suit flying out behind him. He collapsed onto his knees in front of the boulder and reached his hands toward Jesus.

"Jesus!" The man paused to catch his breath. "I have followed all the commandments ever since I was a little boy. Is there anything else I can do to make sure I go to Heaven?"

The man was confident in his holiness, but Jesus sensed he wasn't fully committed to the Lord. He wondered if the man loved money more than he loved God. He decided to give him the ultimate test.

"If you want to be perfect, go sell everything you own and give it to the poor. Then come and follow me."

"But I have millions," the man said after a disbelieving pause. "I give way more than the tithe. Isn't that enough?"

"All of it," Jesus said solemnly.

"And you want me to follow you like your disciples? How can I do that? I have a family back home that needs me and hundreds of employees that depend on me for a paycheck."

"You asked me what else you can do, and that is my answer," Jesus said.

The man shook his head, got to his feet, and brushed the dirt from his pants. The crowd watched him walk away in tears.

"It's hard for the rich to enter Heaven," Jesus said as the man got into his Lexus and drove away. "They cling to worldly possessions and worship them like idols. Honestly, it's easier for a camel to go through the eye of a needle than for a rich man to enter the kingdom of God."

"So money is evil?" someone asked.

"Money itself isn't evil, but the love of money is. Money can be used for good, but it can also take a person's focus away from God."

The questions kept coming until late afternoon. At that point Jesus slid off the rock and invited anyone who wanted to be baptized to join him at the water's edge. When the baptisms were over, Jesus heard a woman singing a beautiful hymn from somewhere in the back of the crowd. The melody grew louder as others sang along with her. Jesus stood waist-deep in the water, the music piercing his heart like a warm arrow. His eyes filled with tears.

Philip waded over to him. "It's getting late, Jesus. Let's call it a night so they can get something to eat."

"Why don't you give them something to eat?" Jesus said without taking his eyes off the crowd.

Philip frowned. "You mean order a bunch of pizzas or something? There's no way we have enough money for that. Not to mention it would take hours to get that many pizzas here."

"Go into the crowd and see what you can find for everyone to eat," Jesus said.

Philip looked to the other disciples for help, but they only gave him blank stares in return. "Um, I don't think that's going to work. There's probably five thousand people out there, and I doubt many of them have any food."

Jesus smiled at Philip, feeling the Lord's hand at work. "Go look. For me."

The disciples waded back to shore, mumbling amongst themselves. After wandering through the crowd asking for food donations, they returned to Jesus with five sandwiches and two protein bars.

"So do we order pizza or what?" Bartholomew asked.

Jesus knelt in front of the food. He broke the protein bars into small pieces and tore the sandwiches until they resembled finger foods. He prayed over the food and then sorted the pieces into twelve even piles.

"Have everyone sit in groups of about one hundred. Then each of you take some of the food and pass it around."

Andrew laughed. "Do we tell them to take a crumb and pass it down?"

Jesus knew the disciples thought he was crazy, but they would become believers soon enough. "Tell them to eat as much as they want."

The disciples rounded up various containers while the crowd divided into groups. Phones had been put away, and the moon provided the only light. For a moment, technology had taken a backseat to God's creation.

Jesus watched as Andrew handed his bowl to a man in the closest circle and told him to take as much as he wanted. With a doubtful look, the man took one piece of sandwich, hesitated, and then took three more before passing it down.

Jesus lost sight of the bowl after it reached the fourth person, but it made its way around the circle and back to Andrew after a few minutes. Andrew took the container with trembling hands and stared at it in disbelief. The few tiny pieces had transformed into an overflowing bowl of food. Jesus gave a silent prayer of thanks for God's provision.

"Did someone put more in here?" Andrew asked. His voice was as shaky as his hands.

"Andrew, look at this!" Peter ran up to him with a Tupperware bowl full of sandwiches and protein bars. He saw Andrew's container and froze. "Yours too?"

"How are these full?" Andrew said.

"Full? It barely had anything in it when it came to me," someone from the crowd said.

"Jesus did this! It's a miracle!" came a cry from somewhere in the shadows.

One by one, each of the disciples returned with their abundance of leftovers. There was singing, praying, and weeping throughout the cove; Jesus could hear shouts of praise from every corner.

The disciples brought the twelve containers of food to Jesus and laid them at his feet. He smiled at their bewildered looks.

"Now you can send them home," Jesus said.

***

After the crowd left, Jesus told his disciples to leave without him and retreated deep into the woods. He ascended a hill overlooking the cove and saw his disciples' shadows dancing along the dock.

Jesus watched them with a smile. He loved these men with all his heart. They had stepped out in faith and left behind their families and stable jobs to join a man they hardly knew. Many professed their devotion to God with their lips, but few would be willing to make the sacrifice these twelve had. He watched the boat pull away and then stretched out on a soft patch of grass with his hands behind his head.

He closed his eyes and felt the light, cool breeze against his face. Taking several deep breaths, his grief began to drift away like balloons in the wind. Clearing his mind of everything except for his longing for God, the Lord's presence flowed through his body like a warm current.

***

"I got another one!"

Peter yanked on his fishing pole, the tip of the rod dipping below the edge of the boat. He reeled in a large catfish, plucked the hook from its mouth, and tossed it into a bucket of water with the others. He wiped his hands on the front of his shirt and puffed out his chest.

"Show-off," Thomas said.

"This reminds me of being back home. Man, I miss my wife and daughter like crazy." The thought of them tugged at Peter's heart.

"I know what you mean," Bartholomew said. "I can't wait to see my wife again."

"How much longer do you think this road trip will last?" Judas said.

Bartholomew shrugged. "As long as it takes, I guess."

"It's been months, and all we've been doing is preaching and healing people," Judas said.

"Yeah, *all* we did tonight was save a few hundred souls and magically feed thousands of people. So lame," Andrew said, rolling his eyes.

"That's not what I meant. What Jesus is doing is incredible. I wouldn't be here if I didn't think it was. But don't you guys ever wonder when he's going to start, you know, taking over?"

"Judas is right," Thaddeus said as he cast his line into the water. "Isn't the Messiah supposed to start a revolution and form a Jewish kingdom? I'd say we're a long way from anything like that."

"Exactly!" Judas said.

"Jesus heals people with a single touch and makes food appear out of thin air. You don't think he can take over whenever he wants?" Peter said, frustrated. How could they be so negative after everything they'd just seen?

Judas sulked. "That's not what I said. I just asked how long it's going to take. We all miss our families, and we're living in poverty. I'd like to live like a king and see my kids again, that's all."

"Why don't you ask Jesus about it the next time you see him?" Andrew suggested, narrowing his eyes.

"I think everyone's a little tired and cranky. Why don't we call it a night?" Thomas said.

"And leave Jesus?" Peter asked.

"He told us to, didn't he?" Thomas glanced at his phone. "Besides, it's two in the morning."

"Hey, look over there!" Andrew pointed across the water. "What the heck is that?"

Everyone's eyes followed Andrew's outstretched arm. Something was hovering over the water in the distance.

"It looks like a buoy," Matthew said.

"No way. It's moving," Andrew said.

Peter squinted. "Some sort of bird, maybe?"

"You ever seen a bird that big?" James asked.

Arms, legs, and a head became visible as the object grew closer.

"It's a ghost! That thing is walking on water!" Thomas shouted.

The men cowered against the far end of the boat, some of them screaming.

"Don't be afraid! It's me!" the ghostly figure said.

Peter broke from the group and peered at the figure now less than twenty yards away. It was a man standing on top of the water, the waves lapping against his feet. Peter had a moment of recognition, and his mouth dropped open in shock.

"I . . . I don't believe it. Jesus? If it's you, tell me to join you on the water," Peter said.

Jesus held out his arms. "Come to me."

Peter threw his leg over the side of the boat.

"Peter, what are you doing? You don't know if that's really Jesus. It could be a ghost . . . or a demon," Thomas said.

"It's Jesus," Peter said confidently without looking back.

Peter placed a foot on the lake. It felt like standing on tile buried beneath an inch of water. When he didn't sink, he scooted off the side of the boat and let go. He couldn't believe it; he was standing on water. Becoming more confident, he jumped up and down, landing on top of the water each time. Peter laughed and clapped his hands as the others watched in amazement.

Peter walked toward Jesus's outstretched arms. After several steps, the wind picked up, and small waves rolled across Peter's feet, splashing against his legs. Panic set in as he realized how vulnerable he would be if a storm blew in. He looked down to see the water rising, first to his calves and then to his knees.

"I'm sinking, Jesus! Save me!"

Jesus walked over to him and grabbed his hands. Peter rose out of the lake and stood on top of the water once again.

"You of little faith," Jesus said, guiding Peter back to the boat. "Why did you doubt me?"

"I'm sorry, Jesus. I really believed you could do it. I just got scared with the wind and everything." Peter flung himself into the boat, feeling like a complete failure.

Andrew looked at Judas. "Do you want to ask him if he's powerful enough to start a revolution, or is now a bad time?"

"Shut up," Judas muttered.

CHAPTER 30

The arena roared to life as Jesus stepped onto the stage. Someone began chanting his name, and it spread like wildfire until the entire arena was crying out for Jesus. There were just over 18,000 seats, and there was a warm body in each of them.

Jesus looked down to see Randy Wood and his friends looking up at him from the front row. Randy laughed and mouthed, "You the man," while giving him two thumbs up.

This was the largest crowd Jesus had ever spoken to, and he was eager to get started. The place was full of people just like Randy; people who were far from God but needed him desperately. That morning, Jesus had prayed his words would touch the hearts of every man, woman, and child in attendance that day.

Once the noise died down, Jesus opened with a prayer before diving into a message that was both powerful and straight to the point. There were over 18,000 souls at stake, and Jesus knew every word mattered.

"I'm incredibly humbled and thankful to see all of you here today. I know some of you have been mocked for choosing to follow me. I've even heard stories of temples banning people for defending my teachings. Although these things are difficult, take comfort in knowing they're only temporary. Blessed are those who are insulted and persecuted because of me. Rejoice and be glad, because your reward in Heaven will be great."

Thunderous applause filled the arena. Jesus continued the positive message for several minutes before taking things down a more uncomfortable path.

"You have all heard people say, 'An eye for an eye, and a tooth for a tooth,' but I say if someone strikes you on the right cheek, turn the other cheek to them as well. You should love and forgive others, not retaliate and keep score of their wrongdoings.

"You've also heard you should love your neighbor and hate your enemies, but that goes against what God wants. I'm here to tell you to love your enemies and pray for those who persecute you. What kind of sacrifice is it to only love those who love you back? Even the most sinful people do that.

"And while we're on the subject of love, let's talk about lust. We all know that it's wrong to commit adultery, but let's take it one step further. Anyone who even looks at a woman lustfully has committed adultery in his heart, so be careful to guard your mind from lustful thoughts. If your right eye causes you to sin, gouge it out and throw it away. It's better to lose your eye than for your whole body to be thrown into the fires of Hell."

The arena grew quiet. Most of the people in the front row avoided Jesus's eyes, including Randy.

"If I'm making you uncomfortable, then that means we're getting somewhere," Jesus said encouragingly. "Feel the conviction of your sins and take them to God. Ask him for forgiveness, and free yourself from the chains of sin. You can begin a new life today!"

Jesus paused to let his words sink in. He prayed that hearts were being changed. People were sobbing, and some fell to their knees in the middle of the aisles, crying out for forgiveness.

"Let's talk about righteousness for a minute. All of us should do things that are pleasing to God, but be careful how you do them. Don't do something good just so others will see you. When you give to the needy, don't announce it to everyone like the hypocrites in the temples. Don't take a selfie while helping a homeless person and then post it on social media for attention. Instead, do it in secret. Then God will reward you openly.

"And when you pray, don't be like the hypocrites who love to pray on the street corners to be seen by everyone. Instead, go into your room, close the door, and pray in solitude. Also, don't keep babbling like pagans who think God will hear them because of all their fancy words. God already knows what you need before you even ask him.

"Now, I'm sure a lot of you are thinking, 'At least I'm not as bad as my neighbor, Bob. He's always holding up his offering so everyone can see how much he's putting in the basket. Oh, and Jenny always prays for at least ten minutes before we eat. I bet God can't stand her.'" People laughed and pointed accusatory fingers at those sitting next to them. "Before you start comparing yourself to others, let me talk to you about judging people." The crowd groaned. "Don't judge others, or you'll be judged as well. Why do you focus on the speck of sawdust in someone else's eye and ignore the plank in your own eye?"

"Burn in Hell, you liar!"

A man leapt onto the far side of the stage and rushed Jesus. Security guards intercepted the man and brought him to the ground before he could do any harm.

"You're a false prophet, Jesus!" the man yelled from underneath a pile of muscular men. "Your kind needs to stay in their own country! You're nothing but trouble!"

Security slapped a pair of handcuffs on the man and dragged him away. The audience booed him off the stage.

Jesus shook his head at the crowd, sighing inwardly. It looked like his message wasn't sinking in yet. "I know you're upset with him, but please don't act like that. Fighting hate with more hate will not soften his heart or change how he feels about immigrants and minorities. It will only strengthen his convictions even more. We must love this man and pray for God to change his heart."

Jesus led the crowd in a prayer for the attacker's soul and then dove back into his message as if nothing had happened. By the time he finished preaching, people were crying, clapping, smiling, and kneeling. The atmosphere was electric. The spirit of God was alive in the arena.

Inflatable swimming pools were stationed throughout the building, with a disciple and several helpers at each one. When Jesus asked those who wished to commit their lives to God to come forward, a surge of people made their way to the nearest pool. Six of Randy's friends stood up to be baptized, all of them holding hands.

Randy watched them go with a smile. Jesus invited him up on stage, and Randy shook his hand.

"You put on a good show, Jesus. I might not believe in God, but a lot of what you said up there makes sense. A small part of me was even hoping you'd get to me." Randy held up his thumb and index finger an inch apart and winked. "But just a small part. At least you got to some of my girls, which is still impressive. I don't think they've even been inside a temple before."

Jesus placed his hands on Randy's shoulders. "I'm not giving up on you, Randy. I'll be praying that God finds his way into your heart. If not today, then someday soon."

Randy nodded. "I know you will, buddy."

***

The disciples gathered backstage, exhausted but gratified. They had never baptized so many people at once. It had been an amazing day.

Volunteers brought the offering buckets into the room and placed them on a table. Judas stared at the piles of cash with a lustful greed. Taking an offering was a common practice for Jesus and his disciples. Offerings kept their vans full of gas and their bellies full of food as they traveled from city to city. What was unusual this time was the amount. Judas estimated there were tens of thousands of dollars on the table. With money came power, and with power came God's kingdom. Judas was certain this was the start of Jesus's revolution.

CHAPTER 31

The disciples gawked at the towering home in front of them. The white pillars along the front of the colonial mansion were wider than they were.

Judas let out a long whistle. "Would you look at this place? How much do you think it cost? Ten million, maybe fifteen?" He couldn't help but think they would all soon be living in similar mansions.

Jesus rang the doorbell. A melodic chime echoed deep into the house. The door opened, and a Sadducee stood smiling in the doorway.

"Jesus! I'm so glad you and your friends could make it. My name's Martin. It's a pleasure to meet you. Please, come inside."

The men gathered in an open foyer that served as the central hub of the mansion. Archways opened into adjoining rooms and hallways all around them. A massive staircase in the middle of the room split in opposite directions at the top, winding to parts unseen.

"Is this your place?" Andrew said, his wide eyes working their way around the room.

"It sure is. Well, it's my wife's too. I designed it, she decorated. You know how that goes."

"It's beautiful," Andrew said.

"I bet this set you back a pretty penny," Judas said. Peter elbowed him in the side, and Judas cried out, rubbing his ribs while giving Peter a dirty look. "Sorry," he muttered.

Martin chuckled. "It's fine. A house like this sort of invites those kinds of questions. Let's just say it wasn't cheap."

"It's impressive, isn't it?" A handsome man, who appeared to be in his early forties, entered the foyer and stopped in front of Jesus. "I'm Jordan Larson, member of the Sanhedrin. It's a pleasure to meet you."

Jesus shook his hand. "Thank you for inviting us to dinner."

"It's our pleasure. After seeing your amazing performance at the arena yesterday, we just had to meet you and your followers."

"Disciples," Jesus corrected.

"My apologies. It's an honor to have you and your *disciples* as our guests for the evening."

"I think an uninterrupted meeting between us was long overdue," Jesus said.

"Absolutely. If you gentlemen will follow me, I'll introduce you to the rest of the group. Dinner's not quite ready yet, but we have plenty of wine to hold us over," Jordan said.

The wine was expensive, but the dinner was even more elaborate. They enjoyed a five-course meal over the next two hours. Judas couldn't remember the last time they had eaten so well.

The conversation during the meal was cordial. Everyone avoided subjects likely to cause tension between the two groups in lieu of topics of shared interest. However, the Sadducees pushed the envelope during a round of after-dinner drinks.

"Jesus, I believe we should worship God above everything else, and nothing should come before him. Would you agree?" Jordan asked.

Jesus sipped his wine and nodded. "Like it says in the Ten Commandments, 'Thou shalt have no other gods before me.'"

"Then what's your opinion on taxes? Should people pay taxes to support a pagan government and the various religions they follow? Isn't that putting other idols before God?"

Judas realized the fancy dinner was just another ploy to discredit Jesus. He couldn't wait to watch Jesus tear them apart.

Jesus pulled a quarter from his pocket and tossed it across the table. It bounced off Jordan's plate and landed on the napkin in front of him.

"Whose face is on there?" Jesus asked.

Jordan took the quarter, flicked away a speck of food with his thumb, and examined it. "History is admittedly not my strong suit, but I believe that's George Washington."

Jesus raised his eyebrows. "And he was?"

Jordan shot him an annoyed look. "A rhetorical question, I'm sure. He was our first president."

"Exactly. Give to the government what is the government's and to God what is God's."

Jordan smiled and pointed a finger across the table. "You're good, Jesus. I thought I could stump you with that one."

"You mean get me to say we shouldn't pay taxes so you can frame me for inciting a government rebellion," Jesus said matter-of-factly.

The smile on Jordan's face transformed into a scowl.

Martin cleared his throat and leaned over the table. "Since we're already talking about God and theology, let me ask you another question. What if a husband dies, and his wife marries someone else? Then the next husband dies, and she marries a third guy. Whose wife will she be in Heaven?"

"I'm afraid you don't understand the scriptures very well," Jesus said.

Judas wiped his mouth with a napkin to conceal his smile. Jesus was putting them in their place, and he was loving every minute of it.

"Excuse me?" Jordan said, his eyes narrowing. "I take offense to that accusation and can assure you we know more about scripture than almost anyone else."

Jesus shrugged. "Then perhaps it's simply an oversight on your end. Regardless, at the resurrection people will neither marry nor be given away in marriage. They will be like the angels in Heaven. But you didn't really want an answer, did you? You don't believe in the resurrection and are trying to prove me wrong by finding a logical fallacy."

"I was just curious what you thought, that's all." Martin's words were as icy as his stare.

"The resurrection is real, and it will happen," Jesus said.

"Okay, Jesus. Let's cut to the chase. What we're really after is some sort of proof of your divinity. Something that will convince us you're more than just a normal guy trying to undermine us and everything we stand for," Jordan said.

"Show us a miracle," Martin said, spreading his arms out wide. "Something just for us. Right now."

"He's not a magician that does party tricks for your entertainment," Thomas said, his voice full of anger.

Jesus laid a hand on Thomas's forearm. "The wicked ask for miraculous signs, but none will be given except for the sign of the prophet Jonah. Just like Jonah was in the belly of a fish for three days and three nights, so the Son of Man will be in the earth for three days and three nights."

"I'm not sure I understand what you're trying to say," Martin said.

"You've already made up your mind about who you think I am. Nothing I do here tonight will change that."

"No offense, but that sounds exactly like something a fraud would say." Jordan leaned forward and sneered. "A little convenient, don't you think?"

"Show him, Jesus. Put this clown in his place," Judas said, knowing one incredible miracle would shut them up.

Jordan feigned a hurt look. "Clown? And Jesus called us wicked? Hardly the words of the righteous. Why are you all so angry?"

"What angers me is the way you abuse your position of power," Jesus said. "You tell people they have to follow countless religious laws, but you don't even follow them yourselves. Then there's the fact that your temple taxes overburden the poor just so you can afford your own ridiculously lavish lifestyles. You're all a bunch of hypocrites."

Jordan's mouth twitched; his face reddened. "It's this type of rhetoric that gives you a bad name with the Jewish leaders. You constantly berate us in public and undermine everything we do."

"People deserve to know the truth," Jesus said.

"You know, John the Baptist had a similar problem with his words. It didn't work out so well for him," Jordan said.

Peter jumped to his feet. "Is that a threat?"

"Of course not. Sit down," Jordan said with a devilish grin.

Jesus pushed back his chair and stood up. "I think we should go."

"Maybe you're right. I'm afraid this evening took an unexpected turn," Jordan said.

"I somehow doubt that. I think we both know what this evening was really about. Now, if you'll please excuse us, we'll see ourselves out," Jesus said.

The disciples followed Jesus through an archway leading into the adjoining living room.

"Hey, Jesus. Wait a minute." Jordan plucked the quarter off the table and flung it at Jesus, who snatched it out of the air with his hand. "Don't forget your change. I'm sure you'll need it."

The Sadducees roared with laughter. Judas looked at the quarter in Jesus's hand and then at his magnificent surroundings. With his head down, he followed Jesus to the front door, the hearty laughter of the Sanhedrin trailing behind him.

"Why didn't you do something?" Judas said as the van door slid shut. "You could have turned the silverware into snakes or made blood rain from the ceiling. Now we're just a joke to them."

Jesus sat in the passenger seat with his eyes closed. "Who do the crowds say I am, Judas?"

"I'm serious. Why did you let them treat you like that? You should be king!"

"Who do the crowds say I am?" Jesus repeated.

Judas sighed. "I guess it depends on who you ask. Some say you're a phony, some say a reincarnated prophet, some say the Son of God."

Jesus turned around. "But what about all of you? Who do you say I am?"

"The Messiah," Peter said.

Jesus nodded and turned back around, staring into the darkness. "Let others think whatever they want, but there is something all of you must understand. The Son of God must suffer many things and be rejected by the elders, chief priests, and other teachers of the law. He must be killed and on the third day be raised to life."

"Are you crazy? We'd never let them kill you!" Peter said.

Jesus jerked his head around. "Get behind me, Satan! You're in my way because you think like everyone else and not like God!"

The disciples recoiled. It was the first time they'd ever heard Jesus raise his voice. Judas wished he would direct his anger at the Sadducees instead of his loyal disciples. None of this was making any sense to him.

Peter slouched in his seat. "I'm sorry, Jesus. We just love you, that's all."

"And I love all of you as well. That's why it's so important you understand that God's will is above everything else."

Later that night, when Jesus left them to pray, the disciples discussed the day's events. What was all this talk about death, and what did Jesus mean about Jonah being inside a fish for three days like the Son of God? Jesus had a knack for speaking in parables they didn't always understand, and they knew from experience that asking him for clarification was a fruitless endeavor. You would understand the meaning when the time was right, if you were meant to understand it at all.

In the end, they gave up on trying to make sense of it and called it a night. At breakfast the next morning, Jesus was back to his normal self, the events of the prior evening forgotten.

"What's on today's agenda?" Thomas asked.

"I thought we'd go see our families for a couple of days," Jesus said through a mouthful of oatmeal. He smiled at the shocked faces around the campfire. "That's right. We're going home."

CHAPTER 32

"Gin," Mary said, placing her cards face up on the table.

"Again?" Jesus said in disbelief.

"We could try something else if you're tired of losing. Do you want to play Monopoly?"

"Let's go again. I'm not quitting until I win at least one of these."

Mary checked her watch. "Then you're in for a long night."

Jesus laughed and took her cup. "I think we're going to need some more coffee."

"How about some pie to go with it?"

Mary followed him to the kitchen and grabbed some plates and silverware while he brewed a fresh pot of coffee. Jesus leaned against the counter and watched his mother. The past two days had been wonderful. She'd tended to him just like she had when he was a boy. She had done his laundry, taken him shopping for new clothes (according to her, the Son of God should not be seen in the rags he was currently wearing), fed him three meals a day, and trimmed his hair and beard (both out of control in her opinion). The love of his mother had pulled his thoughts away from the troubles of the outside world. His mind and body were rested.

"I can't believe it's already time for you to leave again," Mary said.

"Me either. These last two days have flown by. I just wish I didn't have to go so soon. I hate leaving you here all alone."

Mary slapped him on the arm with a dish towel. "Would you stop it? I'm not *that* old. Not yet anyway. Besides, the other kids are always checking up on me."

"I know. It's just James—"

"Let me guess. James told you about the doctor?"

"Well, yes."

Mary sighed. "That boy. I pray to God every night that he'll come around. He just can't get it out of his head that you're nuts, and I am too for believing you. I wish your father was still around to talk some sense into him. James always listened to him."

"But you went to the doctor?"

"Of course, but only because your brother forced me to. They ran all kinds of tests on me because he's convinced I'm mentally unstable. Did he tell you they didn't find anything wrong with me?"

"He said it was inconclusive." Jesus was relieved to hear his brother had misinformed him.

"That's his way of saying he didn't get the answer he wanted." She tapped the side of her head. "There's nothing wrong up here, Jesus. James is just trying to make you feel guilty for leaving. You ignore him and stay focused on what God wants you to do. I shouldn't have even told him you were home."

"Stop it, Mom. It was great having the whole family over yesterday."

Mary pushed a plate of pecan pie into his hands. "Even James?"

"Even James. It was good to see him, sarcastic jabs and all. I'm going to swing by his house in the morning to see if I can make things right between us."

"It'll take a miracle."

Jesus kissed her on the cheek. "That's kind of my thing."

***

Olivia was fast asleep in her father's arms. She had snuggled up against Peter as he had read her a bedtime story, and then cried herself to sleep, begging him not to leave again. She had promised to clean her room every day for the rest of her life if he would stay.

Her sobs had become small whimpers, and then she'd fallen asleep against his chest. Now, as he listened to her rhythmic breathing and felt her heart beat against his, he stared at the family picture on the nightstand and cried. He'd already missed a dance recital, her school play, a parent-teacher conference, and her first sleepover with friends. How much more would he miss? How much more would he have to sacrifice?

He untangled himself from Olivia's arms and slid out of bed. She stirred but didn't wake. He pulled the covers around her shoulders, brushed the hair out of her face, and kissed her goodnight.

Annabelle turned off the television when she saw him coming down the hall. "How'd it go?"

Peter's shoulders sagged. "Awful."

"Poor guy." She patted the sofa cushion next to her. "Come over here and let me rub your shoulders."

Peter sat on the couch and sighed as her fingers dug into his tight muscles. "I'm failing as a father."

"Stop it. You are not. You're an amazing father."

"I haven't seen Olivia in months, and then I show up just long enough to break her heart all over again. She deserves better. So do you."

Annabelle turned him around and put her hands on his cheeks. "Don't ever say that. We're lucky to have you. When Olivia grows up and fully understands what you're doing, you'll never meet anyone more proud of their father. She'll tell all her friends about the amazing things you did."

"And what about you?"

"I brag about you every chance I get. I'm the only girl in town whose husband is on TV every week. You're a big deal around here, mister."

"So you won't leave me for someone else?"

Annabelle laughed. "And who would I leave you for?"

"What about Gary? He's young and buff."

Annabelle squeezed his arms. "Look at those muscles. You're the only man I need, Simon."

"Excuse me? It's Peter now," he said with exaggerated seriousness.

"Listen, when you're with Jesus, they can call you whatever they want, but at home you'll always be my Simon."

***

"You're seriously going to leave us again?"

Judas continued piling things into his suitcase without looking up at his wife. "I don't have a choice, Karen. Jesus said it's time to go."

"Well, Jesus doesn't have three kids or a wife who's raising them by herself."

Judas stopped what he was doing and looked at Karen with a mixture of exasperation and pity. "I'm sorry, okay? What do you want me to do? We both agreed this was the right thing to do. I can't back out now. Do you know how that would look?"

"What we agreed to and what's actually happening are two very different things."

"It's just going to take some time."

"Time? Judas, we can't afford more time. The bills are piling up, the kids need new clothes, the pantry's almost empty. You need a paying job, not more time. I thought Jesus was supposed to make us rich?"

"The guys say it'll happen when Jesus is ready. Until then, there's not a lot I can do. I don't even know how much longer I can keep skimming from the offerings without getting caught."

"And how long are you willing to keep this up? Until the kids cry themselves to sleep because they're hungry? Until we lose the house? Until I have to sell myself on the streets to get by?"

"Don't be so dramatic."

"It's not dramatic, Judas. It's reality. While you're hanging out with your friends all day, I'm at home fighting off the bank and collection agencies." She grabbed a handful of bills off the dresser and held them in front of his face. "It's bad. It's really bad."

Judas pried the papers from her hands and set them back on the dresser. He wrapped his arms around her and pressed his forehead against hers. "Okay, I'm sorry. I know things are tough. I'll figure something out."

"Promise?"

"Promise."

CHAPTER 33

"Your plan has been an embarrassing disaster," Caiaphas said.

The rest of the Sanhedrin nodded in agreement. Jordan stood before the table of Jewish leaders like a man in front of a firing squad.

"I completely agree, Your Excellency. Every attempt we've made to discredit Jesus has blown up in our face. I think we underestimated him," Jordan said.

"He has made a mockery of our religion, and I grow tired of seeing him all over the news. I assume the dinner did not go well either?"

"Not exactly."

"Perhaps you are not the man for the job, Jordan. Jesus needs to be silenced, and my patience runs thin," Caiaphas said.

Jordan was humiliated. This was his big chance to put himself at the top of the Sanhedrin ladder, and he was failing miserably. Jesus had been a much bigger problem than he'd expected. It was time to take off the kid gloves and finish this once and for all.

"Your Excellency, I humbly ask for another chance. I assure you I can deal with him."

"What do you have in mind?"

Jordan placed both hands on the table and looked each member of the Sanhedrin in the eye. "Death."

Caiaphas shook his head. "Millions of people love and worship the man. Killing him will only make things worse."

Jordan paced the room. "Not if it's handled carefully. It's complicated, but not impossible. It will be easier if we get help from the inside."

"And how do we go about doing that?" Caiaphas asked.

"One of his disciples isn't like the others. He was enamored with our wealth and seemed more interested in us than his own cause," Jordan said.

"That sounds promising. What is his name?"

Jordan relaxed. He was going to get another shot at this.

"Judas."

Part III
The Death

For even the Son of Man did not come to be served,
but to serve, and to give his life as a ransom for many.

-Mark 10:45

CHAPTER 1

Lazarus's sisters, Mary and Martha, called Jesus with the heartbreaking news that his best friend had died of a massive heart attack. Jesus immediately dropped what he was doing and drove to Lazarus's home. Although none of the disciples knew Lazarus, they knew how much he meant to Jesus and had insisted they come with him for emotional support.

Martha ran out the door and fell into Jesus's arms as he exited the van, tears rolling down her face. "Oh, Jesus. I can't help but think Lazarus would still be alive if you had been here to heal him."

Jesus felt the power of God burning inside him. "Lazarus will rise again. He that believes in me will live, even though he dies, and whoever lives and believes in me will never die. Do you believe this?"

"Yes, Jesus," Martha said. "I believe it with all my heart because I know you're the Son of God."

"Where is Lazarus?" Jesus asked.

Martha pointed toward the house. "He's in his bedroom. We made them wait to take the body since we knew you were on your way and would want to see him."

"Can we go inside?"

Martha nodded and called to her sister as they approached the house. Mary stuck her head out the door and bounded down the porch steps when she saw Jesus. She hugged him tight and looked up with the same beautiful blue eyes he remembered from their childhood. Her red lips were in stark contrast to her flawless porcelain skin. The freckles that had dotted her nose as a child were faded, but not gone.

Inside the house, the living room was packed with grieving friends and family Jesus hadn't seen in years. Sadness hung in the air like a thick, invisible fog, and his heart was heavy with sorrow. Jesus wept.

Mary and Martha each slipped a comforting hand into one of his and walked him to the bedroom. In the dim light of the lamp on the bedside table, it looked like Lazarus was only sleeping.

Jesus looked at the lifeless body of his longtime friend and reflected on all the good times they'd had together in their younger years. Through good times and bad, they had always been there for each other. Jesus sat on the edge of the bed and placed a hand against Lazarus's forehead.

"Lazarus, wake up!" Jesus commanded.

His booming voice disrupted the silence of the room like a bomb detonating in the still of night. Mary and Martha jumped.

Lazarus's eyelids fluttered and then opened wide. Mary and Martha screamed loud enough to bring the rest of the house-guests running.

"What's wrong?" one of them asked.

"It's Lazarus!" said another.

Lazarus was up on his elbows, looking around the room. Martha leapt onto the bed and hugged her brother hard enough to knock him back against the pillows.

"Praise God! You're alive!" Martha said as she covered him with kisses.

The room filled with cries of wonder and delight. People swarmed the bed, touching Lazarus's warm body with their own hands. It was a miracle that had to be felt to be believed.

"Let's give him some space," Jesus said. "We don't want to overwhelm him."

"What's going on? Where am I?" Lazarus said.

"Jesus brought you back to life! He really did it! Praise the Son of God!" Martha said through fresh tears of joy.

"What do you mean? I was dead?"

"How do you feel?" Mary said.

"Really confused. When did all these people get here?"

"Don't worry about that right now. We'll explain everything later." Mary turned to Jesus. "Can you and your friends stay the night? We *have* to celebrate this."

"That sounds wonderful," Jesus said, happy to have brought such joy to the people he loved.

Lazarus looked befuddled. "Can someone please tell me what the heck is going on?"

***

They held an extravagant party the following night in Jesus's honor. Laughter floated throughout the house, a much different sound from the crying and hushed voices from the day before.

Jesus and Lazarus sat at the table, reminiscing about their childhood. Jesus rarely spoke about his past, and the disciples seemed fascinated to learn about his younger days. As the evening wore on, the discussion turned to the drama surrounding Jesus's ministry.

"You know, I'm sure the Sanhedrin have already heard about you raising me from the dead, and they aren't going to like it one bit," Lazarus said.

"What else is new? They don't like anything I do," Jesus said.

"Listen to me. You need to be careful with them. Don't let those robes and Torah fool you. They can be ruthless when you cross them."

Jesus's heart constricted as he thought of what God had shown him in the desert. "I know what they're capable of, but I'm not worried about it. My only concern is that God's will be done."

Lazarus patted him on the back. "Spoken like the true Son of God."

Mary approached the table with a large bottle of perfume, and without saying a word, knelt before Jesus and removed his shoes and socks. Everyone watched as she unscrewed the top of the bottle and poured the perfume onto Jesus's feet. The fragrant smell was overpowering.

"What are you doing?" Judas said, waving the air in front of his face. "Do you know how much that costs? Why would you waste it like that? You'd be better off selling it." The rest of the disciples stared him down. "I meant sell it and give it to charity. Think of all the good that money could do."

Jesus knew what was really in Judas's heart, and it saddened him. He hated seeing Judas always so consumed with money and other material things. "Why are you bothering her? She's done a beautiful thing to honor what I've done for Lazarus. Let her show reverence however she wants. You will always have the poor with you, but you won't always have me."

"I'm starting to understand that," Judas mumbled.

The houseguests coughed and gagged as the overwhelming aroma grew stronger by the second. Martha ran around the house, opening all the doors and windows.

Judas left the table amidst the commotion and spent the rest of the evening sulking in a corner by himself.

CHAPTER 2

The restaurant was empty except for Jordan, who sat alone in a corner booth. The neon sign in the window said *closed*, and the only light came from the electric candle burning in the center of his table.

Judas watched him through the window in the kitchen door. Jordan had requested a private meeting between the two of them, insisting it would be very beneficial for Judas, both personally and financially, to hear what he had to say. That had been enough to pique his curiosity and convince him the meeting was worth the risk. Taking a deep breath, he walked through the kitchen door and slid into the booth across from Jordan. His eyes darted around the room.

"Relax. It's just us," Jordan said.

"Does anyone else know about this? If this gets out, my life is over." If Jesus found out about the meeting, it would be the end of his discipleship, and if he returned home with nothing to show for it, possibly his marriage.

"Nobody knows we're here except for the owner of this place, and he's oblivious. I asked him to leave the key out back so I could let myself in. He owes me a few favors."

"What do you want with me?"

"I like you, Judas. I could tell from the moment we met that you aren't like the rest of your friends."

"How so?"

Jordan leaned in; the candlelight gave his face a devilish glow. "We both know this whole Messiah thing is a facade. I'm sure you believed it in the beginning, and who could blame you? Jesus puts on quite a convincing show. But come on, it has to be obvious to you by now."

"I *know he's* the Messiah," Judas said plainly.

Jordan chuckled. "You're not being recorded. This is just you and me talking. It's in your best interest to be honest with me tonight. I think you'll find it very lucrative to do so."

"He brought a dead man back to life. I saw it with my own eyes."

"I heard about that. Let me ask you something. Are you positive he was dead? Did you check for a pulse?"

"Well, no, but they were Jesus's friends. They wouldn't lie about something like that."

Jordan slapped the table. "Friends! Well there you go! Collusion among friends makes more sense than a corpse coming back to life, don't you think?"

"I've seen other miracles too. He doesn't fake them."

"Have you seen that guy on television who claims he can talk to the dead? The one who's always doing a little song and dance for the gullible?" Judas nodded. "He's got a ton of people convinced he's the real deal, and nobody's been able to debunk him. But do you honestly think he's legit?"

"No."

"Of course not! The guy's a total hack, and every rational person knows it. It's the same with Jesus. I don't know how he's doing it, but I know it's not real."

Judas was tired of talking in circles. Jordan didn't believe in the miracles, but Judas did. They were wasting each other's time.

"Why aren't you talking to Jesus about this? I don't understand what any of it has to do with me."

"You could be very useful to me, Judas, and I can make it worth your time. Do you like money? Do you want to be on the winning side of history? I know that's what you're hoping for with Jesus, but I can do more than make you hope for it. I can give it to you."

"How much?"

"How much do you want?"

A question like that coming from a wealthy man like Jordan opened all kinds of financial possibilities. "Depends on what we're talking about."

"I won't beat around the bush. We want Jesus to go away, but we need to be very careful about how we do it. I need you to be our eyes and ears inside that little group of yours. Tell us what he's talking about and what we can use against him."

Judas shifted in his seat. "I don't know. That's a pretty tall order."

"Name your price."

Judas drummed his fingers on the table while searching the ceiling for an answer. "What about thirty thousand dollars?" Jordan erupted with laughter. He leaned back against the booth while holding his stomach. Judas instantly regretted being so greedy. "Or maybe twenty thousand?"

Jordan waved a hand at him. "No, no. You're going the wrong way. Your ask shows how small Jesus has you thinking. Ask me for a hundred thousand dollars."

Judas's eyes grew wide. "What?"

"Come on! Ask me for a hundred thousand dollars."

"Okay. I want one hundred thousand dollars."

Jordan smiled and shot his hand across the table. "Make it a hundred and twenty, and we've got a deal."

Judas was dumbstruck. That kind of money would be life-changing for his family, but could he really be disloyal to Jesus? A thought suddenly occurred to him. What if this was all part of God's plan? If Judas helped the Sanhedrin attempt to get rid of Jesus, then Jesus would have to fight back, thus beginning the revolution. It was a win-win situation for Judas: be the catalyst for Jesus's rise to power, and make a lot of money doing it. It was perfect.

Still, as Judas shook Jordan's hand, a small part of him felt like he had just made a deal with the devil, and in a way, he had.

CHAPTER 3

During Passover, a week-long celebration commemorating the liberation of the Israelites from Egyptian slavery, Jesus traveled to one of the largest temples in the United States. The temple was famous for its Passover festivities and hosted Jews from all over the country. It was the perfect place for Jesus to reach thousands of people with the word of God.

The temple itself served as the holy epicenter of a Jewish town square. Meeting centers, a Jewish library, rabbi housing, a large park, and a private school surrounded it.

Jesus and his disciples worked their way toward the temple, where an afternoon service was scheduled to occur. A crowd formed around them as people recognized Jesus. They reached out their hands for healing, shouted questions at him, and some threw hateful names and accusations in his direction.

The disciples did their best to keep everyone back, but the crowd was overwhelming. Despite the disciples' growing concern, Jesus made no attempt to pull away from the people trying to touch him. He simply smiled and waved, even stretching out his hands to those who couldn't quite reach him.

His demeanor changed the moment he walked through the temple doors. He saw booths lined up against the walls, selling everything from essential oils to temple souvenirs. A coffee kiosk in the middle of the room offered overpriced drinks and pastries. There was also a local priest near the temple doors, providing financial blessings to anyone who forked over enough money.

There was even a well-known Jewish actor in a corner booth, selling autographed headshots for an outrageous fee.

Jesus was fuming. "You pervert the house of God! Passover is a time for praising God, not turning his house into a flea market! All of you get out!"

He marched to the nearest table and flipped it on its side. The woman sitting there ran away, her homemade prayer candles rolling across the floor. Jesus marched to the coffee kiosk and grabbed the decorative umbrella hanging over it. He snapped it in half and threw it on the ground. Pushing past the barista, he grabbed a pan of warm cinnamon rolls and hurled them across the room.

Then Jesus's eyes fell on the famous actor. The man leapt from his chair, tripped over the legs, and fell to the ground. He crawled toward the nearest exit as Jesus began tearing his autographed headshots in half. He tossed them in the air like oversized confetti.

The chief priests of the temple watched in horror from the safety of the upper balcony. One of them was recording the event on his phone.

"Send that to Jordan," another priest said. "He'll want to see this."

CHAPTER 4

That evening Jesus held a Passover feast for his disciples at a local restaurant. The owner, a devout follower of Jesus, gave them a private room in the back where a huge buffet was waiting for them.

With their plates full of kosher meats, breads, and vegetables, the disciples joked with one another between mouthfuls of food. The mood was light, Jesus's outburst at the temple far from their minds.

Jesus was quiet during the meal, content to listen to his friends' good-natured banter. However, as dinner gave way to dessert, Jesus cleared his throat and spoke.

"This evening I wanted to have one last supper with you because I won't eat again until it finds fulfillment in the kingdom of God."

"What do you mean?" Thomas asked. The rest of the disciples looked confused as well.

It was going be difficult for Jesus to explain this in a way his disciples would understand. He prayed for God to give him the right words so it would all make sense to them. He took a piece of bread from the basket in the middle of the table and prayed over it.

"This is my body given for you. Do this in remembrance of me." He broke off a piece, ate it, and passed the rest to Andrew.

Andrew looked from the bread to Jesus. "You want me to eat this?"

"Yes. One piece and then pass it down," Jesus said.

The disciples sat in silence as the bread made its way around the table. Next, Jesus grabbed an empty glass and filled it with wine. He took a sip and handed it to Andrew.

"This cup is the new covenant in my blood, which is poured out for you."

"Jesus, I don't understand. You're worrying me." Andrew looked around the table at the other disciples nodding their heads. "Worrying all of us."

Jesus understood this was going to upset them, but it had to be said. They were running out of time. Jesus motioned for Andrew to take a drink. After the glass made its way around the table, Jesus met the eyes of every disciple.

"What I'm about to tell you will be difficult to hear, but it's the truth. One of you is going to betray me."

There was an uproar of denials. The disciples threw accusatory glances at one another.

"Who is it?" Peter demanded.

"Surely it's not me?" Judas said.

Jesus closed his eyes and bowed his head in pain. What he was about to reveal would tear the group apart, and it broke his heart. "Yes, it's you."

"I'll kill him!" Bartholomew hollered.

Matthew threw a half-eaten roll at Judas. "What'd you do? Did you steal the money, you little thief?"

Peter jumped out of his chair. "Let's take him outside and search him!"

"Stop!" Jesus said. The room froze. "Leave him alone. Judas, go quickly and do what you have to do."

Judas took a wide berth around the rest of the disciples, hugging the wall until he reached the door. He started to say something, reconsidered, and then left the room.

"Why'd you let him go? We could have stopped him!" Matthew said.

"Don't interfere with God's will. Listen to me. I will only be with you a little longer," Jesus said.

"Where are you going?" Thaddeus asked.

"Right now you can't follow where I'm going, but you will follow me later," Jesus said. It sounded cryptic even to him, but sometimes the Holy Spirit spoke in a way that didn't translate well to his disciples.

"Why can't I follow you now?" Peter said. "I'm not afraid to go. I'd lay down my life for you."

"Would you really lay down your life for me, Peter?"

"Yes! I'm not afraid of death."

Jesus shook his head sadly. "No, you won't. In fact, you will deny me three times before the rooster crows tomorrow morning."

"That's not true! I would never deny you! Now, will you please tell us what's going on?"

"You will know when the time is right. For now, let's enjoy our time together and not worry about it," Jesus said, knowing that would be easier said than done.

"You're the one who brought it up." Peter slumped in his chair with his arms crossed over his chest.

"Fair enough. What do you say we head over to that beautiful garden we saw on the way over here? I think it would make for a nice change of scenery," Jesus suggested.

Peter threw up his hands. "I give up. If you don't want to tell us, then fine, but I stand by what I said. I would *never* deny you. I love you, Jesus."

"And I love you." Jesus looked around the table with tears in his eyes. "I love all of you."

***

Judas stood in the shadows of an alleyway between a hardware store and computer repair shop, both closed for the night. He was starting to think this was the worst idea he'd ever had, but it was too late to back out now. Jesus was already onto him. He might as well finish what he'd started.

A black sedan pulled in front of the buildings and flashed its headlights. Judas darted across the street and hopped in, slamming the car door behind him.

"He knows I'm up to something! I don't know how, but he knows!"

"Are you sure?" Jordan said.

"Positive. Did you tell him?"

"Don't be stupid. Why would I do that?"

"Well, you better do something tonight because he's onto us. Or at least he's onto me."

"After that stunt he pulled in the temple, the Sanhedrin gave me the green light to move immediately, but we can't do it in public."

"That's why I called you. I think he's going to that garden a few miles up the road later tonight. I doubt anyone else will be there at this hour."

"The Garden of Gethsemane?"

Judas shrugged. "If that's the flower garden we passed, then yeah. He said we should check it out after dinner. If you want him, now's your chance."

Jordan smiled. "Perfect. Let me call our security team, and we'll be on our way."

"We?" Judas said, feeling panicked. "I don't want to be anywhere near Jesus when this goes down. I've done what you asked. I just want my money."

"Don't worry. You'll get your money. I just need you to identify Jesus for us when we get there."

"No way! You know what he looks like. You do it." Judas remembered the disciples' reaction at dinner when they found out he was going to betray Jesus, and he dreaded the thought of facing them again when they discovered who he was working with.

"I'm afraid that won't work," Jordan said. "It's going to be dark, and I might not be able to tell which one he is. We'll hide somewhere until you point him out. Then we'll jump out and grab him. Piece of cake."

Judas leaned his head against the window. How had he gotten himself into this? "I think I'm going to be sick."

Jordan patted his knee. "It's almost over. Just a few more hours, and that money is yours."

***

It was after ten o'clock when Jesus and his disciples entered the Garden of Gethsemane. The place was deserted except for a group of crickets calling to each other across the foliage. Jesus led them through a winding stone path lit by solar garden lights. He stopped when they came to an open area surrounded by benches. With his hands behind his back, Jesus observed the flowers blooming all around him and took a deep breath.

"Magnificent," Jesus said.

"It certainly is," Matthew agreed.

Jesus motioned toward the benches. "You guys sit here and keep an eye on things. I'm going to see if I can find a place to pray."

"You want some company?" Peter offered.

"Thank you, but I'd like to be alone right now. My soul is overwhelmed with sorrow to the point of death." Jesus dreaded the events that were about to unfold. Anxiety coursed through his body like a poison, causing him to feel weak and ill.

After disappearing into the shadows, Jesus strolled off the path and found an overgrown and undisturbed area. He fell to his knees, lowered his head, and prayed, his voice little more than a whisper.

"Father, I know you're all-powerful and can do anything you want, and it's with that belief that I ask you to take away the suffering I'm about to endure. If there's any other way for this to happen, then please let it be so, but only if it's according to your will, Lord. Despite my sorrow, I pray for your will to be done instead of mine."

Jesus meditated on the words he'd spoken and felt the overwhelming presence of God descend upon him. Despite the knowledge of the horrors to come, Jesus found a sense of peace that gave him a renewed strength. With his burdens lightened, he returned to his disciples and found them dozing on the benches, nestled against each other like baby puppies.

There was a rustling in the bushes behind him. He turned to see a figure cloaked in darkness walking toward them.

"Wake up!" Jesus's words jolted the disciples from their sleep. "The time has come!"

The shadows pulled away from the man's face. Judas walked into the center of the circle and stood before Jesus.

"Hello, Jesus," Judas said. His voice trembled, and his body shook.

"It's okay, Judas. Do what you came here to do." As much as it hurt to know Judas had stabbed him in the back, he understood that it had to be done.

Judas hugged him and kissed his cheek, avoiding Jesus's eyes as he pulled away. Jesus's stomach churned at the knowledge of what was coming next.

"Now!" a voice cried from the darkness.

A group of men dressed in black rushed out of some nearby trees. With weapons raised, they surrounded Jesus and his disciples. One man removed a pair of handcuffs from his utility belt and approached Jesus.

Peter leapt off the bench, pulling a steak knife from his back pocket. With eyes full of rage, he swung it at the man holding the handcuffs. The blade sliced through the man's ear, carving off the bottom half.

"Peter, no!" Jesus said.

The injured guard clutched at his mangled ear with one hand while pointing his revolver at Peter's head with the other.

"Don't shoot! Lower that weapon right now!" Jordan stormed into the middle of the fray, waving his arms above his head. "Anyone who fires their weapon answers to Caiaphas. Understood?"

"Peter, drop the knife. Where did you even get that?" Jesus asked.

Peter held the knife in front of him like a madman. "I took it from the restaurant. I knew something was about to go down."

"Don't you think I could call on God to bring down thousands of angels to save me if I wanted to? Please, put it away."

Peter spat at the feet of the man he'd struck and threw the knife into some nearby bushes. He glared at Jesus. "Happy now?"

"Alright, let's cuff him and get out of here," Jordan said.

One man slapped a pair of handcuffs onto Jesus's wrists. He winced as they dug into his flesh.

"Am I so dangerous that you have to capture me in the middle of the night with guns? Why didn't you arrest me during the day when I was preaching out in the open?" Jesus didn't get a response. "It doesn't really matter. All that matters is this has taken place so that scripture can be fulfilled."

"Whatever you say, Jesus." Jordan pointed at the disciples. "I suggest the rest of you get out of here unless you want to join your leader, which I can assure you will not be a pleasant experience."

The disciples hesitated, but outmanned and outgunned, they relented and left the garden. Only Peter stood firm.

"It's okay, Peter. Go with the rest of them," Jesus said.

"I'd listen to your boss. He's a wise man," Jordan said.

Peter balled up his fists. "I'll call the police. They'll put you away for life."

Jordan gestured at the armed men surrounding him. "No need to call them. Several of them are right here."

"Shut up! Just shut up!" Peter said. "I wish I'd saved my knife for you."

Jordan rolled his eyes. "So brave."

"Go," Jesus said. "No police. This is God's will."

"I'll find a way to get you out of this." Peter pointed at the man he'd attacked. "You're lucky it was just an ear. Next time it'll be your neck."

Although Jesus didn't care for Peter's violent temper, he appreciated his loyalty. Peter looked at Jesus one more time and then disappeared into the night.

CHAPTER 5

Jesus sat between two guards in the back of an SUV with his hands cuffed behind his back. As the vehicle pulled into the courtyard of Caiaphas's elaborate mansion, Jordan saw the crowd of people waiting for them and cursed under his breath. News of the arrest had leaked, and Jesus wondered if it had been his disciples.

The crowd sauntered toward the SUV like mindless zombies. The vehicle veered around them and drove through the security gate leading to the back of the house. From there they dragged Jesus out of the vehicle and led him inside. The size and grandeur of the mansion made Martin's house look like a bungalow. Jesus saw room after room of extravagance; it disgusted him.

The guards shoved him into a large sitting room with a roaring fire that gave it a hellish glow. A variety of people filled the room, wearing everything from priesthood robes to street clothes.

Caiaphas sat in an oversized chair across from the fire. Jesus thought the flames reflecting in his eyes made him look more like the devil than a priest. With a groan of effort, Caiaphas pulled himself out of the chair and walked over to Jesus. He stroked his wiry, gray beard as he examined Jesus's face like an artist inspecting his latest work. He smiled, the wrinkles in his face becoming more defined.

"So this is the man who has caused us so much grief," Caiaphas said. "I have been looking forward to meeting you for a long time."

***

Outside, a fire had been lit in the courtyard's stone fire pit. Peter, wearing a navy hoodie and a Boston Red Sox baseball cap, approached the pit and warmed his hands in front of the flames. After learning that Jesus had been taken to Caiaphas's home, Peter had gone there himself to see if he could help Jesus. He hadn't expected the large crowd, and it was making him uncomfortable.

A young girl standing nearby looked up at him with interest. Peter felt her gaze and pulled the hat lower over his forehead.

"Hey, mister. Aren't you that guy that's always with Jesus? I've seen you on TV."

"I don't know what you're talking about, kid. You must have me confused with someone else."

The girl ran to her father, tugged on his coat, and pointed at Peter. Peter turned his back on the girl and walked away.

***

Caiaphas had paid false witnesses to come and testify against Jesus. Although Jordan had a very promising future, it was clear he still needed hand-holding in bigger situations like this. After watching Jesus repeatedly outsmart Jordan, Caiaphas had decided to take matters into his own hands to make sure Jesus got what was coming to him.

One by one, the witnesses came forward and lied about things they had seen. They said Jesus had performed fake miracles, incited acts of violence, and claimed to be the Son of God.

After the last man had testified, Caiaphas turned to Jesus. "What do you have to say about the things they have brought against you? Are they true?" Jesus ignored the question. "Do you understand the seriousness of this situation? These accusations could lead to severe punishment if proven true."

Jesus continued to sit in silence, even in the face of a threat that was very real. The legal system of the Jews had existed in the United States for a long time. However, following the violent reign of President Alexander Herod, their power had been expanded to ease the heightened tension between the Jews and the government. Jews now had the authority to handle almost any crime, as long as it only impacted their community. As long as the Jewish leaders didn't step on the toes of the United States government, they were happy to let the Jewish community govern themselves. It wasn't without its flaws and controversy, but overall the system had been beneficial to both parties.

Jordan grabbed Jesus's face and squeezed. "When Caiaphas asks you a question, you answer him."

"Let him go, Jordan." Caiaphas gave a devilish grin. "One way or another, he will answer me."

***

Peter kept to the outskirts of the courtyard as the crowd continued to grow. A latecomer bumped into Peter while trying to get closer to the action.

"Sorry buddy," the man said, patting Peter on the shoulder.

"You're good," Peter said. He was growing more uncomfortable by the minute.

The man's gaze lingered for a moment. "Hey, you're one of them, aren't you? One of Jesus's disciples!"

Several people nearby turned and looked at Peter.

"No, I'm not! I don't even know the guy!" Peter was getting scared. If the Sanhedrin realized Peter was out here, they'd probably arrest him too.

The man put up his hands and took a step back. "Okay, man. Take it easy. I just thought you looked like one of them, that's all."

Peter pulled the hood of his sweatshirt over his head and left the courtyard. There was a grove of trees on the other side of the gate that would hide him from the crowd while letting him continue to keep an eye on the house.

***

They had thrown questions and accusations at Jesus for hours, but he still refused to speak. The frustration in the room was growing, but Caiaphas remained calm. He respected Jesus's resolve, but he knew Jesus would eventually break. They always did.

Caiaphas paced back and forth in front of Jesus. "The most condemning thing I've heard is that you claim to be God's son. Why are you so afraid to respond to that? Is it because you're a fraud? Has the whole Messiah thing been a big lie? Speak up! Are you the Son of God or not?"

Jesus locked eyes with him. "I am."

Relief washed over Caiaphas. They finally had him. "You all heard this blasphemy! What do you think?"

"Punishable by death!" Jordan cried.

The room echoed Jordan's decree. The verdict was death.

***

As the doors to the second-story veranda swung open, Jesus was shoved to the edge of the guardrails overlooking the courtyard. Peter was relieved to see Jesus was still alive. He risked returning to the courtyard in order to hear what the Sanhedrin had to say.

Caiaphas stood next to Jesus while addressing the crowd. "I am sorry to have kept you all waiting, but I wanted to make sure we had everything in order before making a formal statement." Caiaphas nodded toward Jesus. "This man has been perverting our holy religion long enough, and his violence at the temple was the final straw. His actions have escalated to the point where the safety of the religious leaders and their faithful followers are now at risk, and we will no longer tolerate it.

"We brought Jesus here tonight hoping to reach a peaceful resolution, but he was unwilling to cooperate. He claims to be the Son of God and refuses to apologize for his vandalism at the temple. He also continues to lie about the validity of his supposed miracles. We have a room full of witnesses that can attest to all these things.

"The crime of blasphemy alone is sufficient for the harshest sentence under Jewish law, but Jesus is guilty of other crimes as well. After everything we've heard here tonight, the Sanhedrin have unanimously agreed that the only appropriate sentence is death."

The overwhelming majority of the crowd voiced their displeasure. Peter was in shock. He removed his hat and ran his fingers through his hair.

"Hey!" someone standing next to Peter shouted, startling him. "I knew you looked familiar. You're Peter."

Others murmured their agreement.

"Yeah, I think you're right."

"Definitely looks like him."

"Where's the rest of your crew?"

Peter shouted a flurry of obscenities; he couldn't afford to be recognized, especially after they had just condemned Jesus to death. "I'm not Peter!" He pointed up at Jesus. "I've never even met that man!"

A rooster crowed somewhere in the distance. Jesus turned and looked straight at Peter. Jesus's words from the restaurant crashed through his mind like a battering ram. *You will deny me three times before the rooster crows tomorrow morning.*

Remorse flooded Peter's body, draining his strength. He pushed through the crowd and stumbled into the street. His sobs could be heard even as he disappeared around the corner.

***

After the disturbance in the courtyard had subsided, Jordan watched in disbelief as the people began shouting up at the Sanhedrin. The crowd was turning on them.

"No questions at this time," Caiaphas said quickly. He motioned for the guards to take Jesus inside. When the doors were closed behind them, Caiaphas slapped Jesus and spat in his face. "Do you see the trouble you have caused us? You deserve everything you are about to get."

"What are we going to do?" Jordan asked. "You saw their reaction. They'll turn on us if we kill him." He couldn't believe the crowd was supporting Jesus. What was it going to take to get rid of this guy?

Caiaphas nodded. "Yes, it seems we underestimated how much they love Jesus, but those outside the Jewish realm are not quite as enamored with him. We'll turn him over to Pilate. That way our hands will be clean." Caiaphas spat on Jesus again and moved toward the door. "I'll be in the car when you're done with him. Take your time."

Jordan came up behind Jesus and punched him in the kidney. It felt good to take out his frustration on the troublesome man. Jesus cried out and stumbled forward. A second man punched him in the stomach and then ducked behind the others.

"Who hit you, Jesus? Prophesy to us, Son of God. Who was it?" the second man said, laughing.

Jesus fell to floor, coiling into the fetal position as everyone took turns beating him.

"Alright, that's enough," Jordan said. "We don't want him too messed up when Pilate sees him. Let's get him out of here."

CHAPTER 6

There was a knock on the bedroom door. Pilate pulled the covers over his head and wrapped an arm around his sleeping wife. A second, louder knock rattled the door in its frame.

"What is it?" Pilate said from underneath the covers.

"Sir, we have a situation out here that needs your attention."

His wife stirred. "Go see what they want."

Pilate groaned. "One of the few days I get to sleep in. Are you kidding me?"

"Sir?" came the voice from behind the door.

"I'll be down in a minute."

"Very well, sir." Footsteps faded down the hall.

Pilate kissed his wife's forehead and rolled out of bed. He loved being the governor, but sometimes he wished for a normal nine-to-five job. This morning was one of those times.

He threw on a white button-down shirt and slipped into a pair of navy slacks. He considered a tie and jacket but decided against it. Anyone calling on him at this hour would have to settle for business casual.

"Will you turn off the light on your way out?" his wife said. She nestled her head deep into the pillow.

"Rub it in, why don't you?" He gave her a wink and flipped off the light.

Pilate's assistant, Greg, was waiting for him in the downstairs entryway. His hands were clasped in front of him so tight that his fingertips were white.

301

"I'm sorry to wake you, sir. I told them you couldn't be disturbed, but they insisted on seeing you." He glanced at the door. "And there's a lot of them."

Pilate peeked out the nearest window. Several men in robes were standing on the front porch. Behind them were at least a couple hundred people loitering on the front lawn.

Pilate sighed. "Jewish priests. This can't be good."

He'd dealt with the Jewish leaders on many occasions, and none of them had been pleasant. The only time they came to him was when there was a problem, and Caiaphas had always been a particular thorn in his side. Caiaphas had connections to President Herod and had filed multiple complaints against Pilate. At one point President Herod had even called Pilate to ask if he needed to find a more competent governor to manage the Jews. The message had been clear: one more strike and Pilate was out.

Pilate opened the door, doing his best to offer a welcoming smile. "Good morning, gentlemen. Is everything okay?"

Caiaphas stepped aside so a guard could shove Jesus to the front of the group. "This man claims to be the Son of God, and we have found him guilty under Jewish law," Caiaphas said.

"So?" Pilate said.

"He is also defying this country's laws by refusing to pay taxes, and he is telling others to do the same. He is trying to start a rebellion."

"Come on, Caiaphas. That hardly warrants you bringing him to my doorstep," Pilate said, studying Jesus's bruised and bloodied face. "Or roughing him up like this."

Caiaphas stiffened. "It is not just taxes. He claims to be the king of the Jews, and as you can imagine, it's causing us all kinds of problems."

Pilate looked at Jesus. "What do you say? Are you the king of the Jews?"

"That's correct," Jesus said.

"You see? There is your proof right there. He just admitted it to your face." Caiaphas turned to the crowd. "You all heard what he said, right?"

Many shouted in agreement. Pilate recognized some of them as members of the Sanhedrin. It was no surprise to see them supporting their leader.

"Then judge him by your own laws. You don't need my permission," Pilate said. Why on earth were they bothering him with this?

"We are not here for your permission. We are here to hand him over to you."

"Me? I haven't seen any proof he's trying to start a rebellion, and you can take it up with the IRS if you want to get him on tax evasion. I don't have time to deal with this."

Caiaphas leaned in close and whispered, "We have sentenced him to death, but we cannot be the ones to do it. He has too many followers. Executing him would cause too many problems in the Jewish community."

Pilate laughed. Now it all made sense. "So you want me to do your dirty work for you? I don't think so."

"Governor, he is a criminal, and we demand that you punish him accordingly," Caiaphas said.

"I already told you. I don't see anything that requires my involvement."

"You are being unnecessarily combative about this situation. Perhaps we should ask President Herod what he thinks."

Pilate's stomach lurched. A call to President Herod would be the end of his governorship and kill any future political aspirations. A sudden flash of ingenuity sparked in his mind. He stepped onto the front lawn and addressed the crowd.

"I'll arrest Jesus and charge him as Caiaphas has requested. However, I'd like to remind you that as part of the government's continued goodwill toward the Jewish community, the governor can pardon one prisoner of your choosing during the Passover celebration each year. Since I haven't received this year's request, do you want me to release Jesus so we can be done with this?"

The crowd discussed their options, muttering amongst themselves. Pilate looked over at Caiaphas and smiled.

"Give us Barabbas!" someone shouted.

"Yeah! Let Barabbas go!" another one said.

"Barabbas! Barabbas! Barabbas!" The chant spread through the crowd like a contagious disease.

The smile dropped from Pilate's face. Somehow, the Sanhedrin supporters had convinced the crowd to choose a convicted murderer over Jesus.

Barabbas had made national headlines the previous year when his wife had been brutally murdered inside their home. Although Barabbas had been the initial and obvious suspect, police couldn't find any evidence tying him to the crime. Despite a thorough investigation, there were no additional suspects, and as a result, the police honed in on Barabbas even more. They eventually pieced together enough evidence to support an arrest, and a jury sentenced him to twenty-five years in prison. The trial was extremely controversial, and polls showed about half the people believed he was innocent.

"Do you seriously want me to release him instead of Jesus? Do you hear what you're saying?" Pilate said, incredulous.

"You asked for a name, and they gave it to you. Now release Barabbas, and arrest Jesus," Caiaphas said.

"And what am I supposed to do with him? Give him a life sentence for tax evasion?"

Caiaphas turned to the crowd and raised his clenched fists in the air. "Crucifixion!"

Crucifixion was the most barbaric form of corporal punishment still in existence, and it was reserved for only the most heinous crimes. Crucifixions took place in a public venue as a crime deterrent, but the actual effectiveness of it was widely debated.

Pilate stood horrified as the previous chant of "Barabbas" was replaced with "Crucifixion." The crowd had been worked into a frenzy and was out for blood.

Pilate returned to the front porch and stood next to Caiaphas. "You realize President Herod will have to sign off on this."

"Merely a formality," Caiaphas said.

Pilate knew he was right. There was a law that allowed states to carry out punishments on behalf of the Jewish community as long as the Jewish leaders requested it. The law's intent was to assist the Jewish legal system whenever unique circumstances prohibited them from carrying out the punishments themselves. Execution requests had to be approved by the President of the United States, but Pilate knew it wouldn't be an issue. No president wanted to be responsible for worsening the relationship between the Jews and the United States government, especially President Alexander Herod's son. Jesus was a dead man.

"This man's death is on your hands, not mine," Pilate said.

"I welcome it," Caiaphas said.

Pilate shook his head at the hypocrisy. "Aren't you supposed to be a man of God?"

"Just do your job," Caiaphas snapped.

Pilate sighed. "Greg?"

"Yes sir?"

"Call the prison and have them send some guards to the house. Tell them it's for a crucifixion."

CHAPTER 7

Jordan,

I'm writing this letter to confess that I was wrong and so are you. Jesus is the Son of God. He is the Alpha and the Omega. The beginning and the end. You may have the upper hand today, but he will have the upper hand when it's all said and done. We are on the losing end of this battle, and that is not a good place to be.

I let greed get the best of me, and in doing so, I betrayed an innocent man. I doubt God will forgive me for what I've done, and I know I can never forgive myself. It's tempting to blame you for what I did, but the blame is mine and mine alone. I will answer for my sins just as you will answer for yours.

I've wired all the money back into your account. I almost left it with my wife, but that money is cursed, just like me. I don't want it anywhere near my family.

I can't live with what I've done. I know it's the coward's way out, but I've never seen myself as a noble man anyway. Repent for what you've done or be destined to join me in Hell.

Judas chugged the last of his beer as he stuffed the letter into an addressed envelope and placed it next to the one he'd left for his wife. Tossing the beer can into a pile with its empty friends, Judas got up from the table and stumbled over to a chair in the middle of the one-room cabin he'd rented earlier that day. An elastic exercise band hung from a wooden beam along the ceiling, one end fastened into a noose. He stood on the chair and slipped the noose around his neck, pulling it tight until he could feel the elastic digging into his throat.

His eyes drifted to the television, where the news of Jesus's death sentence had been playing for the past several hours. Judas thought he had been starting the revolution by helping the Sanhedrin arrest Jesus, but he had been wrong, very wrong.

"I'm sorry, Jesus. I'm so sorry."

Taking a deep and final breath, Judas kicked the chair out from underneath him. The noose tightened around his neck like an iron fist, and his body jerked in the air like a puppet on strings. He soon became unconscious, and death was not far behind.

CHAPTER 8

Jesus stood naked and soaking wet in front of a group of soldiers, shivering so hard it looked like he was having a seizure. He'd been transported to the local prison and thrown into a concrete holding room on the basement level, where they'd stripped him down and tied his hands to a pipe hanging above a floor drain. The soldiers were now taking turns blasting him with a stream of icy water from a hose.

Although every prisoner ended up on a cross at the end of the crucifixion process, soldiers were given free rein when it came to the torture leading up to the grand finale. They were the artists, and each prisoner was a fresh canvas on which they could create their sadistic masterpiece.

Most soldiers looked forward to these events. Day-to-day life in the military was a far cry from the flashy brochures and testosterone-fueled videos they wooed you with at the recruiting centers. In reality, military life could be very monotonous. Being able to crucify someone was a welcome break in the routine, and there was no shortage of volunteers willing to carry out the barbaric duties.

"Alright, that's enough. Shut it off." Seargent Dickerson stepped away from the wall and stood in front of Jesus.

"Ah, come on, Sarge. We're just getting started," said the soldier with the hose.

"I said shut it off, Mathers!" Dickerson looked at Jesus, shaking his head. "King of the Jews, huh? I was expecting someone a lot tougher. Someone that could at least handle a little cold water." Dickerson had been through enough of these to know civilian prisoners were all the same. No matter how tough they thought they were, they always broke once the torture started.

Jesus looked at him with glazed eyes that seemed to stare right through him. His teeth chattered like a machine gun, and his lips were an unhealthy mixture of purple and blue.

Dickerson marched over to a table near the door and surveyed the various instruments on top of it. His fingers ran across a pair of pliers, a baton, and some jumper cables attached to a car battery. All of these typical tools of torture bored him. He wanted a new toy to play with. His eyes lit up as his hand rested on a whip near the end of the table.

He let the whip uncoil from his hands like a venomous snake and began circling Jesus like a tiger stalking its prey. He cracked the whip above Jesus's head, causing Jesus to flinch. The soldiers roared with laughter.

Dickerson continued walking in circles, taunting Jesus with the whip as he went. He relished the intense fear he saw on Jesus's face. After the tenth time around, he cracked the whip again. This time it struck flesh.

Jesus shrieked and went limp. The rope around his wrists was the only thing keeping him upright. Dickerson whipped him a second time, and Jesus let out a cry that sounded more animal than human.

Two bloody stripes formed an X across Jesus's back like a gruesome treasure map. Dickerson nodded his approval and offered the whip to Mathers. One by one, the soldiers took their turn with it. Jesus drifted in and out of consciousness as the whip slashed across his backside time and time again.

"Cut him loose," Dickerson said once everyone had their turn.

Jesus collapsed to the ground in a gruesome heap. His back looked like raw hamburger meat, his legs like bloody drumsticks.

Blood ran down his sides and pooled onto the concrete underneath him. The only sign of life was the almost imperceptible rise and fall of his back with each labored breath.

***

Jesus opened his eyes and groaned. The surrounding noises were muted like a distant dream, and pain coursed through his body like a million needles stabbing him at once. He lifted his head and saw a man kneeling beside him. The name, Dickerson, was stitched across the right breast of his uniform.

"We lost you there for a minute. Welcome back," Dickerson said.

Two soldiers grabbed him by the arms and yanked him to his feet. It felt like his back was being torn apart and lit on fire. Jesus howled.

Mathers stepped forward and handed Dickerson a ratty, purple robe and a bunch of thorns woven into a circle. Dickerson draped the robe over Jesus's shoulders and placed the crown of thorns on his head. Using the butt of his pistol, Dickerson smashed the thorns into Jesus's scalp. Tiny rivers of blood ran down his forehead and seeped into his beard.

"Hail, king of the Jews!" Dickerson said.

The soldiers knelt before Jesus in mock reverence. They spat at his feet and laughed. One of them grabbed Jesus by the shoulders and kneed him in the stomach. He vomited a putrid mixture of bile and blood onto the concrete.

Jesus silently prayed for God to make it all stop while holding up a trembling hand. "No more. Please."

"Oh, we have a lot more in store for you, buddy." Dickerson grabbed him by the hair and looked him in the eyes. "A lot more."

***

Jesus lay in the back of a military truck traveling toward a place known as The Long March. Each bump in the road sent a fresh bolt of pain surging through his body.

The Long March was a stretch of dirt road that wound its way up a large hill overlooking the city. Those being crucified were placed at the bottom of the hill and forced to drag a wooden cross all the way to the top. After the grueling trek, the prisoner was hung from the cross and left to die.

By the time Jesus arrived, hundreds of people were already gathered at the foot of the hill. Crucifixions were a public event, and such a horrific punishment attracted all kinds of onlookers. Friends and family of the prisoner were regular attendees, along with those affected by the prisoner's crime. Some people brought their kids to see the negative consequences of a life of delinquency, and others simply had a perverse fascination with torture.

The soldiers dragged Jesus out of the truck and flung him to the ground. Dirt clung to his bloodied face like a red mask.

Dickerson placed a boot on top of a wooden cross lying in the dirt next to him. "Get over here and pick this up."

Jesus slowly got to his knees. The skin on his back stretched, pulling open the wounds. He groaned and fell to the ground. Dickerson cursed and marched over to the truck. He grabbed the whip out of the back and cracked it in front of Jesus's face.

"Get up and carry that cross, or we go back to square one."

Jesus tried to stand, but the pain was too great. Stars exploded in his vision, and he collapsed. The whip struck his back. Jesus screamed and thrashed from side to side. He placed his hand on the new gash, and a second strike caught his wrist. Many in the crowd turned away in horror, but none of them said anything. Although everyone was encouraged to watch a crucifixion, anyone who interfered risked their own punishment.

"Somebody drag him over there. I'm sick of watching him cry like a little girl," Dickerson said.

The soldiers carried him over to the cross and held him upright until he could support his own weight.

"Now, pick it up," Dickerson said.

A mixture of sweat and blood stung Jesus's eyes. "I can't."

Dickerson clasped his hands behind his back and stood toe-to-toe with Jesus. "Well, you better find a way. And fast."

Jesus attempted to bend down, grimaced, and shook his head. The pain was too intense. It was all he could do to stay conscious. "I can't do it."

"Then let me help you."

Dickerson snapped his fingers and pointed at the cross. Two soldiers lifted it and lowered it onto Jesus's back while supporting most of the weight themselves. Dickerson grabbed Jesus's arms and wrapped them around the horizontal beam, ignoring Jesus's cries of pain.

"Alright, let it go," Dickerson told the soldiers.

They released the cross, and over 100 pounds of wood came crashing down onto Jesus's back. He took three stumbling steps forward before falling to the ground. Hundreds of splinters dug into his wounds as the wooden beam scraped the length of his back. A woman in the crowd fainted.

Jesus lay in the dirt, whimpering like a wounded animal. "Father, help me," Jesus said. He tried to hold on, but the pain was unfathomable.

"Your daddy's not here." Dickerson smashed the heel of his boot against the crown of thorns. "I'm your daddy now."

Mathers exited the cab of the truck and approached the sergeant. "Sir, the guys up the hill want to know how much longer we're going to be. They've already started hanging the other two prisoners."

"Alright, let's speed this up." Dickerson surveyed the crowd and pointed to a young, muscular man. "You. Get over here and carry this thing."

The man's eyes widened. "Me?"

"Yeah, you. What's your name?"

"Tyler, sir."

"Tyler, I'm not giving Jesus the satisfaction of watching my men haul this cross up there for him. Now, let's go."

Tyler knelt in front of the cross and lifted it with ease. With the horizontal beam resting on his broad shoulders, he started up the hill. The soldiers threw Jesus into the back of the truck and crept along behind Tyler, the rest of the caravan following close behind.

A large group of soldiers and onlookers were waiting for them at the top of the hill, along with two other prisoners already hanging from crosses standing tall against the brilliant sky. Tyler lugged Jesus's cross to the designated area and dropped it with a grunt. His shirt was drenched with sweat.

The soldiers placed Jesus on top of the cross, pinning his arms against the horizontal beam and crossing his legs over the vertical one. Dickerson knelt beside Jesus and dropped three iron stakes next to his head while waving a large mallet in front of his face. Jesus was terrified.

"You ready?" Dickerson spat in his face and laughed. "Hold him tight, boys."

He took the first stake and placed it against the soft flesh of Jesus's inner right wrist. He raised the mallet high above his head and brought it down with violent force. Jesus screamed as the stake tore through his wrist and dug into the wooden beam behind him. He didn't think there could be anything more painful than what he'd already experienced, but he had been dead wrong.

Dickerson hopped over to Jesus's other side and placed the second stake against his left wrist. Another scream echoed over the hill as the stake pierced his flesh. Tears ran down his pale face. His breathing was rapid and shallow.

Dickerson moved to the foot of the cross with a stake much longer than the other two. Mathers held Jesus's feet together, one crossed over the other, while Dickerson pressed the stake into the flesh where the foot meets the leg. Mathers fought to keep Jesus still while Dickerson hammered away until the stake went all the way through. Jesus fainted.

***

Jesus was vertical by the time he regained consciousness. The soldiers had connected the cross to a support pole already cemented into the ground, and Jesus was now hanging several feet in the air. Gravity soon became Jesus's worst enemy. With his head lower than his outstretched arms, it was impossible to breathe without using his pierced arms and legs to pull himself up. The coarse wood shredded his back like a cheese grater with each breath.

The soldiers allowed the crowd to move in closer. Some of them wept, some prayed, and others mocked him. Even in the midst of incredible agony, Jesus still felt compassion for the people who loved him enough to come all this way to support him. He focused what little energy he had left on thanking God for them while ignoring his haters.

"Look at this imposter!" one of them shouted. "He allegedly saved others with his miracles, but he can't even save himself!"

People ridiculed him as he fought for each breath. Many took selfies in front of the broken Messiah. A few dared to get close enough to spit on him. They did everything they could to get a reaction out of Jesus, but he ignored them.

"Hey, man. Are you really him?" the prisoner on his left said. For whatever reason, the guards had been kinder to him. His body wasn't as bloody and broken as Jesus's. "Yeah, you're him. You call yourself the Son of God, right?"

Jesus winced as he took a deep breath. "Yes," he rasped.

"Dude, what are you doing? If you're the Son of God, then why don't you save us? Do some of that magic of yours and get us out of here."

"I can't," Jesus said.

"I knew it. You're a phony just like they say, huh?"

"Just ignore him. He's no better than the ones on the ground," the other prisoner said.

Jesus looked to his right. "What's your name?"

"Andy."

"You seem like a good man, Andy. How'd you get here?"

"One too many bad decisions." Andy shifted his weight and groaned. "Can I ask you for a favor?" Jesus nodded as he fought for another breath. "Will you remember me when you get to Heaven? I know I don't deserve it, but I really need God right now."

"Andy, I promise that today you will be with me in paradise, and all your sins will be forgiven."

"What a load of crap," the first prisoner said.

"It's not too late for you either," Jesus said.

"Get me down from here, and I'll be your biggest believer. Otherwise I'm good."

Jesus prayed that God would change the man's heart before he took his final breath. Nothing would make him happier than to see both men standing next to him in Heaven.

The crowd continued to mock Jesus. The soldiers entertained themselves by placing bets on when he would die, and they humiliated him at every opportunity. At one point they offered him a sponge soaked in vinegar, disguising it as water. It was the first and only drink Jesus received on the cross.

Death from crucifixion was an unpredictable process. Some people lasted for days, some only hours. A lot of it came down to the mental determination of the victim. Many gave up right away, while others fought to live as long as possible.

The prisoner on Jesus's left was the first to die, and Andy passed away a couple of hours later. Then all eyes turned to Jesus to see how much longer he would last.

As the afternoon gave way to evening, Jesus saw his disciple, John, escorting his mom up the hill. Although he was happy to see her, a part of him wished she hadn't come. He didn't want her to see him like this.

315

Mary sobbed when she laid eyes on him. Jesus felt like crying as well, but he didn't have the strength. She ran to the foot of the cross and reached out to him.

"My baby! Not my baby!"

A soldier stepped in front of her. "Please don't touch the prisoner."

"He's not a prisoner! He's my son! What have you done to him?" The soldier took her by the arm, and she slapped him. "Get your hands off me!"

John wrapped his arms around Mary and pulled her away before she could strike him again. Overhearing the outburst, Dickerson interjected himself into the situation.

"Ma'am, I'm sorry you have to see this. I know it must be difficult," Dickerson said.

"Don't you apologize to me. You did this," she hissed.

"I understand you're upset, and you're more than welcome to say goodbye to your son. All I ask is that you refrain from touching him or any of my officers. Do you understand?"

"She'll behave," John said.

"Behave? They're torturing my son, and I'm the one that has to behave?" Mary's voice was shaking.

Dickerson nodded at John and walked away. John put an arm around Mary and led her back to the cross.

"Mom," Jesus said. His voice was barely a whisper, but it took all his strength just to manage that much.

"Oh, my poor baby. What have they done to you?" Mary started crying again. "I'll get you down from there. I promise."

"Mom, look at me." Mary looked at the blood-stained face of her son. "This is God's will. Let it be."

"What can I do for you? Please tell me what I can do."

"Stay with me until it's over. I don't want to be alone."

Mary placed her hand on the cross. "I'm not going anywhere, sweetie. I promise."

Jesus struggled for another breath and looked at John. "Thank you for bringing her."

"Of course. She called me when she heard about your arrest. I got her on the first available flight and rushed her over here as fast as I could."

"You did good, John." Jesus lowered his head and closed his eyes. Exhaustion was taking over his body.

Over the next hour, Jesus's legs gave out. No longer able to use his legs to help himself breathe, he was forced to pull himself up with only his arms.

Mary spoke to him the entire time. She reminisced about her favorite memories of him as a child and reminded him repeatedly of how much she loved him. Every now and then she would interrupt the one-sided conversation to sing some of her favorite hymns. Her presence comforted Jesus in a way that nothing else could.

At one point Jesus grew still and appeared to stop breathing. Mary knelt in front of him and prayed, one hand on her heart and the other against the base of the cross. An unsettling hush came over the crowd.

Just when everyone assumed he was dead, Jesus pulled himself up and took a deep breath. "My God, my God, why have you forsaken me?" He couldn't feel God's presence, and it was too much to bear on top of everything else.

Mary jumped up and touched Jesus's feet; this time the guards didn't stop her. "It's okay, Jesus. I'm still right here."

"It is finished," Jesus said, and he exhaled for the last time.

***

Mary clung to John and cried into his shoulder. Her sorrow was excruciating. A mother should never have to bury her own son, and she wished God had taken her instead.

A sudden earthquake shook the ground, interrupting her grief and sending people stumbling into each other. Mary and John hugged the cross as everything around them rattled. The earthquake stopped as suddenly as it had started. Car alarms blared in the distance, and dust floated from the buildings and bridges in the city below them. Mary thought the earthquake had been God mourning the death of his son.

A soldier approached Mary, a look of awe on his face. "He really was the Son of God, wasn't he?"

"Is," Mary said, looking up at the sky with tears in her eyes.

"Excuse me?"

"He *is* the Son of God."

CHAPTER 9

Although Pilate had refused to take part in the crucifixion, the news of Jesus's death, along with the subsequent earthquake, had brought him to the top of the hill. He watched the soldiers lower the cross and yank the nails out of the wood. They rolled Jesus's broken body onto the ground like an afterthought. His eyes were wide and vacant. His mouth hung open in a grotesque yawn. Pilate felt ashamed for having played a part in Jesus's gruesome death.

"Load him in the truck with the others," Dickerson said.

"Hang on a second." Pilate approached Jesus's mother. "I understand this is your son. Would you like for us to leave the body with you?"

Mary nodded and looked at the man standing next to her. "John, how are we going to get him home?"

"I'll call the airlines and see about getting him on a plane." John turned to Pilate. "Can you hold him for a day or two? I don't have anywhere to keep him."

"I'm afraid I can't do that. We have to cremate the bodies if loved ones don't claim them."

"I'm claiming him right now. I just need you to hold him until I can arrange a flight. Can't you put him in the morgue or something?" John asked.

Pilate considered the request. He could make an exception to the rule, but he didn't want to deal with the headache that would come with holding Jesus's body.

"Excuse me." A man stepped out of the crowd. "I think I can help."

"Who are you?" Pilate said.

"Just a fan of Jesus's teachings." The man looked at Mary. "Your son saved my life. I was on the verge of losing my family. I even thought about killing myself. Then one night I came across some of Jesus's videos online. I stayed awake all night watching them, and I ended up giving my life to God as the sun came up. Now, my family's stronger than ever, and it's all because of Jesus. I've been praying that God would show me a way to repay him, and I think he just answered my prayers."

"How so?" John asked.

"I have a place you can keep his body until you make proper arrangements. This might sound weird, but I had a tomb built after I gave my life to God. I wanted a place where my family could be buried together someday. A lot of people thought it was creepy, but I don't know, it just made sense for us to always be together, even in death. Anyway, it's just sitting there empty if you need it."

Pilate agreed it was creepy, but he was more than happy to let someone else handle the body.

"Can I have a word with you, Pilate?" Caiaphas stood several feet away, surrounded by other members of the Sanhedrin.

Pilate sighed. "Will you all please excuse me for a moment?" He shot daggers at Caiaphas as he approached him. "What now? The man's dead. Isn't that enough for you?"

"You cannot let that man take Jesus," Caiaphas said.

"Oh, I'm sorry. Did *you* want to give him a proper burial?"

"What's to keep his crazy followers from stealing the body and claiming he rose into Heaven or some other nonsense? Rumors like that could make a dead Jesus more bothersome than the live one. I want his body burned in front of everyone."

"The law is the law, Caiaphas. If the family wants the body, they can have it. Your little vendetta against Jesus is over. You crucified an innocent man. That'll have to be enough." He turned to leave, but Caiaphas wasn't finished.

"Then at least have some soldiers guard the tomb, and put a big rock or something in front of the door. That way none of his followers can take the body, and none of his haters can vandalize the property. It's a win-win."

"Fine. If it'll shut you up, then I see no harm in it, but then it's over, okay? You leave me alone after this." Pilate couldn't wait to be done with the hateful man.

Caiaphas held up his hands and smiled. "You won't hear another word from me."

***

Lucas and Austin guarded the front of the marble tomb, both of them leaning against a large boulder blocking the entrance. A crane had brought in the rock, which was almost as tall as the tomb itself.

"This is stupid," Lucas said, taking a drag on his cigarette and watching the embers burn against the darkness. "Nobody's going to come out here, and even if they do, there's no way they're getting inside."

Austin plucked a stone from the ground and tossed it into the woods behind him, listening to it crackle through the branches. "At least the weather's nice." He thought the cemetery was a peaceful place to be as long as you didn't dwell on the hundreds of decomposing bodies underneath you.

"Everyone else got to help with the crucifixions, and we have to guard a dead guy. We got hosed."

"Could be worse. We could be in a foreign country getting shot at by terrorists," Austin said.

"Always the optimist, huh?"

A blinding light exploded around them like a flash of lightening. As it dimmed, Austin saw a man in white standing on top of the boulder. The light seemed to come from both around and inside the man's body. Austin, numb with fear, aimed his rifle at the stranger, and Lucas followed suit.

"You can put those down. I am not here to harm you. I am an angel sent from the Lord," he said.

The angel stepped off the rock and floated to the ground. Both guards took several steps back, their rifles shaking between their hands. The cigarette fell from Lucas's mouth, creating a shower of sparks as it hit the ground.

"I think it is time for you to leave," the angel said.

Austin looked to his left in time to see Lucas disappearing into the woods. Without a word, he turned and chased after him.

CHAPTER 10

Lazarus's sister, Mary, paused at the end of the stone path weaving among the graves. She shifted the flower bouquet to her other arm and studied the tomb in the distance.

Mary had arrived with her siblings the day after Jesus's death. Lazarus and Martha had visited the tomb yesterday with Jesus's brother, James, who had flown in to be with his mother. Mary, not quite ready to confront her friend's death, had stayed behind at the hotel. This morning, however, she'd woken with the resolve to say goodbye. She'd crept out of her hotel room before dawn and made her way to the cemetery.

Now, as she stood among the headstones, she wondered if she could go through with it. Jesus had always held a special place in her heart, and this was proving to be more difficult than she'd imagined.

Mary looked at the tomb and frowned. She didn't see any soldiers guarding it. In fact, the entire cemetery was empty. As she drew closer, she saw the entrance to the tomb standing wide open. A soft glow was coming from inside. She thought perhaps it was a lantern or some candles that had been lit to mourn Jesus's death. Deep grooves ran through the dirt where the boulder had been shoved aside. Mary marveled at how many men it must have taken to move it.

"Hello?" she called into the tomb as she hurried forward.

Only her echo responded. She shivered and hugged the flowers against her chest. Fighting the urge to run, Mary stepped inside the tomb and screamed. The crude, wooden casket in the middle of the room was open and empty. Sitting on the edge of it was a man dressed in white. The light radiating from his body filled the room. Mary trembled and took a step toward the open door.

"Do not be afraid, Mary," the man said, smiling. "Jesus has risen! As you can see, he is no longer here."

"Where is he? Who are you?" The words were hard to form. Her tongue felt like it had been glued to the top of her mouth.

"I am an angel sent from God. Go and tell the disciples that Jesus has risen from the dead. Hurry! Today is a glorious day!"

Mary dropped her flowers and ran to the rental car. She tried to make sense of everything that had just happened. Had she really seen an angel? What would the others think when she told them?

She was so absorbed in her own thoughts that she didn't notice the man standing next to her car until she was almost on top of him. She pulled up short and stared in disbelief at the man in front of her.

"Hello, Mary."

She put her hands over her mouth. "Jesus? It can't be."

The world swam around her like a murky dream, and she fell to her knees. Jesus knelt beside her.

"Take some deep breaths, Mary. I didn't mean to frighten you."

"You're dead," Mary said, her heart racing.

Jesus smiled. "I was, technically speaking."

"I don't understand. Are you some sort of ghost or actually back from the dead?" She squeezed his arm to confirm he was real.

"It's a little more complicated than that, but it's not important right now. How do you feel?"

"I'm okay. I just got dizzy for a second. I think I can stand up now." Jesus helped her to her feet. "Does anyone else know about this?"

"Not yet. That's why I'm here. I need you to tell the disciples what you've seen. Tell them to get together as soon as possible."

"Where?"

"It doesn't matter. I'll find them. Can you do that for me?"

"You know they won't believe me." Mary was still trying to believe it herself.

"Maybe not at first, but they will soon enough."

***

"He's gone! He's really gone!" Peter said over the video chat on his phone.

"John?" Thomas asked.

"Peter's right. Jesus isn't here. Nobody is."

Mary had called John from the cemetery to tell him what she'd seen and what Jesus had said. John had got in touch with the rest of the disciples, and within the hour they had all gathered together in a conference room at the hotel where Jesus's family was staying.

John and Peter had volunteered to go to the tomb and check it out. Although the disciples wanted to believe Mary's story, they couldn't bring themselves to accept it unless they saw it firsthand.

John and Peter had raced across the cemetery and seen exactly what Mary had described. The soldiers were gone, and the stone had been rolled away from the door. John had hesitated at the entrance, remembering what Mary had said about the angel inside, but Peter had stormed through the door like a man with nothing to lose. The angel was gone, and so was the body.

Now, Peter held up his phone so the rest of the disciples could see the tomb. There was an excited murmur on the other end as the camera scanned the empty coffin. Peter turned the camera back to his face.

"See? I told you. Gone!"

John's face appeared over Peter's shoulder. "We're heading back to the hotel. We'll be there in fifteen minutes."

***

When Peter and John returned, the rest of the disciples were sitting around a large conference table with Jesus's brother.

"James?" Peter said, surprised.

"Mary told Mom and me about her little adventure at the cemetery. Mom got pretty worked up about the whole thing, and now she's convinced Jesus is going to visit her. I finally had to give her something to calm her down."

"It's all true, James. Peter and I saw it for ourselves. It's empty," John said.

James shrugged. "So what? Maybe someone stole his body. Was it one of you?"

"He's alive!" Peter said. After everything that had happened, how could James still not believe Jesus was the Messiah.

James laughed. "Of course. That makes more sense than someone stealing the body or the government destroying it in the middle of the night."

"James has a point. All we know for sure is the body's missing," Thomas conceded.

"Mary wouldn't lie to us," Peter said. "She saw him."

"Look, I want to believe it, but isn't it possible she was hallucinating? Being in a creepy cemetery all by yourself can jack with your mind," Thomas said.

"Jesus brought Lazarus back to life. You don't think he can bring himself back too? Where's your faith?" Peter demanded.

Thomas slammed his fist on the table and stood up. "Don't talk to me about faith! I'm not the one who said he didn't know Jesus. Three times, wasn't it?"

Peter could feel the anger bubbling up inside of him. "At least I was there! What hole in the ground were you hiding in?" He pointed at the other disciples. "Where were *all* of you cowards?"

"Cowards?" Andrew said. "Who was the one crying like a baby when he sank in the water? 'Help me Jesus! I'm sinking! I can't swim!'"

"I didn't see any of you get out of the boat," Peter said.

"Care to step outside and see who the real coward is?" Thomas threatened.

"I'd love to!" Peter said, marching toward the door.

"Stop!" a voice thundered from behind them.

Everyone turned to see Jesus standing in the far corner of the room. The bruises on his face were gone; his hair was no longer matted with blood. The disciples huddled together against the table. Thomas and Peter stood shoulder to shoulder, their argument already forgotten.

"Why are you fighting? Mary told you I returned. Why did you doubt her?"

"It's a ghost," Thomas whispered. "It's got to be a ghost."

"Oh, Thomas. Always the doubter. Touch me and see if I'm real." Jesus held out his wrists. "Put your fingers on my wounds and believe."

Peter nudged him forward. Thomas slowly made his way across the room. He took Jesus's outstretched hands and slid a finger inside one of the wounds. Thomas shuddered and pulled back.

"My Lord and my God!" Thomas dropped to his knees and buried his face in the carpet next to Jesus's feet.

Shame and guilt weighed on Peter's conscience like a stone mill around his neck. He ran across the room and fell on his knees next to Thomas. "I'm so sorry, Jesus! I'm a coward just like they said. Please forgive me."

Jesus placed a hand on Peter's shoulder. "Don't dwell on the past, Peter. All has been forgiven."

One by one, the other disciples knelt before Jesus. Joy replaced their fear as they celebrated the return of their Savior.

After embracing each of the disciples, Jesus went to his brother, who was sitting alone at the table with tears running down his face. James lunged forward and hugged his brother tight.

"What have I done?" James said. "God forgive me. What have I done?"

Jesus held his brother. "I love you, James."

"Don't say that! I don't deserve it. You don't know half the things I've said about you."

"I don't care. This moment right here is all that matters to me. I've waited a long time for this."

Jesus and James sat at the table and had their first genuine conversation in years. Afterward, Jesus explained to his disciples the reason for his supernatural visit.

"I need all of you to continue my work while I'm gone. Go and make disciples of all nations, baptizing them in the name of the Father, the Son, and the Holy Spirit. Teach them to obey everything I've commanded you, and know that I will always be with you, even when things get difficult."

Peter was overcome with emotion and determination. He would bring the story of Jesus to people all over the world, no matter the cost.

***

That night the disciples returned home to say goodbye to their families. Several days later, they would each embark on their own separate journeys to preach the word of God and share the good news that Jesus had risen.

James left the family business and began traveling the country as a new disciple. He would become one of Jesus's biggest advocates and lead thousands of people to God before being murdered for his beliefs.

The rest of the disciples would encounter similar hardships. Most of them would meet gruesome and painful deaths, including public hangings and even crucifixion. Only John would live long enough to die the graceful death of old age.

Others would pick up where the disciples left off, spreading Jesus's message around the world. Despite countless attempts to discredit his legacy, the words of Jesus Christ would live on forever. And someday he'll return. Will you be ready?

ABOUT THE AUTHOR

Dan Hambright believes the best books are the ones that stay with you long after you've turned the final page, and as an author, he strives to influence his readers in the same way with each of his novels. When he's not writing, you can find him hiking through the state parks of Oklahoma, playing sports with his son, having deep, philosophical conversations with his daughter, or spending time with his beautiful and amazing wife. He lives in Yukon, Oklahoma with his wife and two children.

You can follow Dan
on Twitter at @DanHambright,
on Facebook at @AuthorDanHambright,
and online at www.danhambright.com.